THE HOMICIDAL HAIRSTYLE OF THE VIRAL VIDEO VIXEN

a psychic barber mystery

PHILLIP MOTTAZ

Not As Bad Books

The following is a work of fiction. That means it's made up, and any resemblance to real people — alive or dead — is strictly coincidental.

And so a special thanks to everyone who loaned their names, whether they realized it or not. Many yearbooks, phonebooks and old conversations were scoured to pull authentic sounding names. If a name sounds familiar, please know it only happened because it sounded great, and not as any comment on your personal lives.

Names are hard.

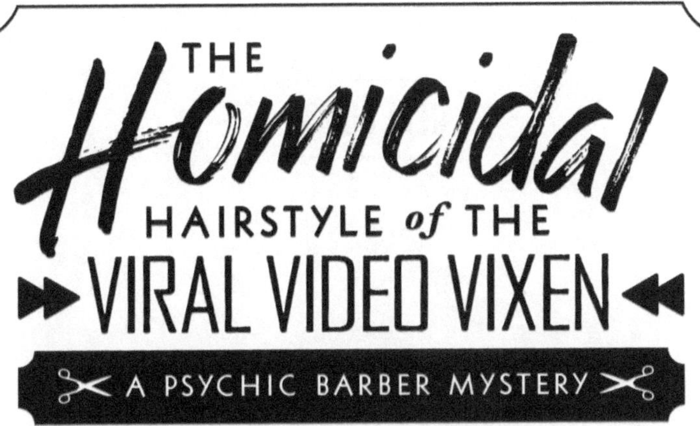

THE
Homicidal
HAIRSTYLE of THE
VIRAL VIDEO VIXEN
A PSYCHIC BARBER MYSTERY
· PHILLIP MOTTAZ ·

REAL QUICK...

Consider signing up for the newsletter!

Go to **phillipmottaz.com** and sign up for freebies, contests, and very, very little spam.

Or email **phillip.mottaz.author@gmail.com**.

Or follow **@phillipmottaz** on Twitter and Instagram.

Furthermore, I'd like to provide a **trigger warning**: this book contains scenes of violence as well as some awkward discussions of racism and homophobia.

While I try to be a co-conspirator in the fight for equity and justice, I recognize that I make mistakes due to my personal biases. Please feel free to reach out and hold me accountable, and I promise to do better in the future.

To my friends, supporters, spell-checkers, parents, Beta readers, ethical shoppers and all the otherwise attractive people I'm lucky to have in my life, thank you. So attractive!

To my Rachel and Henry, another extra thank you. I am blessed to be in your proximity.

CHAPTER ONE

Wednesday, January 14, 2009, 4:07PM.
Interstate 40, West of Seligman, Arizona.

Danica Luman had a problem.

Well, several problems. Collecting problems had become a hobby of hers since the previous fall, when she'd helped solve a murder in a way only a working hairstylist with secret psychic abilities could. Her unique ability allowed her to see visions from people's minds by touching the backs of their heads. Most those visions were dull or concerned a desired hairstyle, but on the rare occasion where those visions illuminated criminal plots with seedy attempts at circumventing the law — as they had mere months prior — Danica allowed herself to try and solve the case, despite her lack of detective experience, putting herself in danger, getting shot at, nearly burned to death, and spilling blood all over her barber chair.

You know: normal stuff.

She'd given herself recuperation time in Illinois, spending the holidays with her step-father. Her time in the Midwest had been the good kind of dull, allowing her wounds to heal in relative comfort. But after a couple months of resting and eating too much, she became restless to return to Los Angeles. She was ready to get back cutting hair at Earl's World of Curls, and to resume whatever kind of life she'd built for herself. She packed her stuff, buzzed her hair back to its classic peach-fuzz level and left snow-bound Illinois once again, hoping that this time she could keep her problems in the rearview.

Yet as she sped through the desert towards Los Angeles with her pale fingers strangling the wheel, Danica kept working out one of her problems. The title of "Danica's Main Problem" depended entirely upon who you asked.

If you asked the mechanic at the Fast Lube in Seligman, Arizona, her main problem was "Her Car's Fan Belt." The PT Cruiser she'd acquired from a friend of her step-father was said to have no issues. This held true for most of her journey until middle Arizona, at which time growls and smoke farted from under the Cruiser's hood. The Fast Lube tow-truck found her on the side of the road, then found a way to dig into the money she'd squirreled away that Christmas.

If you asked her roommate Gabby, then Danica's main problem was "Time Management." Gabby called Danica on New Year's Day, asking for her résumé. She called back the next day telling her she'd lined up work for her styling hair for headshots. Work was contingent on Danica getting into town by that evening. Danica had pledged to be back in time, but her car troubles were putting that punctuality to the test.

If you asked Andrew Luman, his step-daughter's main problem was "Leaving Illinois So Soon." Her LA doctor had ordered her to rest, and she'd done so by chewing on the walls and scanning TV channels for something tolerable. Andrew cared for Danica and promised to support her no matter what. He didn't throw a fit when she told him at Christmas that she wanted to return to Los Angeles. Andrew didn't have to throw fits for his disappointment to register.

If you asked some anonymous internet gargoyle, her main problem was "Nosing In Where She Didn't Belong." A month ago, her manager Carla had forwarded a link to a blog called ForWhatItsWorth. Its headline read: "AMATEUR DETECTIVE ACTUALLY CUTS HAIR." The blogger gave disparate details from the prior fall's events, mentioning the death of Drake III, a little bit about his family and so on. It mainly focused on how little detective training Danica had, and how lucky she had been to solve the case *and* survive. The ratio of praise to criticism went 1:5, including passages such as: "It's not every day a hairstylist solves a major crime, nor should it be."

If you asked her lungs, her main problem was "Her Smoking Habit." True, she'd given it up years ago, but her lungs had bitter memories.

But if you asked Danica herself what her main problem was — and to be certain, she was asking this very question as she drifted into the passing lane — it was "White Stuff on the Bottom of a Pipe."

While Danica was paying, she'd caught a glimpse of the woman in the waiting room. The mechanic was showing her a part from her busted car: a pipe-shaped object, dirty and greasy. Running along one end of the pipe, in a kind of misshapen triangle, was a collection of white stuff. Danica knew nothing about cars (and judging by the confused expression on the other woman in the Fast Lube, neither did she) and knew less about what discoloration to metal might mean. Yet the white stuff owned her attention.

A nagging voice interrupted her thoughts, returning her focus to the highway. The voice let her know that if she asked Officer Freddie Ford what her main problem was, he might agree with the blogger troll guy. Freddie had always been careful to show his concern in such a way as to not appear patronizing or creepy. He was, to date, the only police officer she truly trusted, yet he did not endorse her recent foray into the do-gooder lifestyle of solving murders. Plus he had a nice smile.

And they were just friends, added Danica's more considerate voice. Just friends. That was all.

If they were friends — *just* friends — then why hadn't she told him she was coming back to LA?

Because friends who were 'just friends' didn't share every intimate detail about their lives, Nagging Voice. Sometimes 'just friends' floated in and out of each other's orbits. Her return to LA qualified as nice-to-know information, not need-to-know. The fact that she hadn't talked to Freddie since just after exiting the hospital last fall was further evidence of this just-friends status.

Many of these problems had coalesced during Danica's foray into the solving of mysteries. One mystery, actually. One case. A murder case, though. One which had almost gotten her killed, too. Enduring and surviving that trial had illuminated a deep-down spot within her. The part of her that paid attention to weird, out-of-place things. She'd always considered herself an observant person. But her last case — sure, her *only* case — had permanently activated that trait. It mutated odd events and danger into puzzles to solve. The trait had made her antsy in Illinois, forcing her to seek more excitement elsewhere. She couldn't deny the fact that, aside from the near-death parts, and the lingering-pain-in-her-wrist-after-being-attacked part, the idea of solving mysteries had become kind of, sort of, almost... fun.

Hence, the fixation on the white stuff.

The woman at the garage with the pipe problems drove a Ford Explorer with Arizona plates. She must have been from around Seligman, but not such a local that she knew a better place for service. She probably drove on these same highways as the 40-West, wide open and bone dry.

Danica checked her clock to refocus herself. If she pushed a little, she'd make it with plenty of time for Gabby's gig. The road was all hers, with mountains lining the distance.

Mountains without snowy peaks.

That white stuff wasn't snow. It would have melted. But it seemed so familiar and winter-like.

'Stay out of it,' said the Nagging Voice.

'You should just try to relax,' added an Andrew-like voice.

She passed the spot on the road where her car had crapped out, where the Fast Lube tow truck had just so happened to have found her.

No snow around there, either. Just dust and dirt.

Before the nagging voices could even start again, Danica instructed them to shut up, pulled off at the next exit, turned around and headed back east.

She rolled into the lot and stopped short of the garage. The Explorer with Arizona plates was still elevated as one of the garage's lackeys gave it a go with a wrench.

Danica gave a quick look to the side of her own car, kicked her imitation Docs at the grey discoloration lining the wheel well. She zipped up her hoodie and beelined to the waiting area.

The woman hadn't moved and had no company around her. She was white, with opossum-colored hair coifed into a helmet. On the floor next to her Reeboks was the pipe with the white junk stuck to the end.

Danica's fingers twitched as she stared at that hair. She hadn't thought out a way to convince this uptight woman how to allow her to touch her head. It would have answered so many questions, avoided so much awkward conversation.

Looking at the woman clutching her purse to her lap like she was riding the New York subway at two AM, Danica gave up on reading her mind and blurted out, "Exhaust issue?"

The uptight woman nearly jumped out of her mom jeans. "I'm sorry. I don't know what you mean... are you... are you talking to me?"

Granted, it hadn't been Danica's best opening line. But the look on the woman's face showed something close to fear. Rather than traumatizing her further, Danica left the woman and headed for the garage, set on doing some investigating on her own.

'Investigating.' The thought felt less foreign. Half a year ago, the notion of doing some sleuthing would have felt like it belonged to someone else and she'd borrowed it for the night. But there, in the Fast Lube with justice at her side, she sensed a kind of rightness.

Behind the desk was the man who had talked to her. His name tag said "Hoss," leading Danica to assume he either had a sense of humor or was the type of person she should not be messing with.

"Help you?" said the presumably-named Hoss. "Again."

"Yeah, I was in here a little while ago and... I got down the road a bit and heard another noise. Could you check one more time? Just to make sure nothing's loose?"

The Man Presumably Named Hoss barely contained his enthusiasm at this request, a thin sigh slipping through his fat lips. He pulled up from the desk and slid his ample stomach through the gap, his coveralls remaining mercifully intact.

They walked to the PT Cruiser and he knelt next to the front grill.

"I think it came over here," said Danica, pointing under the driver-side door.

"Well, you had a fan problem earlier. That's near the front."

"Then what if I heard something here? It was kind of a

whap." She watched the idea dance through his eyes, another opportunity at performing repairs.

Hoss slid over to the door and leaned down to take a look.

The hair on the top of his head was all but gone, but he'd left the sides thicker than an untended garden. As Danica squatted next to him, she reached out her fingers and touched his hair, glancing his scalp. She closed her eyes and hoped that if he felt anything touching him, that he'd assume it was just his collar sliding up.

That familiar whoosh swept beneath her mind, drawing Danica into the darkness. Lights danced as she connected to Hoss' thoughts. She saw the dark grey undercarriage of a car. It didn't seem like her Cruiser — this one seemed cleaner. More uptight. The view slid toward one end, the rear, to the exhaust.

A swarthy hand reached out and pulled at the pipe, dark grey with no discoloration. With a little help from a hammer, the hand pulled the pipe free.

Satisfied, Danica pulled her hand back and joined the real world, then joined Hoss in his inspection of her car. She scraped her finger along the wheel well.

"Lots of this white crap on here, huh?"

"I'm not finding anything loose," said Hoss. "Better get it on the lift again just to be safe."

"I said," Danica repeated, sure to land this killer blow, "there's a lot of this white crap on my car."

Hoss shrugged.

"Know what it is?"

The man looked again. "That there? That's road salt."

"Yes!" Her enthusiasm peaked. Four months of Illinois weather mixed with four months of Illinois boredom had finally paid off. Icy evenings followed by morning visits from snow plows who spread salt everywhere. Andrew never stopped griping about it; the stuff stuck to cars.

"Road salt's not something you see in, y'know, Arizona."

Hoss pulled his head out from beneath the car long enough to stare at Danica and say, "Wha?"

"You swapped my part for hers," said Danica. "You took my exhaust part — obviously older — and showed it to that woman in there, told her it was hers and it was worn out, so you'd have to do the work."

The squinting continued, as Hoss scratched the back of his head.

"You're scamming that woman. You probably did it with me, too. What, do you set up some kind of trap on the road so people have 'car trouble,' then you just *happen* to stop by with a tow truck 'cause you just *happen* to know a place that will do the work?"

Hoss stammered something else, but Danica took the win. Charged with righteous confidence, she rushed back to the waiting area.

"Excuse me, ma'am. You are being robbed."

"Oh, god," said the woman. "What... what did you do? How did you... what did you do?"

Obviously, this woman had been stunned stupid by Danica's incredible discovery and investigation skills.

"No, not by me," said Danica. "By these guys. The garage guys are scamming you." She grabbed the pipe and ignored the woman's recoil. "See this? It's salt corrosion. It happens when cities throw salt on the streets to get rid of the ice. But there isn't any ice here, or where you live, is there? 'Cause you live in Arizona."

"I... I don't understand..." The woman pulled out her phone.

"Call the police right now. We should get our money back."

The woman talked to her phone, cupping her mouth.

"Hello. There's a woman at the Fast Lube who is harassing me.

Danica ran the woman's words back again. Clearly, the woman had lost control of her faculties. Like a stroke victim, this woman — in her excitement at seeing Danica in action — had mispronounced 'heroic.'

She stepped closer. "Ma'am, please. He scammed us. Both of us."

"Shaved head and a red hoodie," continued the woman to the phone. "About five-eight. White. Early thirties and big black boots."

While Danica litigated being mistaken for 'early thirties,' she reiterated their position. "Ma'am... miss... I'm telling you. They're ripping you off. I'm on your side—"

"How do you know?" said the woman, venom behind her voice. "We're in the middle of nowhere and you're just going to... you open your big mouth and... how do you know?"

That part, Danica had not fully worked out. She had the salt corrosion, sure, but as far as seeing the act, she'd seen it by using a method which Danica normally kept secret from the world.

Hoss charged into the waiting room, huffing and puffing from the fifteen-foot marathon.

"What's going on?" he said between gasps.

"It's fine. This woman is... I'm calling the police," said the woman.

"Good," said Hoss. "I think she touched my head back there."

And just like that, the 2-against-1 teams had set. Danica made an excuse, backed to the door and rushed back to her PT Cruiser.

Heavy traffic met her at the edge of LA, delaying her arrival even more. As she rolled into the parking space for Island Estates, she clung to the hope that she would still make it in time. That hope expired when she opened the apartment door to the darkened apartment. Then the failure set in. Gabby hadn't waited; she couldn't have. Danica had screwed up the whole affair.

As she brushed her teeth for bed, Danica thought back to that poor, uptight Arizona woman and how she'd rejected her free help. While making up her bed sheets, she remembered back to Hoss' face. The cruel stupidity hanging out and open for all to see, so dumb he didn't even realize he'd been caught. He got away with it just because he got away with it. The cops were even called, but on Danica, all for sticking her neck out for another person — for a stranger.

Her pillow smelled like her car and her bedding felt lumpy. An itch grew in the back of her mind. She'd had it since Illinois; she thought it was for more detective work, and being honest with herself, it was. But as the failures piled on mistakes, Danica made a promise to herself:

"No more drama. Keep your head down, help your friends, that's it. No more snooping, no more drama."

She had enough problems already without searching for more.

CHAPTER TWO

THURSDAY, JANUARY 15, 2009. 9:00AM. ISLAND Estates Apartments, #213.

In the light of day, the apartment appeared suspiciously clean. Plopped onto Hazeltine and Oxnard, the busy street provided a coat of dust atop everything Gabby and Danica owned. But after half a night's sleep following a full day of driving, the place was practically spotless.

Danica knew Gabby had been busy working, auditioning and all the other-ing's around Hollywood, so maintaining the war on dust couldn't have been easy. Yet the results of that war were clear, as were the bookshelves and chairs.

As Danica stumbled out from her old bedroom, she saw her roommate hard at work in the kitchen, her blonde hair in a sloppy knot, an actual dust rag in her hand. Some things had changed since the fall.

"How was the shoot?"

Gabby continued cleaning and it didn't take a secret psychic to feel the tension in her pause.

As she pulled the old toaster from the wall and wiped at the crumbs, Gabby finally found her words. "These opportunities are usually so, like, few and far between."

"I know."

"No. You don't know. *I* know." She ran a rag-covered finger over the edge of the stove, reminding Danica that Gabby had interesting manifestations for her stress. Sometimes she made up stories to set her mind at ease. Other times she cleaned. Judging by the cleanliness before them, things had been stressful for a while.

"I appreciate it, Gab. Really. Maybe it's for the best. I'm not much of a fan of movie sets anyway."

This stopped her. "First of all, you're in the wrong town for that kind of talk. And second, these aren't movies. They're internet shoots."

"OK. So if another one comes along—"

"You blow one, there's a chance you blow them all. These people talk. They talk about you and blowing them off and you're done. Maybe me, too."

Danica offered no response. The trip back to LA had delivered serious blows to her finances and the sting of Gabby's words hurt all the way down to her empty wallet.

Gabby stopped torturing the sink. "Sorry. I'm stressed. I'm glad you're back, but we're gonna need some cash from somewhere and soon. I can barely keep myself going and—"

"Yes. And I should be chipping in. I will be. Soon."

"The salon, you mean?"

"Yeah. I'm gonna go back over there soon, get back on the schedule and... you'll see."

"...OK."

"And, seriously, if you see anything else for me, I'd appreciate it."

"Sure, sure." Gabby nodded to her rag. "'Cause you love moonlighting."

"Hey." Danica took offense for the half-second her brain needed to realize that this statement was correct. Despite encouragement from Carla, Gabby and the world at large, the idea of hopping from place to place, wishing each job would last a little longer than promised but knowing they never would, Danica had never cottoned to the idea. Wherever she picked it up — from her step-father, from her midwest upbringing, or from the American Capitalist Dream as portrayed in every movie ever — the ideals of having a steady paycheck from one job warmed her up faster than hot cocoa.

The whole genre of gig hopping included private detective work. Very much so. With a thin CV containing all of one case solved, opportunities for pay-to-play detective work remained a fiction. Somehow, her experience the previous fall had shown her just enough of that lifestyle to understand how little earning power it could offer, even for someone possessing her unique abilities.

"I'll sweep," she said, not that the floor needed it. Judging by the hospital-corners look of the tiles, maybe things were even rougher than Gabby had said. Danica thanked the universe for a stomach capable of running on lean peanut butter sandwiches.

Three floor-swept rooms later, Danica's phone received a text. It read only: "YOU'RE HERE YAAAAAAY!"

Gabby saw Danica's smile. "That Carla?"

"You know it." She wrote a quick response, then said, "You go there while I was gone?"

"Yeah sure."

Gabby's answer was very brief. Short. Almost curt.

Carla's next text came with an invitation to come just after opening.

"You going over there?" said Gabby.

"At opening."

"OK." Again, curt. Gabby handed over the keys. "Alone? You want me to... I mean, you gonna be OK?"

Danica giggled a little. "Yeah. Why?"

"I mean... nothing. You'll be fine." Not suspicious at all.

"We OK, Gab? I really am sorry."

Gabby looked up from her tile scrubbing and smiled. "Uh-huh."

Danica headed for the garage, still working over their exchange in her head. Four minutes later, when her Cruiser let out the distinct call of in-operation, she returned to face her roommate.

"Can I borrow your car?"

"Yeah sure," said Gabby. Still short. And almost curt.

<hr>

Danica parked Gabby's Prius in a nice spot, one where she could keep an eye on it. Not that it was in jeopardy of being hit, touched, or even breathed on by another person; the entire lot was devoid of customer cars. A tear in the awning sagged the corner, reducing the establishment's name to "EARL'S WORLD OF CU___." Danica focused on the familiar tan Corolla in the far corner, the one Carla had sworn would outlive her.

Two steps from the door, Carla burst through the entrance carrying a large box. It slipped a little when she yelled, after which she quickly gave up, put the box down and gave Danica a grizzly bear hug. It lasted longer than would be conventionally polite and Danica appreciated every second. Carla's blue plastic frames creaked in Danica's ear. She waited as a truck barreled down Sepulveda before speaking complete words.

"Oh my gawd, it's good to see you! How's your arm? Did

you eat? Was traffic bad? Your step-dad OK? Dear lord, seeing you feels so great."

Danica tried to return the enthusiasm, though her hug was no match against Carla's. The traffic, smog and general urban cluster during her drive had served as her unofficial return-to-city greeting, but being back in Carla's presence meant she had returned home.

After a few more hugs, the grip released and they entered the salon.

The same smells of dry shampoo and clipper oil remained. The low volume adult-contempo lite rock fit perfectly. Mixed with Carla's Liz Claiborne perfume, all the right memories triggered.

Yet the calm reminders distressed her. Something was either different and she couldn't explain it, or it was all so undifferent as to imply no time had passed.

"Gene in today?"

"Tonight," said Carla. "He's dialed karaoke way back. You'd barely recognize him. I haven't seen sequin one since Christmas. True, that's only a few days ago, but still... for him, that's impressive."

Gene and Danica enjoyed a relationship which bounced between playfully adversarial and just-shy-of-openly hostile. Typical of children vying for their mother's approval. And work hours. Gene's de-sequin-ing likely came from a recommitment to the salon, snatching up the available chair time during Danica's vacancy.

This worry gave way to the nagging sense of displacement. That calmness again. The sinks sparkled, the register sat in the same location. She searched and searched, milling about like a high school graduate pretending to be interested in her old school, looking for some out of place thing.

The lack of customers may have been a culprit. The

empty parking lot mixed with the just-as-empty salon, whose appointment log held all of one name.

"Been slow?"

"Pfft. Slow ain't the word. I had to start selling more product and side crap just to make ends meet and they don't hardly meet at all." Carla shuffled her feet. "I read that blog."

"Yeah, that's just..." She recounted the snotty way it mentioned her 'complicated' relationship with the police along with how stubborn she could be. How, despite performing a public service and uncovering a murderer, she remained an amateur. The words 'cosplay' had been used.

"Hey, don't worry about that troll internet person," said Carla. "I don't know how these people find these things out, or why they care or what, but it's none of your concern."

As Danica said she'd try not to worry, Carla moved to the side wall, to a plastic shelf against the supply closet door. A collection of odd looking bottles lined the two top shelves. At closer look, Danica read the labels: Olive Oil Spray-All-Day and Butter-Tonight. Below them were large boxes, each a different cooking appliance. Every item had the same smiling spatula logo under the words 'HAPPY SPATT.' A couple had fallen to the floor and Carla huffed as she reset them.

There. *These* were the new elements in Earl's World of Curls.

"That stuff's, like, Amway things?"

"Happy Spatty, yeah. The cooking supply sales and marketing, um...." Carla's shoulders sagged under her yellow sweater. "We're supposed to say 'opportunity,' but I can't do it yet without barfing. But, hey: gotta do what you gotta do."

"Thing's will pick up again. Winter's usually slow, right? We're just coming out of the holidays now and..." Danica's denials ran out of gas.

"Even if it did, I'm not sure I could ever satisfy Lorena."

Danica couldn't be sure, but she thought she saw Carla

mumble a curse at the wall. On the other side of the wall was Madame Lorena's Psychic Readings and Tarot Enterprise, run by none other than Carla's landlord, Lorena Baronette. At least twice a month, Lorena plagued the renters of the Sepulveda strip mall: one time for rent checks, the second time (Danica believed) just to mess with people. Everything with Lorena was transactional; how to get money, find money, trick her customers out of their money. Carla claimed to have never met a bigger capitalist in her life. Any time Lorena stood outside Earl's World of Curls, she swore the old woman was measuring the place to sell, envisioning ways to entice a lucrative tanning salon into its spot.

Instinctively, Danica checked the parking lot.

"She's not here," said Carla. "Damn miracle, too."

"Lorena keeps odd hours. How's she manage to make any money?"

"Don't know, but it's all she cares about, so she must make something. Landlord, psychic and opportunist — she's got it all." Carla sighed, then added, "She's raising the rent."

"Oh?" Danica's optimism held out hope for this information to not be as bad as it sounded.

As if she could tell what Danica's optimism was doing, Carla added, "And it's bad."

On came the desperation, which ran through Danica's mind. It grasped at any and all straws it could reach.

"Maybe she could cut you a break. With the economy being what it is and..." Recent blurbs of what could liberally be referred to as news joined with that desperation to form a kind of super desperation, taking the form of random fact-like sounds shaped into sentences. Instead, Danica trailed off. Having never used the phrase 'the economy being what it is' in her entire life, she had no way to follow through.

Carla shook her head. "We talked a couple times about it. Says her taxes and prices are too much. Same as everyone, but she won't hear that. She even blames Obama already! Guy hasn't even been sworn in yet and she's laying it all on his lap."

Danica checked the parking lot again, but with a different intent. She wanted to corner Lorena, slug her and persuade her to ease off the rent hike. Society generally frowned on younger people striking older women, but if society got to know Lorena, it would understand.

"That Happy Spatula bastard." Carla swiped toward the shelf. "He isn't exactly flying off the shelves, lemme tell ya'."

"We could advertise."

"With what money? And what would we say? Come to 'World of Cuu's?' We can't even fix the sign!"

"Reach out to local places? Schools or parks maybe? To get some families through here."

"All the energy we'd spend doing events and stuff, it'd take us away from actually doing the work here."

Danica's burgeoning tight-wad habits sent her eyes darting around the salon. Perhaps Craigslist had a booming marketplace for used shears.

Finding nothing, she continued. "Gabby keeps pushing internet film stuff on me."

"That's great."

"Well, one of them. I haven't done any yet. I was hoping..."

She sunk while standing. Danica regretted it as soon as it happened, but couldn't help herself. Guilt consumed her and Carla could tell. She put her arm around her shoulders.

"I know. I want you back here, too. But I can't do it yet. So take the work when you can get it."

"Really? Anywhere I can get it?"

"Anywhere but that. Your step-papa wouldn't be OK with more... you know...."

To say Carla disapproved of Danica's detective work would be an understatement. Only Freddie matched her level of distaste for the dangerous position Danica put herself in a few months ago. They both cared a lot. Or seemed to. Or used to. Because they were friends.

"I get it," said Danica.

"Just keep your eyes open and you'll be fine — We'll be fine."

She looked into her sort-of-former manager's eyes, then away before she started crying. Her mission of getting back on the schedule and avoiding drama had already failed so spectacularly that the one person she most wanted to help ended up taking care of *her*.

Danica sucked at this.

CHAPTER THREE

THURSDAY, JANUARY 15, 2009. 11:45AM. EARL'S
World of Curls.

Danica's manager (TBD) loaded some unsold kitchenware into her trunk. Carla had mentioned something about getting to trade some of it in for newer stuff, but her tone held no confidence. More like acceptance, like a work horse understanding it would never run the Preakness.

Since Danica was an available body who still had her key and nothing better to do, she offered to watch the salon. Alone in Earl's for the first time in a season, the first time since solving Drake Alberts III's murder, tickled her skin. A blood vessel blurped in her right hand and rose up her arm as Danica moved to the sink. One of the scenes of one of the crimes.

Gene had removed her old toolkit from the mirror area, replacing it with his plastic purple Kaboodle. The counter sparkled with alien cleanliness. Two crisp aprons hung from the hooks — hooks she didn't remember existing last August.

The worst day of her adult life had been scrubbed away. Or got supplanted. Or just plain forgotten.

The chair was the same though. She touched the leather carefully, afraid to discover that she had a telepathic connection with furniture involved in a traumatic event. Though her breath caught for a moment, no such supernatural occurrence occurred. She sat and reality sat next to her.

She'd been naive, even for her. Expecting to jump right back into work after being away for months? Maybe she was naive about returning to LA at all.

The morning ticked by, customerless. No money came in, only went out. After a good forty minutes of lonely self-pity and without a better plan to follow, Danica turned off the hallway and bathroom lights. At this point, every buck counted.

She took a big gulp of pride and swallowed it whole. She could act all bad when she had money, or at least had options. But without money or those options....

Phone in hand, she texted Gabby. "I'm sorry. I'm in. For real this time. Won't be late again."

In record time (even for Gabby, an Olympic-level text responder) a message returned: "Will keep eyes open."

Done. Good. It would be good. She could make a little cash and spare Carla the trouble of babysitting her.

A few minutes later, Gabby wrote again. "You can do reality, rite?"

"That's what I do already."

"Reality TV. Like makeup and hair for documentary type stuff."

Danica paused, considering the question. She could do hair, obviously, and perform standard makeup maneuvers. However she'd never done any honest-to-god work in the realm of reality television. She'd barely watched it. She understood enough about makeup to know there had to be subtle differences in application for the variety of performances being filmed (Stage makeup wasn't good for film, film makeup was different from TV, TV wasn't right for dates, all that), but that meant she only knew she didn't know anything.

So she wrote, "Totally."

"Perf," said Gabby. "BRB."

More time slid out of the day. Fifteen minutes became twenty, then thirty, all in the empty Earl's. She'd just started a daydream about styling a drag queen for a global race show when a car parked in the lot. A gray Escalade, clean and new looking. She stood, hopeful this was a walk-in with deep pockets and friends. When the driver did not emerge, she sat back down and resumed her musing.

She weighed how terrible her punishment might be for lying about her reality TV qualifications. Worst she could imagine: they wouldn't hire her again. Which meant she'd be right back where she was, but with a day's pay.

After a minute, a man exited the Escalade. He slipped into shadow while heading to a neighboring door, so Danica could not get a good look at him. He quickly disappeared from sight, but then returned just as quickly, appearing in the window of Earl's. His face at last in full sight, the man's gaze went straight through the glass pane and caught Danica's.

It should be well-noted that Danica was not the type of person to go gaga over anything, let alone anybody. She had gone weak-kneed for a few celebrities here and there (her middle-school commitment to the films of Christian Slater bordered on alarming), but nothing reached beyond her control. She had seen clips from "Ed Sullivan" where girls pulled their eyeballs out over the mere sight of Elvis or the Beatles and never understood it. Sure, she could capably recognize beauty and attractiveness, but that recognition never manifested into a physiological reaction.

That was until seeing the driver of the Escalade. His looks

were so classically "good" that Danica's brain system lagged in comprehending the rest of his form. The chiseled chin, sparkling dark eyes and gentle-yet-commanding grin sent beams across the lot, through the door window and straight into Danica's soul. She regarded the face before her with amazement, the kind early humans must have had the first time they saw the Grand Canyon. The man before her was a marvel.

A marvel that walked through Earl's front door.

"Hey there." His voice was neither high nor deep, rather dripping off his lips like chocolate syrup. His smile somehow grew wider when he looked at her.

A second of frozen non-responsiveness passed before Danica managed to speak. "Can I?" She thought she'd added 'help you,' but couldn't be certain of anything any more.

"Can I ask you something?" He leaned against the door frame. Lucky frame.

She might have uttered some form of an answer, anything between "Certainly, sir" and "Muh-m'buhhn."

"Do you know Madame Lorena?"

Full world collapse. Nothing made sense. Why would this apparition of human perfection know of Lorena's existence, let alone sully his alabaster teeth by uttering her name? The grotesquely gorgeous man even pointed toward the neighboring business, toward Madame Lorena's parlor of tarot cards and light chicanery. As if such a motion would help anything to make more (or any) sense.

He moved away from the door and entered the full light of the salon. Once under the unforgiving fluorescents, Danica scientifically confirmed his looks were not a trick of favorable exterior light or window refraction.

"Yes," she said, managing not to drool on herself.

The Grand-Canyon Man nodded. "It's my first time meeting with her. Supposed to be right now, but her place doesn't look open. Lights are off, too." The noontime sun cast a golden glow around the man's head. Somehow this dude knew how to find his light in a strip mall hair salon. That or the light just naturally found him. At this point, anything seemed possible.

With a kind of strength she didn't know she possessed, Danica looked beyond the man's incredible nose and magnificent cheeks to deliver a coherent sentence.

"If I see her, I'll let you know. If you want to leave your number."

Not half bad compared to the prior two minutes.

"Nah, that's okay. I'll just keep waiting. Thanks." He waved and turned away, confirming Danica's suspicions about his backside.

He reached his car and disappeared from her sight, thereby breaking the spell. Her head ached at the mere memory of his looks. His features appeared almost touched up, but in real life! It fractured Danica's brain. His eyes lingered the longest; they'd appeared disappointed at the delayed appointment, but worried as well. Worried about what, Danica could not venture to guess. Good looking people had problems, she supposed. Good-looking problems. Something was distracting this guy.

Her phone buzzed with a Gabby text.

"Tonight," it said.

Danica re-read the preceding exchange before responding, "Tonight like you found a job for tonight? As in today at night?"

"Yep. 9."

"That was fast."

"Online content moves quick. No costumes or blood or fx or anything. You heard of Sofi Starr?"

She had not, but wrote, "Yep."

"Great. Hair n make-up. You in?"

The phone grew heavy, waiting for an answer. Danica typed, "In," and sent it.

Plan, settled. Pride, swallowed. Keep surviving. Keep eating. No drama.

Danica told herself these things as she put her phone away and resigned. She couldn't expect Carla to do everything for her when she had her own stuff to sort out. Gabby sent a follow-up about prep related to some other Sofi Starr videos. The links were all videos with "Sofi Tries" as their first words in the titles. Danica added them to her mental to-do list and took one more glance at the Escalade in the lot. Its tinted windows shielded the world from the radiance in the driver's seat.

She turned from the door to the salon stations just in time to meet eyes with a 60-year-old woman and scream.

The woman wore a thin scarf, a thinner smile and a Member's Only jacket over a flowing dress. She stood beside the reception desk, looked to be about the same height as Carla, but was definitely *not* Carla. This woman had tanner skin, with deep creases in her cheeks. Her hands were out and open, as if to signal 'I'm not here to kill you.' Danica remained unconvinced.

"Easy, dear," said the woman. She wiggled her right hand. A set of keys hung from the forefinger and her bony wrist cracked when she gave them a jingle.

"I entered through the back. Didn't think anyone was here."

Danica's breath finally exhaled as she stared at Madame Lorena Baronette in the flesh.

They'd first met years earlier, when Danica became a full-timer at Earl's. Lorena would often stop by to pick up the rent check, but more often to complain about things like trash not being handled properly. Sometimes she popped over between palm readings, often through the back door. Lorena owned the building and acted like it, much to her renters' chagrin. After a few of these uninvited visits, Danica had made a habit of keeping some distance between herself and the would-be mystic.

Danica held the door handle for support and glanced through the window. "You've got a client waiting for you."

Lorena joined her at the door and peered through the window. "Indeed I do. You've seen the boy, I trust?"

Her voice hissed when she spoke, words sliding through her teeth, transforming into smoke. "How could you miss him? He is dreamy, but I understand he has little cooking in the kitchen, if you follow my meaning." She leaned in for affect: "I hear he's got money."

This last detail explained so much to Danica. "Yeah, well, he's waiting and you're late."

Lorena squinted at Danica's scalp. "You're Carla's girl, aren't you? The one with the trouble last year."

A prickle zapped through Danica's forearm. "I've been out of town for a few months."

"Out of town." Lorena dragged the words through her incisors. Danica sensed no mockery in this mimicry; it was more akin to how a hypnotist might lull victims to sleep by stretching every syllable into a purr. Danica blinked and reminded herself to stay alert and keep her hand on her wallet.

Lorena's scrutiny released Danica. "I apologize for my intrusion. I arrived after my client. And since I prefer to maintain an air of mystery and magic about my person, such tardiness would dilute that aura."

Danica awaited more explanation.

It finally arrived, with less magical affectation. "I did not want to drive up in my Kia and unlock the door like a common troll."

"So you sneak into the salon? You can't do your seance stuff in here."

"And so I shall not," said Lorena, regaining her performance. "Our two businesses share a wall, allowing me to bridge the gap from this business to my own, maintaining my mystic atmosphere."

Lorena delivered the speech with such authority that it took a moment for Danica to realize she still couldn't put it together. "Come again?"

"I'm sneaking into my place so he doesn't see. My back door's jammed up, so I get in through here." Her formality dropped again, loosening her accent. The faintest regionality hung on Lorena's words — her 'into' very nearly become 'inta.'

With a slight bow and without further elucidation, Lorena glided to the rear of the salon, toward the Happy Spatula products area. She nudged the shelf to the side with unpredictable strength, allowing full berth of the closet door.

Another key unsheathed from her robes, Lorena unlocked and opened the closet with ease. The interior was just as Danica remembered: dirty, junky and a little spooky. A dusty floor held old paint cans, long-forgotten sweaters and some old hairspray bottles. There was stepladder that looked way below code.

Lorena stepped inside the closet and gandered at the ceiling. She wiggled the ladder a bit, hitched up her skirt, stepped onto the first rung and reached up. Her bony fingers grabbed a rope attached to the ceiling tile. Under her weight, a trap door opened and an attic ladder telescoped all the way to the floor.

The ladder invited Lorena up and, after pocketing her keys, she accepted the invitation, ascending rapidly through the hole in the ceiling.

"Close that door for me?" Lorena's voice came from the

hole in the closet ceiling. Danica had moved closer to the closet, as if in a trance. Witnessing a Grand Canyon man with her own eyes was one thing. Lorena's cat-burglar skills sent her head spinning.

Just as the last swath of silky scarf billowed up through the hole, Lorena popped her head back down, spry as ever.

"It was that Alberts family murder, was it not? The one last summer? The case you solved, I mean?"

More head spinning. "I was... I helped, yeah."

"And," said Lorena, again studying Danica's scalp, "you cut hair as well."

"Sometimes. Well, not 'as well.' I do other things... I'm trying to. Cut hair again, I mean."

Lorena nodded, so Danica nodded back, unsure of the proper response to such an inquisition from a woman hanging through a hole in the closet ceiling.

"I'm gonna have to tell Carla about this," said Danica.

"About what?"

"You sneaking around our— her place. It's not right, Lorena."

The woman held up her ringed pointer finger. "Please. *Madame* Lorena."

With that, she vanished into the darkness.

A minute later, Danica heard Lorena's door swing open outside. The older woman's voice announced her arrival with all the glee of someone who could never be accused of abusing her authority.

CHAPTER FOUR

Thursday, January 15, 2009. 8:51PM. Van Nuys Streets

"What a freakin' weirdo!"

Gabby took side streets through the North Valley, cutting across lanes and driving at speeds many would consider dangerous. The added distraction of hearing Danica's account of the morning at Earl's did not help her driving safety improve.

"You tell Carla?"

"Of course." Danica clutched the door handle, allowing her go bag to slide around her lap. "She kinda knew already, but she was still mad. I think that's part of why she doesn't like Lorena."

"You mean *Madame* Lorena." Gabby took a right, her signal blinking all of two times. "She married?"

"Lorena? I heard she was, once. She's got enough rings to be married to an entire hockey team."

Gabby honked at a stopped pickup truck. The go bag

rattled at the sudden deceleration and Danica's stomach rattled along with it.

A lo-fi version of a pop song emerged from Gabby's phone.

"I'll get it for you," said Danica, grabbing the phone before Gabby could think about it, hoping for better on-road safety practices. No name appeared on the caller ID.

"Oh, man. It's only 8:50-something."

"Do you know who this is?"

Gabby snatched the phone back and answered. "Hi... so close... my map thing says I'm only, like, two turns away."

From the dashboard, Gabby's Garmin shouted, "AT. THE. NEXT. STREET. TURN. RIGHT." Gabby covered the mouthpiece.

"I gotta concentrate. Sorry, Tori."

When she hung up, Danica took the phone back.

"That was our production manager, Tori. Your boss for the night. My agent mentioned it had some quirks. I mean, every set's got quirks, but from what she said, this one might have some doozies."

"Could you elaborate on 'doozies?'"

"The whole Sofi Starr thing is a real family affair kind of deal. You saw that in those videos, right?"

"R-right," lied Danica.

"Well, Tori Stornelli is not just the production manager. She's Sofi's sister and she's strict to the point of being paranoid. Sticks tight to schedules. She's her sister's manager, too. Career manager. Runs the shoots, her YouTube pages, socials, everything."

"Was she mad? On the phone?"

"It's hard to say," said Gabby. "She has an accent. She's either Eastern European or furious. Six of one, I think. The thing is that she runs a tight ship and that means — and I'm just gossiping here, it's all stuff I heard from the agent — that she micro-manages the whole deal. Like, micro-micro-manages. Like, I heard that a couple months ago, they fired an entire crew. Just because a couple of them were slacking off. I mean, the *whole* crew, dude."

"So I'm hearing this might not last long," said Danica.

"Don't get your hopes up too high, Miss I-Don't-Do-Side-Hustles. You'll be fine. Work isn't easy. It's work." Gabby took another turn and kept talking. "Weird she knows about you and that thing last year."

"Who knows?"

"Lorena. Do you think she has the place bugged? You think she knows about... y'know...?" Gabby twiddled her fingers, the universal sign for 'psychic powers.' Being in the tiny club of people who knew about Danica's ability to read minds, Gabby was naturally protective of club membership.

"I doubt it. If she did, she would've asked me to perform for her. Make some cash off it somehow. The Alberts stuff wasn't really a secret. She's the landlord. She had to hear something."

"I dunno. She *is* psychic."

"I find that offensive," said Danica, half meaning it. "Lorena *plays* psychic. She is a scam artist who pretends to be psychic. She tricks people, tells them what they wanna hear, looks at some playing cards and takes their money. That's it."

Apartment buildings and shopping centers surrendered to houses, which gave way to office parks, which devolved into storage areas.

"This is pretty industrial," said Danica.

"Crews can rent these places cheap. Cheaper than renting from studios. They've been doing it for years."

"So it's not a studio we're working for? I thought this was a reality show thing."

Gabby's Garmin yelled to turn off the street and into a long parking lot.

"You didn't do the research I sent you," said Gabby.

"I... yes."

Gabby sighed. "Sofi Starr does all kinds of stuff. Like skits and pranks and even stunts. Mostly she learns how to do things and then she fails at it."

"And this is popular?"

"It's the internet, Dan. I don't know how it all works."

"But how is that 'reality?'"

"It's semi-reality. Sofi's herself, but another version of herself. Even reality isn't reality."

Danica let that one sink in as she watched the parking lot path bend. Ahead of them lay a wall of green metal doors, rows and rows of them, all identical, with beige walls framing each. None showed signs of life.

At the end of the line of doors, one was open. It also had the distinction of having a stern-looking woman in an orange jacket standing in front of it. She checked her watch in a performative manner, so everyone could see she was concerned about time. Gabby slowed down and parked.

"I'm guessing that's Tori," said Danica.

"Guess so." Gabby waved. She leaned back into the car and whispered, "Let's get our stuff and move quick."

Danica did. She smiled at the woman, Tori, wanting to make a good impression.

She failed; Tori wore an expression as icy as her white blonde hair. Danica spotted expert dye work, cut short around the neck, pulled back at the ears in a fierce wedge.

"Traffic was tough." Gabby likely meant this for Tori's face, but at best it grazed the side of her shoulder. Tori had spun on her heels, turning back to her crew to shout at some twitchy peon for not doing something to her standards.

Danica chewed her lip.

Gabby grimaced. "It's money?"

They entered.

The viral video industry must have been a boon for owners of uncomplicated, available spaces. Got three walls and a door? Congrats — paint one wall green and you own a studio! Danica imagined what these places would do without fame-hungry twenty-somethings dedicated to the lease and rental game. Did the storage facility owners rent to art shows? Garage bands in need of a garage? Actual storage? The void before her offered little beyond itself.

A crew of eight young men and a couple young women middled about, hanging lights, adjusting lights and talking about where to best hang and/or adjust those lights. They were all white and most wore baggy pants. All of them carried wrenches roped to their belts. Few of them looked old enough to purchase alcohol.

"Here," said Tori, pointing to the front left corner of the room. It had a mirror, a folding table and one light, meeting the bare minimum qualifications for a make-up station. Before Danica could ask any follow-up questions, Tori had left to terrorize someone else.

Gabby dragged two folding chairs toward her. "Found these for you."

She thanked her and continued her scan of the set.

'The Set,' as it were, occupied the space surrounding the green wall opposite the entrance. The most-bearded twenty-something boy directed others to keep the light uniform. He pointed his wrench at the sections of green needing the most help. Two older boys, fresh out of film school if not grammar school, climbed ladders in response. Another arranged a scaffold to the side. They shouted things about keys and fills and pickups and other such things which, when spoken with such confidence, reminded Danica of how little she understood this side of the planet. She had hung around a few filmmaker types before, but never in their natural habitat. She couldn't imagine what it meant to "highlight the hidden tease," and doubted any of these kids would tell her.

The crew's energy picked up whenever Tori stalked nearby. Bolts got a little tighter, chatter got a little quieter, and all eyes stayed on their work. She said nothing to them. She didn't have to. Tori's shoulders hunched and she favored one leg, but these features did not lessen her intimidation vibes. If anything, the features intensified her menace.

Among the hushed crew members, one man continued to speak. He wore the same beard-and-baggy-pants look as those around him, but he also had a tool belt. Danica guessed he must have had fifteen years on every other person around him. He was pale, like he had sun allergies. His beard looked trimmed, his hair thin at the forehead. While he looked capable, his tucked-in flannel shirt revealed a slight-gut, the kind which originated less from poor diet and more from age (*and poor diet*). He wiped his sweaty brow with a wristband and made eye contact with Danica.

To her dismay, he hustled over to her.

"Hi. New here? Make-up, right?"

Danica introduced herself. The man had a pinching handshake.

"Bobby. Good to have you on the team. We're trying to make it like a family here. A working family. Guess that makes me the dad. Or maybe the grandpa. You'll fit right in. Lots of new faces, but that's just fine. No Sofi today, of course, but that's how it goes. Can't always get what you want. But you try sometimes, you get what you need, right?"

He smiled. It seemed a nervous smile. His eyes surveyed the room as he spoke.

Gabby scratched her head. "Is that a Beatles line?"

Bobby scoffed. "No! Rolling Stones."

"This is Gabby Holstrom," said Danica, moving the conversation along. "She's acting today."

Bobby shook her hand, eyes traveling all around Gabby's face, then back to the room.

"How you doing? Good to have you. Remember: no Sofi today. She might come. She might. But just to pop in. We don't need her for this. This is just some pickups and inserts. Like Second Unit stuff, but with A-level talent, right? It's filmmaking. You know? The stuff that dreams are made of."

Bobby went on, mentioning schedules and other such film jargon that Danica wasn't sure she needed to know. He acted like he was running the place. Danica struggled to imagine Tori delegating anything to anyone, let alone the guy with such jittery eyes.

Those eyes found Tori's from across the room. Tori looked down, back to her clipboard. Unless Danica had missed her guess, Tori had tried the classic look-away move to avoid being noticed.

It didn't work. Bobby jogged over to her, saying, "Tori, I wanna run something by you right quick."

Gabby rubbed her fingers. "That dude hurt my hand."

"He's..."

"Odd?"

"I was going to say 'notably older.'"

"Uh, yeah. So odd. And he keep talking about Sofi not being here. Dude, we know. And I just heard you say it, like, five times."

The conversation at the green wall continued, with Bobby jabbering away and Tori nodding along. She appeared to be humoring the man, like a tired mother listening to a kinder-gartener's rambling story from recess.

Gabby sighed. "Some people are their own ducks. Nosing in where they don't need to. Ooo! I forgot to tell you: craft services has yogurt parfaits!" With that, she was off.

Danica joined her a moment later, facing the food spread at the opposite side of the space. She helped herself to what felt like an appropriate level of abundance. If a few granola bars made it back home with her, this production would not falter. She stretched across the table to grab an apple, her sweatshirt sleeve pulling back and showing off the scar on her wrist.

Bobby's one-sided conversation with Tori provided a dull soundtrack as Danica waited for the lauded parfaits. He eventually turned away from Tori and focused on one of the light set-ups. He reached out a gloved hand and moved the light here and there, splashing the beam around the top of the green wall. Satisfied, he removed his glove and chased after his next auditory victim.

As soon as he left, one of the women in the crew pulled on her own gloves and re-set the light to its original spot.

Danica had zero experience in the business of setting up lights, but even she could tell that the young woman's set up was... she didn't want to say 'better,' but that was the most accurate way to describe it.

She reached for a set of crackers when another hand snatched them first.

"Sorry," said the snatcher without a trace of actual apology. She was white and blonde, standing on the other side of the table. Next to her was a Black woman the exact same height. They both had pony tails, were probably the same age, and they giggled to themselves about — Danica assumed — the white one saying 'Sorry' to someone so beneath their social status. If she didn't know better, Danica might have thought they were groupies, with their miniskirts and faded tees. They clacked away in their heavy heels, still giggling.

Suddenly, a clipboard appeared in Danica's face.

"Gabby's part is Veronica," said Tori. "Ambitious snowboarder. British. Competitive with Sofi." Her crisp words did lean toward Eastern Europe, verging on Schwarzenegger.

Danica accepted the clipboard, first examining the schedule:

SKI LESSONS (ser. "Sofi Tries...") - 1.15.09
7:00 - 9:00 — Load In
9:01 — 9:45 — Prep (costume, make-up, etc.)
9:46 — 9:59 — Last looks...

It went on like that, with every detail marked. She flipped the script portion — the part Tori was currently pushing. Danica nodded like it meant anything to her. "OK... uh-huh."

Tori tapped the script with her finger. "British. Competitive. Got it?"

Danica gave a firm nod then rejoined Gabby at the makeup station. "You're supposed to be British."

"'at's roigh'," said Gabby, with a dose of Cockney.

"And 'competitive with Sofi.' How's makeup reflect that?"

"Maybe something with lipstick?"

That's where Danica focused. She decided that if Gabby's character had some personal beef with Sofi, then she was the antagonist. To Danica, this meant dark lipstick.

After that, Danica focused on basic concealer.

"She likes you," said Gabby.

"Who?"

"Tori."

"What in the world gave you that idea?"

"She's only had to tell you something one time. Efficiency. It's a big thing with her."

"If that's 'likes me,' I'd hate to see 'furious at me.'"

Opting to stay on whatever good side Tori had, Danica zoned in on her work. She applied a finishing touch to

Gabby's French braid (braids felt 'competitive') and checked the mirror.

A familiar face smiled back at her reflection.

A familiar, striking face. Standing right behind her.

"Gabby," Danica said. "He's here."

"Who?"

The face moved closer and smiled with even more confidence than when they met at the Earl's parking lot. The Impossibly Handsome Man — the Grand Canyon on legs — stood right there. Right there! Near her. Again.

And he waved, appearing happy to see her. Again!

Danica sucked back the drool and waved at the mirror.

He got closer and said, "We met before, right? From Madame Lorena's?"

She turned to face him and said, "Yes." Danica couldn't remember the last time she'd legitimately giggled, but with those dark eyes pouring into her, she had a difficult time remembering much of anything.

The moment begged for someone to say something, yet Danica's speaking powers faltered. She put her hands on Gabby's, begging for help.

The man looked at her roommate and said, "Hey, Gabby."

Danica's astonishment reached a new, unexpected apex. The man a.) wasn't a dream after all, b.) appeared in Danica's life more than once, proving that lightning *could* strike the same place twice, and c.) seemed to know her roommate by name.

Gabby waved back, calm as could be, like she wasn't dumbstruck by the ridiculous specimen before her.

"Hey, Marty," said Gabby. "She's done with me if you wanna jump in."

"Sure thing."

She tore her hand from Danica's grip, rose from the chair

and offered her seat to the living monument to human perfection which had an actual human name. Marty.

He sat and introduced himself.

"My favorite Pink Lady," said Danica.

"Huh?" said Marty.

A stream of information burned through Danica's brain. It explained how the words 'My Favorite Pink Lady' were not her name, but rather referred to the Pink Ladies girl gang from *Grease*, and that while she always had loved Stockard Channing — the actor who played Rizzo — in general, there was something the character of Marty that set right with her, especially since it would be cliché for a hairstylist to favor Frenchy the beauty school drop out, and in the movie Marty was a girl, but this Marty wasn't a girl, and she was so lucky her mouth stopped working before any of these thoughts came out.

"I'm Danica Luman." The words came out as clunky as imaginable.

She looked around the room and caught Gabby watching them. When she glared at her, Gabby mouthed 'Enjoy' and practically ran away.

Danica turned to her new client — who was just a client, a job, no different than any of the other non-amazing-looking people she had been totally cool with for years and years, no big deal — and stared. Only for a millisecond, but Marty surely noticed. He was probably used to being stared at. Same way he was used to birds starting to sing as he walked through the park.

With what little professionalism she could muster, she asked him for info on his character. And managed this without stammering or blubbering.

"I'm playing myself, so it's basically this." He circled his hand around his face. "I need to be set for lights. Just make me presentable."

She laughed too hard at this casual dad joke, then stopped abruptly when she realized how loud she'd become.

Paranoia and self-doubt came next, as Danica felt the instant pressure of the job before her. Marty's face was already doing great on its own. Her work could only serve to do harm; she only had room for failure. She decided on giving the most basic of basic touch-ups by adding a whisper of powder around his taut cheekbones.

This strategy, while conservative, came with the added risk of putting her face front and center with his. As she stared at Marty (for work), she thought of her past crushes (not for work). Some were from school, which was so long ago that they were all different people now. Most were musicians and celebrities, so those people did not exist in the real world. Marty, by simply confirming his existence on the same mortal plane as her own, stood above these other infatuations. It was like seeing an alien being and not comprehending how anything so fantastic could be real. It sat in a chair. Her chair. Where she could touch it.

As her brush rose up his face, she tried to distract herself with conversation.

"Why'd you see Lorena?" It was an honest question, though perhaps too personal. Asking people about making gross errors in judgment usually didn't generate polite chatter.

"I dunno. I might go back."

"Really?"

"Maybe not. I dunno...."

Danica respected him more. She watched his eyes lower and his arms relax. Carla called these types of customers "chair snoozers," folks who wanted you to do your work and let them relax without chit chat. At least this way, Danica could delay her next verbal embarrassment.

She avoided the proverbial landmines that were his lips and moved behind him, shielding herself from his distracting face. Danica adjusted his hair, thick with loose curls at the end, when a scientific thought came to her: if this actually was an alien being, it would be beneficial — in the name of science — to find out just what made him tick. Wasting an opportunity to observe such a creature would be comparable to a sin in the science world, especially when such an opportunity had been presented to a person possessing the kind of resources Danica had.

Danica let her fingers reach out and touch Marty's scalp. She owed it to the betterment of humanity to peek inside his mind. Just a peek. For humanity.

Her eyes closed and she saw into his mind.

A woman. Young, blonde hair. White. Walking away on a long lawn. The sky ahead of her was dark, a reddish evening sky. The woman turned back. Shoulders back, hips to the side. Everything was hers for the having.

Danica released her grip, retreating from Marty's natural auburn highlights. A girlfriend. Had to be. Of course he had one, and of course she was almost as gorgeous as he was (almost). It seemed more like a dream than a memory, similar to the visions Danica received from children.

It had spiked Danica's curiosity. It was only natural to be interested, she told herself. Pursuing answers was similar to looking inside someone's bathroom medicine cabinet: it broke a societal rule, but everyone did it.

"Think you need any product?" she said, even though he didn't.

Marty's eyes stayed closed. "You're the expert."

She added a minuscule amount of gel to her fingertips. "Need to impress anybody today? Or tonight?" It was a long shot and a little awkward, but she had to try and steer him. For science.

Marty grinned. "The usual crew I guess."

At that, Danica put her hands back onto Marty's scalp. The image returned of the same woman on the lawn.

Only this time, different. Her shoulders dipped. She stopped walking and stood with less poise. Less of this world was hers. Her smile faded.

"You lost me," she said. The voice echoed and grew distant, like it had dived underwater.

"I'm caged. A cage... Marty...

"...Marty...

"I'm lost."

Danica pulled away and rubbed her eyes.

"We need lights set, Marty," Tori called from the green wall.

He stood from the chair and looked at Danica. "All good?"

She nodded and smiled. He smiled back. As he walked toward the set, she noticed the sluggishness of his gait. In his posture. Even that smile, just a moment ago, landed with less radiance than the beams of a million suns. It was easy to miss, given the rest of him, but now that she had seen it — having looked into what his mind held — Danica couldn't unsee it.

It happened at the Earl's parking lot, too. After hearing he had to wait.

It was sadness.

Something was troubling the most handsome man on Earth.

CHAPTER FIVE

FRIDAY, JANUARY 16, 2009, 12:05AM. SAME PLACE.

After the brief work on Gabby and Marty, she hid in the corner to give as much space to the crew as possible, waiting for her name to be called for touch-ups or this-and-that's. It never was.

Once the actors got into costume (a.k.a. ski vests), a sound guy coordinated with a camera operator on the optimal positioning against the green screen. All under Tori's watchful eye.

The only hiccup came when the action began. Gabby ran her lines perfectly. Marty, less so. He apologized every time he dropped a line. He apologized many times.

"I'm getting my head into the right space, you know?" he said. "I just gotta find it."

Danica nabbed a loose script and read the lines. She was no actor, but she didn't see a lot to find in these lines. It was all straight forward, all expositiony and forced humor.

It should have gone:

GABBY

Last night's snow ruined the slope
conditions. I think we should call
this off.

MARTY

Why? You scared of an epic fail?

GABBY

I'm just being sensible. This girl boss
has a career to consider.

MARTY

What-ever.

As filming commenced, the lines went more like:

GABBY

Last night's snow ruined the slope
conditions. I think we should call
this off.

MARTY

...line?

After each flubbed take, Danica studied Marty's face with
more scrutiny. The trouble behind his eyes had planted roots
in Danica's memory, replaying the images she saw of that
woman walking away.

Thought she saw. Danica didn't have facts. She had feelings; ill-gotten feelings at that. Snooping inside that handsome man's handsome head like that — she had no right.

Back at the door, the two young pony-tail women
jabbered away, the white one devouring M&M's. Danica tried

to remember the woman's face from Marty's vision. They resembled each other, but it wasn't a perfect fix; M&M Girl looked like Vision Girl's stunt double.

Filming paused as Tori pulled Marty aside. She certainly wasn't Vision Girl either. Vision Girl didn't slouch, stomp or limp. Both had confidence, but Vision Girl's confidence likely came from self actualization, not from bullying people around.

Gabby grabbed a water and motioned for Danica to follow. "Looks like we're going a little late."

"I got nowhere to be."

"Marty's got a *process* all his own. Whatever helps him work out what he's gotta work out I guess."

Danica believed it. "You know him from somewhere?"

"Acting classes. Some skeezy place in Toluca Lake. He was good. Then. Maybe he went somewhere else and, I dunno, got corrupted."

Marty grumbled to the wall. He held his ski goggles, which had split at the nose.

"Costumes," said Tori.

A woman with baggy pants and no wrench tied to her belt stepped forward. "We don't have any more here. I could tape it."

"That'll send continuity to pot," said Bobby. "Get another one."

"There ain't no more here, man."

"Go to the supply room."

"No," said Tori. "Fix these."

"With what? Tape? It'll show on camera."

"I'll go get another," said Marty. "It's my fault anyway."

He reached out a hand toward Tori, who gave him a key. Then he jogged out of the garage, leaving the set in a weird lurch.

Bobby pulled Tori aside, closer to Danica and Gabby, who

instinctively turned toward their waters as to mask their eavesdropping.

"The guy's not getting it, Tori. He's flubbing his lines and now breaking stuff? It's gonna set us way back. We gotta be like John Ford, right? Move fast, shoot what's written, all the cuts in a shoebox."

"Yes," said Tori. She sounded resigned. "Keep a record of your notes for improvements, but we must keep moving forward today. But send me your notes. Your insights are vital."

Danica couldn't see his face, but she assumed Bobby blushed at this show of respect. The girls near the door giggled again. They were not hiding their eavesdropping, weaponizing their giggle nice and loud for Bobby to hear. He acted like he didn't notice as he stepped back toward the camera area.

"He's dating Sofi, you know." Gabby's eyes twinkled at the gossip.

"Who? Bobby?"

"No. Marty."

A certain relief came upon Danica. Not that people had to love certain types, but sometimes comfort arrived when things made sense. And a celebrity dating Marty, or vice versa, made sense. "Is it a secret?"

"Nah. It's just he's not as big a star as her, so some think he's, like, ladder climbing. Those people are blind, BTDub, 'cause look at him. If he's getting something from her, then she's *definitely* getting something from him. I'd call it even."

Marty returned with a fresh pair of goggles. "They were in those back boxes."

Danica and Gabby stared for the entire four seconds it took Marty to walk back to the green wall area.

"He is, objectively, the best looking human I've ever seen," said Danica.

Gabby mm-hmm'd.

"In person, I mean. 'Cause I haven't seen Beyoncé or Hugh Jackman up close to really compare."

"I saw Hugh at Whole Foods once," said Gabby. "Marty's shoulders are better."

The image of Vision Girl returned. Walking into darkness, getting farther out of reach. Danica remembered the troubled look in Marty's eyes. The one that slumped his better-than-Wolverine shoulders.

"He's got a channel, too, you said?"

Gabby said, "Yeah. Got OK followers. Low thousands. Bigger than most. Bigger than mine, that's for sure. Who knows how it works? It's the freakin' Wild West — you're up and then you're down. Nobody totally knows."

A loud crash at the doorway interrupted them. A tray of fruit lay spilled across the concrete entrance. Standing near it was Tori and the two younger on-groupies. They were hugging each other, the younger women, trying to contain their laughter while Tori chewed them out.

"Sofi would let us," said the Black woman. "She knows how to be cool with this stuff."

"I am not Sofi," said Tori.

They laughed.

"Why is that funny to you?"

"It's nothing," they said together, then started laughing again.

"Stop it!"

This explosion halted all merriment within a mile. The faces of the two younger women went slack, their eyes pointed down, away from the furious volcano standing before them. Nobody moved.

Nobody spoke either. Not even Tori. She stared her prey into mush.

Danica tore her eyes away to look around the garage. Everyone else was watching, too.

At last, Tori spoke. It was low and meant only for the two young women to hear. Whatever it was, the message was received. They nodded, then nodded some more.

Then Tori folded her arms. A moment later, the two young women got on their hands and knees and began cleaning the mess. Neither had dressed for this kind of work — miniskirts and clogs were, in Danica's opinion, rarely helpful in any circumstance — but they set to it and made quick work of the mess. Anything to escape that wrath.

Satisfied with the progress, Tori turned back to her crew. She was composed again and jostled her orange jacket back into shape. At this, work resumed. The hum of the crew returned, as though the last forty-five seconds hadn't happened. Tori's slight limp was the most confident limp Danica had ever seen.

Gabby leaned over with her water bottle. "Yep, you play your cards right and you could do this full time."

Danica tried to look busy in her corner, for fear of everything. She snuck another look at Marty, whose worried eyes almost reassured her.

"Caged. A cage, Marty." The woman from the vision returned.

CHAPTER SIX

Friday, 3:35AM. Outside the Storage Unit. Gabby's Prius.

An envelope slapped the passenger-side window. Gabby waved it in Danica's face.

"Forget this?" said Gabby. "Or were you doing this out of the goodness of your heart?"

Getting money remained priorities 1 through 25 in Danica's life, and would likely remain so for the rest of it. Yet even as she opened the envelope and studied the much-needed check, all she could think about was that young vision woman talking to Marty.

Gabby yawned and started the car. "At least traffic won't be so bad going back." She spoke nice and loud, selling her alibi.

They drove with only the radio making conversation. Danica stared at the check in her hand. The words "STARR & STARR PRODUCTIONS" blazed across the top. No address anywhere. Disparate thoughts searched for a home and found no admittance.

"What's Marty's last name?"

"Dole."

"And he films stuff for Sofi's channel even though he's got his own?"

"Cross-promo stuff. Everyone does it for everyone in the company."

"Starr & Starr?"

"PowerWorks."

Danica held up her check.

Gabby swerved to avoid a bus. "I guess one is under the other. I don't know. I'm not a lawyer."

They rode another block in meditative quiet before Danica said, "He's got money though, right? I saw his car. It's brand-spanking new."

"They're all kinda rolling in it, I think. Some might come from money, too, but their channels are raking it in. Even the smaller ones, 'cause they're all under PowerWorks. That's why I gotta get more content up. Build that library, you know?"

Danica nodded and thought. The dull gray of the asphalt sprawled ahead, picking up a few other cars as they neared their Van Nuys neighborhood.

"Starr & Starr is Sofi along with Tori, right?" said Danica "Sisters."

"Correctamundo."

"But Sofi wasn't here today."

Gabby said nothing.

"Think Marty would be, like, concerned about Sofi?"

Gabby raised an eyebrow. "... Why?"

"Seems strange. To film something for her channel without her there."

"...I guess."

"Where was she?"

"I don't know, *Bobby*. I didn't worry about it, unlike some people."

Danica tucked her feet under her go bag, hoping Gabby wouldn't count it as suspicious squirming. Nobody at the shoot seemed concerned about Sofi's absence. Nobody but Bobby, who had his own world of issues.

And maybe Marty.

"You all right?" Gabby took her hand. "Did something happen?"

Danica shuffled her imitation Doc Martin's against the floor, charging herself up to stay silent, even though she wanted to talk.

"I just... I saw something. In Marty's mind."

"Ooo." Gabby glanced at Danica and read the aura. "Oh, wait. It's not something sexy."

"It's probably nothing, but I couldn't help it and now I can't stop thinking about it." She watched on-coming traffic a bit more, then added. "Earlier today — er, yesterday — he went to Lorena for help. Marty's got something to worry about. It's gotta be this thing, right?"

"Hold on a second," said Gabby. "Are you working another case?"

The question smacked Danica in the chest. Prior to her return to Los Angeles, she had discussed her prior-year's excursion with Gabby, about how she had gotten too deep into a weird web of other people's personal matters, how she'd made their business into her own, and how all that had almost killed her. She had to tell her; they were roommates and friends. They had lease stuff to work out, and, sure, Gabby was concerned about her. In those discussions, Danica thought she'd made it clear that last summer's events would be a one-and-done kind of deal.

Danica's return-trip recommitment to a no-drama life-style had further cemented this notion.

And yet the vision played on and on in her mind, with no amount of shoe fidgeting capable of changing the station. She hadn't gone looking for a 'case' or anything 'case like.'

The radio wasn't answering Gabby's lingering question. Danica owed her something.

"No." Another less-than-solid performance.

"The things you saw, was it another dead body?"

"No. It was a girl. A woman. And she was alive. But the way she talked, this woman... she was walking away from him, calling to him."

"'Save me, Marty, save me?' or 'Kiss me, Marty, kiss me?'" Gabby remained hopeful.

"More like, 'You lost me. I'm in a cage.' Something like that." Danica stared at the side mirror. "If he's dating Sofi, it must've been her, huh? But why would she be talking about cages?"

"So," said Gabby as she turned onto Hazeltine Avenue, "you *are* working a case."

"I am not!"

Gabby faced her friend and Danica felt the full power of her smirk. "Well, are you trying to date Marty?"

"No."

"And you're not, like, dreaming about Sofi Starr?"

"No."

"I shouldn't joke. Sofi's got actual problems with that. I've heard about stalkers and such. But not from you. You're not trying to date him, you're not dreaming about Sofi, so... that can only mean..."

"I'm not working a case. I'm not doing that again. That was too much for me. I'm not going back. I just was thinking about the vision I saw is all."

Gabby pulled into their apartment's designated parking spot and said, "Uh-huh."

She exited the car. Danica chased after her. "I'm not a detective. That was a one time thing. I was compelled. By some weird feeling to, you know, do the right thing or some other stupid reason."

On the stairs, Gabby said, "Uh-huh."

"I'm just curious. I saw something weird and I'm naturally curious. I'm not forcing my way into a case again. Especially when there isn't one."

At the door, Gabby unlocked the lock. "Uh-huh."

"Please stop saying 'uh-huh' like you don't believe me and listen: I am not working a case. And don't say 'uh-huh.'"

Gabby set her keys on the couch and said, "Sure."

They each tossed their purses, bags and jackets in various directions in the apartment, hitting random bits of furniture. It felt too late to sleep, and the haze of the near morning had settled through their open windows.

The two roommates brushed their teeth in a zombie fashion, moving toward a snooze before the sun reached full pomp. Danica slid into her sheets and stared at the ceiling.

She rolled onto her side. Danica didn't think she was working a case. Was she? She'd seen an attractive woman saying weird stuff in the mind of an attractive man. Who wouldn't find that interesting? Who wouldn't want to know more about what it meant? Or who the woman even was?

Her hand moved on its own, entered a quick search into her phone. The images that emerged confirmed her suspicion: the woman in Marty's vision was Sofi Starr.

"Do you really think Marty's troubled with something with Sofi?" said Gabby through the thin bedroom walls. She must have heard Danica rustling around.

"The vision was pretty, I guess... ominous? But it could also just be boyfriend-girlfriend stuff."

"Yeah. *Caged* girlfriend stuff."

A six minute silence followed before Danica spoke again. "And how's Madame Lorena fit in?"

"Yeah. Why *was* he seeing her?"

"I mean... *her!*"

"He could be a believer. And he thinks he can reach her through hoodoo."

"I guess, but... *her?*"

Another sleepy quiet slid between their thoughts. Gabby let out a long yawn, then said, "You know, it'd be fine if you did it again."

"Did what?"

Gabby took this as an invitation to jog into Danica's room. "Take a case."

Danica tore her pillow from behind her and buried her face. "There's no case to take."

"I don't mean to push, but I'm just kinda, like, proud of you and stuff."

Danica removed the pillow. "For what?"

"You looking out for people. You're a do-gooder. I know that sounds lame, but it's true. And cool."

"No, I'm not."

"You are. I mean, you even stuck up for that woman in Arizona and she was awful. You do good things for reasons beyond yourself. Now you have this information — about a woman in danger, a troubled boyfriend, all that — and you're thinking of how to help. You caught the Solving-Stuff Buzz."

"The what?"

"You know? The buzz. It's like that thing that keeps you going on things. I have the acting buzz. You have the solving buzz."

The notion of addiction wrestled in Danica's head. "You really think so?"

"Sure. I saw those wheels turning behind that peach fuzz head. It's what you are. You're a do-gooder."

Danica faced Gabby square. "Actually I'm thinking of how to sell this information to Madame Lorena."

"Oh," said Gabby. Her head pulled back and froze. "OK. Maybe you're not a do-gooder."

CHAPTER SEVEN

Friday, January 16, 2009. 8:04AM. Island Estates, Apt #203.

Danica worked out her plan that night before drifting off to sleep. Convincing herself to go through with the plan took the whole morning. She worked on it at the kitchen table, splitting time between staring at her notebook and staring at an empty cereal bowl. All that time had not improved her plan's quality. It only allowed Danica to flower up the writing.

The plan, as conceived, went thusly:

1. Arrive at Madame Lorena's Friday morning
2. Mention recent acquisition of valuable personal information concerning one of her clients
3. Chart out path for M. Lorena to mention above information during next psychic reading with said client

4. Convince M. Lorena that use of this information would persuade her client of her tremendous powers (note: Lorena does not posses such powers)
5. Remind M. Lorena of client's deep, YouTube-funded wallet
6. Detail great potential of client's gratitude (via wallet, see above)
7. Encourage M. Lorena to show *her* gratitude in similar manner by suspending rent increase on Earl's W.O.C.

She examined Step One and pictured the parking lot in front of Earl's. Her non-employer. Danica re-ran her plan, rationalizing and re-rationalizing it to herself; a sign of professionalism or delusion. Or both.

Hard honesty kicked its way through. She was rationalizing and deluding herself *on top of* being desperate. Lorena had no reason to trust or believe anything Danica had to say, with their entire relationship based on half conversations caught between moments of mild breaking and entering. And if Carla caught her going to Lorena's, she'd ask why she was there, so Danica would have to tell her. This would create an argument — a good and loud one — with Carla yelling about the ethics of stealing (that would be the word she'd use, too) the thoughts of some dumb hot guy to turn him into even more of a patsy for Lorena. And Lorena would hear *this*, hear the plan in its worst possible form, reject it and any notion of charity, then unleash landlord hell upon the block. Earl's would shut down, Carla would move, Danica would have to freelance around forever, flame out and end up living in a hole.

High stakes.

She grabbed her pen and added: *1.a. Don't park where Carla can see.*

Who was to say the girl in the vision was in trouble, let alone a truthful representation of the real Sofi Starr? Danica had no evidence to back anything. She had seen what amounted to a half-dream.

With no set schedule, some deep-seated,-junior-high-English-class need to check her references consumed her; a fear made only more real by the fact that Danica had been waiting until the last minute to do it.

She slid Gabby's laptop and began her search, starting with Marty.

The immediate results pointed to YouTube, reminding her of an encounter years prior at an art exhibition. It was held in some guy's garage. There she'd met a woman who worked in internet marketing, which back in the mid-2000's counted as unique employment. Her name was something like Wanda, but not Wanda, who she wore tight jeans and poured red wine into her beer can without apology. Danica remembered little about the ten-ish minute conversation they'd had standing on the patio of some guy's house in Pasadena, except for one bit, which — triggered by Marty's YouTube home page — returned.

Wanda/Not-Wanda had said, "The internet is forever. And you can market yourself that way."

That woman's words had never been more fully realized than on the YouTube pages belonging to Marty Dole. The tailoring was subtle, yet evident, in his touched-up headshots and banner advertisement; the vibe was "I just whipped up this high-quality ad in my bedroom, whatevs," but with professional teeth whitening. Again, Danica thought back to that patio conversation, about how web presence could mold an *entire* personality. One that looked great, fit into a box, only drove toward success, and may not, in fact, exist.

His YouTube channel was dominated with straight-to-camera testimonials. Shot entirely in Marty's room (or what was supposed to look like his room, she couldn't tell), the same blue door framed his perfect head in the same perfect manner again and again. Danica watched a couple, receiving lectures about self-confidence, public speaking and how to talk to women without being a creep. The titles all contained the word "Act" in them: "Act Like a Pro," "Acting On Your Best Impulses," "How to Act Your Way Out of a Speeding Ticket." Danica struggled to complete any of the videos in their entirety. Not because Marty looked bad. At all. His looks aside, they felt generic and couldn't hold her attention. Of what she watched, she guessed half started with quotes from the Buddha, while the others casually referenced U2.

She chicken-scratched some stats around publishing dates and times. He seemed to drop new ones on Wednesdays. Average comment counts were in the 20 to 30 range per video, with most as long as "LOL." Every comment section had at least two links to other videos. His oldest video was from four years ago.

Marty's "also liked" videos got the tailoring treatment as well; strictly cross-promotional fare courtesy of PowerWorks. Above all, the most-often 'also liked' artist was Sofi Starr.

Danica clicked over to her channel. Like Marty's, Sofi's page exuded polish, but of a different sort. Where Marty's output was regimented but slight, Sofi's was a factory on overtime. She'd loaded fifteen videos this month alone, all with links to secondary pages and behind-the-scenes clips. And Sofi's professional pizazz made all competition seem cheap by comparison.

A few clicks sent Danica to Sofi's main series titled "Sofi Tries..." where, as Gabby'd said, the star attempted new things while almost always falling on her face. Cooking, baking, biking, skating, hockey(ing), Sofi threw herself into every one. She even took her format on the road in 2008, knocking on doors of experts in all manner of fields.

Despite these videos being obviously staged (some experts were "surprised at home," despite the fact that a camera crew was already inside their foyers when Sofi arrived), the charm of the series was undeniable: Sofi herself. In theory, watching a blonde woman laugh her way through messing up an oil change would have never made Danica's list of favorite watches, yet she watched the whole damn thing. And not just in the name of research. Anyone who doubted the allure of star power to hook viewers could get straight by watching a mere two episodes of "Sofi Tries...."

Sofi's comment section was very lively as well, showing a level of fan passion beyond reason as well as beyond Marty's numbers. These were fanatics who wrote more than a simple three-letter shorthand to display their love. And like most passionate fanbases, the cocksure experts were on full display. "This crap just isn't ***OUR*** Sofi!!" one person wrote under the most recent video, a comedy skit titled "Sofi the Judge." A few others agreed, dropping links to blogs promising "the truth without that pollitical correct bs" (their words and spelling). Some commenters fought back while others played like victims. Sofi's videos were an industry unto themselves, generating content to initiate engagement. And clicks. Millions of them, by her count, in just the last few years.

Danica dropped her pen and rubbed her wrist. The doctor had told her to take it easy, not to push. She looked at her notes and wondered how Marty's vision fit.

And a frustration rose in her chest as she realized her own honest truth: the woman in Marty's vision *was* Sofi Starr.

So her plan *did* have some relevance.

So she actually *did* have a reason to talk to Lorena.

CHAPTER EIGHT

Friday, January 16, 2009. 9:50AM. Van Nuys Strip Mall.

Following Point 1.a of her plan, Danica drove beyond the open parking lot and searched for a street spot. The parking meter gods smiled upon her, bestowing an open location around the corner with 49 minutes still left on it.

Maybe it was a sign. Maybe Lorena would be nice. Maybe she would recognize the troubles Marty had within him and steer him toward substantive help. Maybe she'd actually find a way to help his girlfriend, too. Maybe Lorena wouldn't exploit the rich guy with issues.

Maybe trees would start talking about their favorite European artists since the Renaissance.

She stuck close to the side of the building, walking around the corner toward the front doors facing the lot. At the edge of the lot sat a blue Kia hatchback. A pile of flyers lined its back seat, spread as if the car had been the victim of a paper bomb. "LEARN YOUR FUTURE… GUARANTEED," they said.

She reached the front entrance where dark windows greeted her, as though nobody had been inside for weeks. The sign in the window had been flipped to its open side. Danica pressed her face against the glass, between a faded green "A" and "R" in "Tarot."

The place looked dead. She checked to see if Lorena was closed Fridays. If so, then Danica's humiliation could be spared.

The door was cruelly unlocked. It tripped an overhead bell. Danica mustered her courage and pressed forward.

Though the layout appeared similar to that of Earl's, she found herself in a kind of isolated waiting area, with a small wall dividing the front section from the back. The ceiling ran high over this flimsy barrier, with cheap foam squares coursing from the waiting room, clearing the dividing wall by three feet and traveling beyond. The door in the dividing wall was not a door at all. More of a passageway, with a beaded curtain holding the space. Though she'd never visited a commercial psychic before, Danica categorized this decorative decision as basic.

Curtains hung from every light and the place reeked of incense, dust and possibly salsa.

"With you in one moment." This voice came from behind the beaded curtain, from Lorena. Her voice sounded ethereal, no doubt the result of her strenuous and legitimate work. Danica tucked her hands in her sweatshirt pockets to keep them from flipping off the building.

She heard another voice. Low and deep. A man's. A customer's. Not Marty, but someone else.

One promised moment later, Lorena poked her head through the beads.

"Well, well… even *I* was not expecting to see you here."

She looked Danica over with a different kind of scrutiny than when they last spoke, then withdrew back to her inner sanctum. She and her customer murmured a few short exchanges. Then Lorena returned to the curtain.

"My dear, would you please turn to the wall while my client exits?"

"Is he shy?"

"It is for his protection, darling. For both of you. To protect your privacy. Maybe pull your hood over as well, yes?"

Danica did not trust Lorena, but she couldn't argue that one of her customers might suffer from the embarrassment of being seen in this place. She abided the request, pulled her hood up and faced the wall.

An assortment of framed newspaper clippings faced her. Most were from local rags mentioning Lorena's parlor either opening, thriving, or managing to still be open. "Could anyone have predicted it?" asked one gag-ready tag line. In the middle was a clip highlighting Kirk Gibson's home run in the 1988 World Series.

Footsteps moved behind Danica as she kept staring at the wall. The beaded curtain click-clacked, the front door opened. Lorena said, "Bye-bye," then, "All is well now."

Danica turned to face Madame Lorena in her full glory, wrapped in thin silk scarves with a rope indicating her waist. She held up her arms, posing with the restraint of a drag queen. Her wrists twisted to aim her rings toward the stars as her gray lips cracked into a smile. She bade Danica to follow her to the back.

The smell of incense grew thicker with every step. A single candle on a table in the center of the room offered the only light. Even in the dimness, Danica could see haze floating through the air.

Two cabinets ran against the back wall. Lorena sat at the candle's table, fitting into a curious half-couch, half-chair kind of seat, the kind of thing normally found around the corner table at a diner.

"Please," said Lorena, her hand in a grand gesture toward the open space on the diner couch. The vinyl farted as Danica put her weight on it.

Lorena extended her hands across the table, palms up.

"I'm not here for a reading," said Danica.

"Mmm, I know this, of course. However," Lorena wiggled her fingers, "my place, my rules."

Why fight indignity now? Danica held out her hands and Lorena took them.

She inhaled, deep through her thin nostrils and lowered her heavy lashes.

In a long, drawn-out voice, Lorena said, "Youuuuuuuuu waaaaaaaaant ssssssssomething...."

Danica tried to consider Lorena's performance positively, as one from a professional dedicated to her craft. Like an actor or a magician. On the other hand, Danica's gag reflex had been put on high alert.

Still, she played along and said, "Yep."

"Mmm," said Lorena. "Mm-hmm... Something from... someone." Lorena didn't chew scenery; she devoured it, smearing vowels all over the place.

"Yes. I actually met—"

"Do not tell me, my dear."

"You prefer to guess?"

"I do not guess." She scolded from behind closed eyes. "This concerns... a man, correct?"

"In a way."

"A man for whom you have... feeeeeeeeeeelings."

"It's about Marty Dole. I don't have feeeeeeeelings for him."

"No, not Marty." Lorena opened her eyes and ran a finger-nail down Danica's palm. "Your heart dwells elsewhere. For another. A man you have not spoken to for, oh, months. Not since autumn."

Danica lacked a snotty retort.

Lorena went on. "You feel for this man. He feels for you and yet you deny his affection."

An image flew into Danica's brain, but she fought it away. She pulled back her hand and stuffed it under her leg. Creepy accuracy was just one of Lorena's tricks. Not that it was accurate at all. Lorena had only said "a man" — she didn't even mention Freddie by name.

Not that Freddie was on Danica's mind. They were friends. Friends thought about each other and missed each other. It wasn't more than that.

Just friends.

Who hadn't spoken for a while. And maybe she had ignored his calls at New Year's.

Danica realized she had let silence reign for too long. She met Lorena's gaze and started again.

"I'd like to keep this professional, please, Lorena."

"As you wish," she said, though she didn't act like she believed Danica's request.

"Marty is a client of yours. A new one, right?"

"I'm not sure I should disclose the terms of our arrangement."

"You told me last week that he's your client. I'm fuzzy about your confidentiality policies."

"It is at the discretion of the customers. For their security."

"Your door is unlocked and you have a beaded curtain. How much security are you after?"

"Firstly," said Lorena, "you knew about Marty already. I did not initiate the sharing of any details. He told you of his meeting with me. Second, a client's request for anonymity should be their own business. They have the right to change their minds any time they want. I honor that."

Touché. Danica had let her buttons get pushed and for that, she'd been bruised. She pulled up her big girl pants and reset herself to act like an adult. Professional. Calm and professional.

"About Marty. I've recently come into some information regarding him that I think you would find very interesting."

Lorena said nothing, listening with folded arms.

"He's troubled."

"Indubitably."

"Would you like to know why?"

"If you wish to share."

"Well," said Danica, losing her momentum. "It might be financially beneficial of you to know. This information. It's *inside* information. And I thought, if it was helpful to you, financially, then, you know…" No great negotiation ever ended with 'you know….'

The left eyelid on Madame Lorena's face crept upward, supported by a suspicious eyebrow.

"Are you blackmailing me?"

"What? No."

"Are you blackmailing Marty?"

"No."

"Then I am afraid you have lost me, dear. You came to talk about someone you don't have feelings for, who you are not blackmailing. You say you have information that would benefit me, which means money, but I see no money. Add to that your disparaging remarks about my professional conduct when it is you who may have broken several laws."

While she mounted her comeback, Danica couldn't help but trace Lorena's accent; the mystic slid to the side, replaced by something else. Boston maybe? Occasionally her t's landed like d's.

"When is Marty scheduled for another appointment?" said Danica.

"That is, again, confidential."

Okay. "I think you should take my information and then call him. Tell him you had a dream that concerns him. And his girlfriend. Do you know about her?"

"I have not met the girl."

"She's Sofi Starr. She's a YouTube celebrity." Judging from the dull look in her eyes, this news meant precisely jack squat to Lorena.

"I'm sorry, my dear, but I do not see how this is helpful for anyone, including yourself."

"He's worried something will happen to her. When he was here, did he talk abou—"

"I cannot reveal any of that to you."

"Fine! I *think* that's why he came to you. He's worried about her and he's desperate. Has he come back here since then? Or made a new appointment? I'm guessing not. Maybe he didn't get what he needed from you."

Danica sensed her infraction. The face staring back at her shot a well of emotions across the table, but mostly rage. The hippy-dippy dream weaver persona broke around the edges, replaced by a stare hard as granite. Danica didn't mean to insult Lorena. At least, not to her face.

Lorena took a deep breath. "How do you acquire this 'information' regarding Marty?"

"Doesn't matter."

"It matters to me."

"It's confidential. I can do that, too, right?"

"'Confidential.' Except you are here selling secrets. This is a negotiation, is it not? We are negotiating terms for something. Negotiations require some form of trust. We must give to each other in order to get from each other."

Lorena's wisdom put Danica on her heels. She hadn't planned on giving any sources. That wasn't on her plan list!

Madame Lorena grinned, almost friendly. "Marty has told me that he has concerns. I assumed it related to his girl-friend, because why would it not? Most concerns for young men do. And, no, he was not overwhelmed by our first session. I would like to have him come back. On a regular basis.

"Now your turn," said Lorena. "How have you acquired this information?"

"I work in the industry." Not one-hundred percent fact or fiction. She did, for now. At least when she saw the vision. She had a check stub to prove it. "I do hair and make-up. And we talked."

Lorena sniffed out Danica's hesitation. Her hedging. Danica could tell she wanted more.

"And I'm a detective."

Danica maintained her gaze, but internally judged herself. She should have rehearsed saying that word — 'detective.' She'd so rarely said it out loud, the thing stumbled over her own teeth.

Lorena, for her part, did not laugh her out of the building, though her eyes crooked a little.

"And what is this inside scoop you have so fabulously detected?"

"It's about a dream. She is walking away from him and says she's lost. No, she says *he* lost *her.* And she feels, well, trapped."

This word vomit had three effects. Firstly, it made Danica's embarrassment reach a new level.

Secondly, it helped her realize that her capability to lie had not improved with time.

And thirdly, it got Lorena's attention. Her thin lips scrunched at the ends and her head tipped back. She might have been reacting to the embarrassment thing, too, but Danica held on to that last shred of optimism.

"For all this," said Lorena, "for this valuable information, what is it you want in return?"

"I want help with the rent you're charging Carla."

Lorena's lips de-scrunched. "Free rent? You must be delusional."

"Not free. Just help. You're raising it too much. Carla's a friend and I don't think asking you to hold off a few more months is too much to ask."

"How long is 'a few months?'"

"Like, let's say... eight?"

Danica watched the older woman's brain spin, calibrating some incongruent thing in her mind. What, Danica could not guess.

After a horrible quiet, the bescarved woman rose from her seat. "I would like time to consider your proposal."

Her performing accent had returned to full throttle. Danica opened her mouth to protest, but Lorena continued.

"Marty is a dear boy. A believer, at heart. But as you have deduced, he is not yet a devotee. If your information strikes a chord within his soul, motivating him to return to my counsel, then we may have a deal."

Danica marveled at Lorena's ability to make a scam sound close to legitimate. She wrote her number and email address on a piece of paper and handed it over.

Then Danica said, "How do I know you won't take this info, call Marty, and, um..."

"Screw you over?" said Lorena. "You don't. That, my dear, is where the element of trust comes in."

Danica knew there was a reason why she didn't do shady, back-alley deals more often. The lack of guarantee placed her on very wobbly ground. She couldn't ask for a receipt. There wasn't a manager to complain to. All her white-girl problem solving techniques fell to pieces when faced with a pure, raw transaction. She would leave Lorena's place with little beyond half a palm reading.

As she pulled her butt free from the vinyl diner cushion, Danica accepted Lorena's hand to shake goodbye. The older woman clasped her left hand on top and held tight.

"He's thinking of you, too," she said. "He may seem gruff sometimes, but he holds you in high regard."

Lorena let go and threw in, "That one's for free."

Danica retreated through the beads and front door, set on getting away from any of those thoughts as fast as she could.

CHAPTER NINE

SUNDAY, JANUARY 18, 2009. 1:05PM. EARL'S WORLD of Curls.

Nearly two days passed and Danica lived in doubt for every minute. Sitting in a barber chair, slowly spinning around, all she could do was replay her meeting with Lorena and worry about how much she'd tipped her hand. She had no collateral, no guarantee, no nothing. Even the hair-and-make-up gig economy had dried up. Gabby lined up with PowerWorks for the coming Friday, with the prospects of Danica working again, only to have it cancelled. As listless minutes compounded without customers, the tension in Danica's chest worsened.

Gene's arrival did not help matters. Upon seeing her in the chair — his chair — he offered his usual amount of friendliness. "Two things: what's she doing, and why's she doing it here?"

Carla shouted from the back, "I told you she's back in town."

"Not back on the ticket though. Or are you here for a trim? 'Cause the ticket ain't as big as it used to be, which wasn't exactly huge to begin with, but your sideburns could use some work."

"I'm just visiting. Friends." Danica added that last word to remind Gene. He returned no indication that it registered.

"Outta my chair."

Carla said, "Be nice."

"Please," he added, shooing Danica toward the old magazines in the waiting area.

Temptation rose in Danica's throat, readying a haughty response about how she'd planned to save the business through a cavalier deal with their evil landlord, but she kept it to herself. Better to surprise him when it worked out.

If it worked out. She barely believed in it herself and she was the mastermind who'd conceived of the stupid thing.

Gene wouldn't hear the news of saving Earl's as good news anyway. He'd shoot it down on sight, seeing as it came from Danica. That didn't matter. Carla mattered. It was her place. She might be suspicious of Lorena's business practices, and even more suspicious of anyone aligning herself with Lorena, but once the deal went through, she'd understand and appreciate the effort.

If the deal went through.

Until then, Danica would keep it all to herself. She watched Gene wipe down the sink as Carla returned from the office to straighten Happy Spatula products on the shelf.

"Are we gonna watch the inauguration?" Gene spoke to the mirror, but addressed the room.

"Free country," said Carla.

"Yeah, but I mean in here. We don't have a TV."

"True."

"It's happening during open hours. It's a historic event."

Carla turned and put her hip to one side in response.

Gene put up his hands. "Not saying you have to buy a TV. Just saying we'd need one to watch is all. And one would look perfect right about there, in that corner where plants die."

Danica had never found bickering to be charming, but she had missed this. She might have even missed Gene, something she never thought she'd ever do. A sense of calm belonging sunk her deeper into the waiting area chair. Andrew Luman's house felt like the place she'd grown up, but it never felt quite like a home. The Valley had more home-like elements. Less cold weather. Friends who understood her. And forgave her.

She hoped.

Lorena using Freddie to manipulate her still gnawed at her brain. The woman must have bugged the salon, or peeped through the windows when he came over. But if she had, how would she know— *guess* that they had feelings for each other?

She thought he had feelings for her. The more Danica considered the situation, the more it felt very standard. She and Freddie were friends. He was a customer who was friends with Danica, and Carla, and maybe even Gene (it was possible). Freddie visited when he needed a cut and sometimes hung out after. He was a Black man who got his hair cut by a white woman in the Valley.

Nothing that strange about it.

They hadn't spoken since Christmas Eve and the conversation had been stilted thanks to the sounds of a party on Freddie's end. How dare Lorena bring him up. "Dirty pool," Andrew called it, to go after an open wound like that.

But she hadn't brought him up. Not by name. Lorena had used that old trick where she gave details with just enough space to allow the customer— the sucker — to fill in the blanks. Were Danica's feelings so obvious that a hack fortune teller could exploit them with ease?

Did she have actual feelings for Freddie? Like, *feelings* feelings?

Some bitter corner of her heart shook the Hallmark Channel out of her. The wifi from the nail salon smiled upon her phone, releasing a bountiful flood of spam email upon her inbox. Danica settled deeper into her chair and skimmed, ready to while away the day. She would be patient to work it out with Freddie, and for Lorena's answer to come.

And if the answer didn't come, what would be the harm? If Lorena never got back to her, then Danica wouldn't have to deal with such an unsavory person again. One less thing to worry about. She could help Earl's in other ways, ways she should have considered prior to jumping into some half-baked scheme of subterfuge and secret selling.

Amid the mishmash of movie promotions and Facebook updates, Danica spotted an email from MLBaronette47@aol.com.

Subject line: "YOU WERE RITE!!"

The typo intrigued her and she opened it:

"Amazing. Come to work and I you. were Right. This is Lorena Signed Lorena."

Lorena's astounding lack of email savvy gave way to excitement. Looking around the salon, watching Carla and Gene argue about the placement of a theoretically-purchased TV, Danica sensed the golden ticket between her fingers. She might pull this off.

A cooler head fought through the celebration to remind Danica that nothing was remotely finalized. Lorena might change the terms or back out of everything all together. This had to remain quiet while the next move got figured out.

"Catching flies?" It was Carla.

"Huh?"

"You're staring. With your mouth open. Just... staring."

"Am I? I dunno."

"That's your thinking face. I've seen it before. Last year, saw it too much. What's cooking?"

"Nothing."

Carla side-eyed her, but resumed her de-cluttering work. Danica considered offering to help, but then drew back; as she'd rarely offered to help clean anything before, an offer to do so at this moment might come across as overcompensation. Which is what it would've been.

She needed to make an appointment to talk with Lorena somewhere far from the strip mall, to go over their next steps. But as the secret swelled inside her throat, Danica realized her top priority was to leave Earl's before giving everything away. Sitting there too long, she could blurt it all out, or her tell-all face and open-to-the-world mouth could spill the story all over. She needed a convincing, casual excuse. Something simple like, "Gabby's dad's horse just died."

As Danica readied a second draft of her terrible excuse, the front door blasted open. Lorena swarmed inside, ignored the actual employees and targeted Danica, holding out her arms.

"You were right! My God, we are set! This is fantastic! Oh, my dear girl, you did it!"

Before she had time to resist, Danica found her head locked in an embrace. She could barely see through the silk shroud, yet Carla's dagger eyes cut through those sleeves and any BS they might have carried.

"Wanna talk at your place?" said Danica, muffled against the sheer.

"Of course!" said Lorena, without letting go or making any motion like she would actually leave. "It was his girlfriend. He was so impressed and you were right!"

Danica extracted her head. "Let's go outside."

"Danica?"

"Be right back." Danica hustled through the door without

looking at Carla, dodging those judging eyes. She swooped Lorena along, her trail filling the doorway like a purple Ring Wraith.

They made it past the Earl's window when Danica had to satisfy her suspicions. "So it was Sofi."

"Who?" said Lorena.

"Marty's girlfriend. Sofi Starr."

"Oh, yes!" Lorena sped into the empty lot, a grand stage for her to command. "Apparently she's of some importance — I think you knew that, too! A celebrity. Even bigger than he is. Oh, you should have seen him. Well, first *heard* him. I called, just like you said and he was very impressed. He seems easy to impress, bless his heart, but when I got him into my sanctuary, in my command? *Bam!*"

The woman did a half twirl.

"So he's a regular now for you?"

"Better than that," said Lorena. "He trusts me implicitly. He's invited me into his inner circle. I should never have doubted you, my dear. Extraordinary work."

Danica's cheeks burned. Blushing around Lorena had not been one of her life's goals, but receiving praise still felt nice despite the source. Midwestern upbringing dictated a deflection, so she said, "It's no big deal."

Lorena turned as though insulted. She stared into Danica's eyes and took both her shoulders in a firm grip. "It was excellent work, dear. Admit it for yourself. I had my doubts, to be certain. Didn't know how you could accomplish such feats, but I was wrong. You really must be a detective."

"Ho. Lee. Crap!"

Carla's voice rang out across the lot. She stood in the doorway, her face lion fierce.

"You're doing it again, aren't you? You're doing detective work again. After... after..."

"No." Danica's tone reached full teen-caught-sneaking-whiskey levels. "That's just what she said. I'm not. There's no detecting happening."

"Do not sell yourself short, my dear," said Lorena, ready to make everything worse. "You put so many pieces together all on your own. You clearly posses a gift."

"Clearly," said Carla.

"I'm not doing detective work. I'm not working a case, there are no clues, no crimes, no danger."

"Then why are you talking to Lorena? And why's she calling you a detective?"

"I can illuminate the situation." Again, Lorena set to ruin as much as she could, helped by putting her arm around Danica. "Our young friend here has taken it upon herself to help us all. Yourself included, Carla. Through her exceptional skills and gumption, this young lady has helped me land a fruitful client. That could mean more income for my shop and possibly act as a rising tide for all boats, if you understand my meaning."

Carla appeared to understand, with her scowl bending a tad toward the nicer side. But when she looked at Danica again, she couldn't help herself. "I just don't want you getting hurt."

"Preposterous," said Lorena. "She'll be safe as a lamb. All we have to do is find a girl. What danger could there possibly be?"

Danica squirmed free of Lorena's grip for the second time. "Hold up. 'Find a girl?' What girl?"

"Why, Marty's girlfriend."

"Sofi Starr?"

Lorena's face went slack. "Who?"

"Same person! Lorena, you have to tell me exactly what Marty said. How it all went down, everything he said. When did you call him?"

"Yesterday afternoon. I called and said exactly what you told me. About how I'd had a vision about him—"

"I never said 'vision!'" Danica felt Carla's gasp in her heart.

"Yes, yes, you said 'dream,' I know, but I prefer 'vision,' my dear. Puts me more in charge of the spirits at play. Anyway, he took the bait and said he could see me the next day — that's today — and he did. Left a few minutes ago, in fact, just before I found you."

"Get to the part about the missing person."

"I did a reading. Tarot. Considering your information, I felt I could utilize it better through the cards. I told him I saw a woman walking away from him and that he was losing her. That she was trapped."

"It was 'caged.'"

Lorena ignored her. "The boy went white, blood rushing from those gorgeous cheeks. I thought he might faint. It was glorious."

An image of Marty's looks diminishing from a 10 to a mere 9.8 flitted through Danica's imagination. She refocused.

"Where do the words 'missing person' come in?"

"I'm getting there. During the reading, I sensed a softening within him. When I landed the final card, I looked up and tears were in his eyes. He reached for my hand. When I took it, he told me he trusted me. His precise words were, 'I can believe in you.' He thought I could help him, since I'd seen so much already. Then he said that his girlfriend has been missing for a few days. And now, he says, he's lucky to have someone on his side."

Danica looked at Carla, almost for permission before asking another question. Then she asked it anyway.

"If Sofi's missing, did the police say anything?"

"Marty said the girl's sister wants her found quietly. Something to do with her 'brand' or the like. So it's all very low-profile. If our search fails, then the police would be contacted as some kind of last resort."

"They must not think she's in too much trouble then," said Carla. "Is it, like drugs or something?"

"I haven't the foggiest notion. It could be drugs, gambling, mobsters — anything!" Lorena's smile lit from big hoop earring to big hoop earring. Bags with dollar signs danced on her pupils.

Danica steered the conversation towards practicality. "When did he last see her? Does he have any ideas or clues or... or anything to go off of?"

Lorena paused her twirling for a moment. "He didn't get into any details. The boy is certainly troubled though. Distraught, poor thing."

She ceased talking as if there was nothing more to say.

Carla raised her hand. "I know I'm late to this thing, but I think I'm following. You—" she pointed to Danica "—helped her with a client. By giving her *inside information*—" those words were laced with cautionary venom "—about some guy and his girlfriend. And now that guy wants Lorena to help find her. Right?"

"Close," said Lorena. "*We* help find her."

It wasn't fear that came first. Or guilt, or anger or any of the usual suspects. No, confusion was the premier feeling consuming Danica's being. A two-factor confusion monster, one part casual (like seeing one of those 3-D posters in the mall) and the other pure mortal terror.

"Who is 'we' in this thing?" Carla said.

Lorena pointed one finger at her own chest and another at Danica.

"Us?" said Danica. "You-and-me we?"

"Yes."

"They want us? Together? Like a team?"

Lorena nodded. "Too good to be true, right?"

"Not how I'd phrase it exactly."

"We have been invited to the missing woman's house where we will search the rooms, gather clues and evidence and try to help find her. And if we help? *Bammo* again!"

"But why, exactly, would they want us both? I mean, why do they think there is an 'us' at all?"

"Teamwork has gotten us so far already, my dear. I could go alone, certainly. It would be possible. However my skills of perception lie in a more limited branch of human interaction. A more direct, personal brand. I posses many gifts, but they are different than your own."

Lorena paused for effect, allowing everyone a moment to grasp how she couldn't do anything worthwhile to help find Sofi. Then she added, "Plus I told Marty you were my assistant."

Mortal terror took full control. "But... why would you... why wou—"

"It seemed a natural fit. He'd met you before, you're obviously skilled. It was perfect."

Danica spiraled, her deal with the devil pushing more and more. Her instincts sent her wobbling toward Carla, searching for protection. Scolding be damned, she needed support. Someone to stand up for her and set her straight.

"Well," said Carla, "if the girl's in trouble..."

"Are you kidding?!" said Danica.

"You did it before, girl. Solved something. And y'know, Lorena doesn't have the experience you have."

"That's not... the point... I solved *one* case."

"Just last year," said Lorena. "Mere months ago. One might argue you are still in the hot zone."

"It's just called 'the zone,'" said Carla.

"Regardless, you have a gift and you must use it."

She could feel a migraine coming. Her eyes closed and her tongue dried. Did she need to put her head between her knees? Have some herbal tea, crawl into bed and survive on whatever pride she had left?

Danica took a step back to allow oxygen to flow. "Madame Lorena," she said, "I appreciate the offer. But our arrangement was for you to use my information yourself. It's a one-time kind of thing. I mean, I'm glad it worked out for you. And yeah, I've solved a case before, but that was a one-time thing, too. I don't know anything about finding missing people."

Lorena's crest fell. Her chin and shoulders sagged, as though the material in her thin scarf dress morphed into rock. Her mouth flapped to build a retort, but rendered only a hushed moment.

That moment passed. "But without you, I have no shot at the reward."

"The reward?" said Carla.

"The reward?" said Danica.

"The reward!" Energy returned to Lorena's body, sending her back into performance mode. "We would go to the house this evening. We have to *help* find her — that is the mandate. We could find clues or dig up information or actually find her herself. If we can do that before Wednesday — this coming Wednesday, the Twenty-First — the reward is one hundred thousand dollars." She went on mumbling something about this wonderful opportunity. None of which registered with Danica; her ears interpreted no words beyond the 'S' in 'dollars.'

This was dumb. The police should've handled this from the jump; should've already been handling it. Sofi was a celebrity. Surely the LAPD had a celebrity peril division all set up to handle exactly such a scenario. Danica could even recommend some names. They had cars and kits and tons of experience. More than a twenty-something with a barber's degree and one prior case, to be sure.

She needed to get Lorena to step back. No reason for wannabe do-gooders — which she wasn't, no matter what Gabby said — to muck up a serious investigation. No need to seek thrills and danger and try to throw herself in harm's way again.

Danica should have said, 'No.'

Instead she said, "I'm in."

CHAPTER TEN

Sunday, January 18, 2009. 6:20PM. Island Estates.

The clock on the microwave to the one in the bathroom and back to the microwave again. Danica circled the apartment, watching time tick away. None of the clocks matched, but none of them had good news anyway.

"I really can drive you, it's not a major deal." Gabby had already offered this charity. She had sunk into the couch with her laptop on her knees. Concern held a place in her voice.

"Lorena said she'd drive. That was the plan."

"So we're trusting her completely now?"

Without a suitable response, Danica said nothing. A glance caught the last of her scribbled notes about Marty and Sofi's view counts. When was the last video Sofi had posted? Danica couldn't recall even checking.

"Did you get a rundown of how this would, like, work exactly?" said Gabby. "I mean, what are the rules?"

"It's not a gameshow."

"Seems like one. A reality show at least. Or a gig — don't hurt me, but it's true. Send me her email."

After the parking lot conversation had wrapped, Lorena forwarded an email she received from Tori, an accomplishment not lost on the two women in Apartment 213. Danica had read it several times already, fighting through Lorena's typed interjections, middle-aged syntax and typos. From these re-reads, she'd discerned a few facts: they'd meet at Danica's place at 5:30PM. Lorena would drive. They were going to Sofi's house in the Tarzana hills. And other people would be in attendance.

"What 'other people' do you think we're talking about here?" Gabby chewed on the ends of her hair. "'Cause, like, I gotta be honest? It sounds like contestants."

"I think they're just other, you know... people like me."

"You mean other detectives?"

"Nnnno."

"Well, you don't mean other hairstylists."

Danica sunk into a dining room chair facing the microwave. 6:29. She found the urge to pack more pens, instead thinking of her notes again. She opened her phone.

The last video Sofi had posted was over a week ago, a content drought definitely noticed by some commenters. A few were antsy, a few were concerned, while others threatened unsubscription — the nuclear option for YouTube — if their free clips remained undelivered.

She gave in and pulled her notebook out of her go bag. What was she going to do — memorize this stuff?

A few ink-stormed minutes later, she had filled two pages with half-cooked research and statistics. The highlighted videos were all in the "Sofi Tries..." series, but buried under them were a few original skits and character scenes. Compared to the "Sofi Tries..." clips, the original skits were under-performers. One view for every fifty. Maybe less. They seemed like flights of fancy, things artists did every now and then to get something out of their system, as opposed to the strategic curation normally seen around her semi-reality series.

Due either to YouTube's limited on-page search power or to Danica's inability to understand the site (even odds really), she found little explanation for the existence of these anomalous videos. She broadened her scope and went to the great wild of Google for more information.

Sofi didn't do many interviews, but she apparently didn't need to. Her media blitz came from fan blogs. Danica began with the link Gabby had shared and spiraled from there. Fans almost exclusively related her to the "Sofi Tries..." series, making special notice of "Sofi Tries to Ride a Bike." Even with this casual search, it seemed "Ride a Bike" was Sofi's breakthrough.

"Oh my g-d, Ride a Bike is where we fell for her, hook line and sink her," said one blog.

"I remember watching it in my bathroom and laughing sooo hard my dad thought I was throwing up. Good thing I was in the bathroom already," said another.

One especially wordy site offered all kinds of statistics and study of Sofi's video world. It listed "Ride a Bike" as "The One," calling it "a spectacular specimen of PPE Sofi." A little more digging translated those initials as 'Pre-Props Era,' another dig at the skits.

That find sent Danica into another odd corner of the internet, with more fan pages cataloging the many, many (many) props and items Sofi featured in her later-era videos. One blog went so far as to count the number of times each prop had appeared, with none more than four times. They also talked trash about each other, particularly of one blog belonging to the unfortunately-named Gasper Kutman.

This guy, Kutman, put in *work*, taking great care to

catalog the entire Starr history. At first, Danica flagged the blog for something to read in case of a nap, but she dipped a little into that deep history and discovered a fanaticism. She found catalogs, rankings, lists and pre-making-it-big clips. A couple showcased pre-Sofi *Sofia* and her sister.

"Ever seen Tori like this?" Danica showed her find to Gabby.

"Whaaaaaaat?"

The two stared at the clip. One sister urged the other to use a zipline. It was tied to a house and ran over an in-ground pool. Sofi spoke to the camera, urging her sister to muster the courage for the stunt. After a minimum of nudging, the young Tori did it, whooshing down the line until she was above the pool, at which time she released and fell into the water, feet first. The camera shook and ran toward the pool's edge as a sopping-wet Tori pulled herself out. Both sisters screeched with laughter and high-fived and hugged. Sofi kissed her sister and they smiled the same smile.

A smile! The clip served as evidence that Tori had, at one time, *enjoyed* herself.

Danica tried to make a note of it when her hand tensed and she dropped her pen, the needles poking from within again. As she rubbed her wrist, she looked at her notes, at the numbers, and considered the fans behind these calculations. The clicks, the sites, the blogs, all of them.

Gabby pointed at her laptop. "This email says it starts at 7:00 in Tarzana. I can totally drive, even if traffic is bad."

"Didn't you say Sofi had a stalker?"

"Huh?"

"At the shoot. Sofi has a stalker, that's what you said."

Gabby nodded. "What I heard. I mean, it makes sense sorta. Well, it *doesn't*. It's totally just patriarchy crap that we have to deal with. But when you're a big star, you cast a wide net, you catch some strange fish."

Danica's eyes glazed over as she thought of her own touch of internet infamy. The level at which strangers felt they owned other people's lives unsettled her, despite the fact that she was participating in that same system. She looked back at her phone and retraced her steps to the Kutman blog. Its tiny font looked like torture, its dark green background screaming 'Free Site.' Its implied intimacy shared DNA with that who-asked-you criticism from the ForWhatItsWorth blog.

"How could someone with such a public life, filming her every move and posting it online all the time, go missing?"

"Sofi's a risk taker. You saw the stunts, right?"

"That's her image."

"Her *brand*," said Gabby. "It's called a brand."

"Either way, the brand has disappeared, and it seems like in order for someone like her to disappear, it would be on purpose."

"Maybe she just had to get away, you know? Like Dave Chappelle."

Danica scrunched her eyebrows. "And not post anything about it? Anywhere? She has a zillion channels. You remember when Sharon was dropping off Facebook? She posted about it. It was like a suicide note, everything explained in detail. But this... I don't wanna say, but hanging around waiting to get picked up isn't helping."

The microwave clock read 6:44.

Gabby stood. "I'll get my keys."

CHAPTER ELEVEN

They only came close to creating an accident twice, with one of those times being not one-hundred-percent Gabby's fault. The Prius still in one piece, they made it to Tarzana in relatively good time. Danica would qualify as late, but not obnoxiously so.

Neither of these facts did anything for her mood.

"Maybe Lorena lives on this side of town and it was, you know, like, a convenience thing. To, um… forget."

Gabby was trying, but Danica was over it. She watched houses drift away as the car drove west. The sprawl opened. There, where two highways crossed, the definition between wilderness and urban life seemed both distant and mixed.

The mountains emerged. Having grown up in the Midwest, Danica still marveled at the very existence of land masses taller than a school gym. The dark gloom of night settled deep into the hills ("hills"; they were bigger than her grandparents' three barns stacked on top of each other).

Lights sprinkled onto their slopes, pinpointing the shadows. Another life ago, Danica might have mistaken those lights for fireflies. Now they signified money and defiance against nature. The will of the powerful placed them on the sides of mountains, covered in trees and surrounded by animals, simply because they could buy it.

"AT. NEXT. EXIT. TURN. RIGHT!" said the Garmin. Its halting speech insisted they leave the 101 and head south, up the mountain. The street twisted. After a few miles, it downgraded to a road.

Danica checked her phone again. No message from that wannabe witch. Was Lorena trying to get the jump on her? If so, why would she tell her about the reward at all? Danica was unsure which outcome was less insulting.

Her driver giggled. When Danica inquired, Gabby insisted it was nothing, so Danica was ready to let it go.

Then Gabby didn't let it go. "It's just, this is kinda classic, right? You're the independent private eye with a secret, can't-miss formula for solving crimes. And you've, like hooked up with a mysterious businesswoman who is a little shady, to inspect a haunted house."

"Haunted house?"

Gabby continued. "Fine, but you've got three days to solve the mystery. All while you're, you know, locked in the house with the kidnapping suspects."

Years prior, the two of them saw a neighbor they'd nicknamed Cowboy Rick swimming naked in the apartment pool. By that evening, Gabby had built his character into an intricate backstory where he (Cowboy Rick) had been part of a sex religion, one which required men to reproduce every year or suffer terrible consequences. "The cowboy hat is part of his piety," she'd explained. "A symbol of his devotion to the Doing-It Religion."

Danica played along with the story despite the likely truth

that Cowboy Rick — who looked like an average dirtbag — was probably *just* an average dirtbag. This happened around the time of a fire in Griffith Park. To keep the smoke out, they slept with the windows closed, making for a murky week. Prior to the Cowboy Rick story, Gabby had been worrying aloud about displaced animals and the homes near the danger zone.

With nothing to clean, Gabby's anxiety fueled her creativity, making up stories to cover for her worries. And it was happening again as they wound through the forest road. The girl was concerned for her, fretting through her imagination that her roommate was walking into something treacherous.

Danica took her hand. "Gab, it's just a missing person. Nobody's used the word 'k-word.' So the other people might just be... other people. There to help. No suspects, nothing suspicious."

"But you'd said earlier. It's a missing *celebrity* person."

"I'm just sticking to the instructions." She waved her print out. "Find Sofi or something that helps find her and collect the money. No drama."

"No drama? That sounds like all drama."

"Well, no *extra* drama from me. Just do the job. That's it."

"Okay, okay."

"Safer that way, too, y'know?"

Gabby nodded.

"RE-CALCULATING... RE-CALCULATING... RE-CALCULATING...." The grey box on the dashboard had its problems, too.

Danica looked around for signs of life, let alone a house. She saw neither. The trees conspired against them to block out the sky.

Gabby swore. "I think we're close, but I don't see anything like an address anywhere."

"Maybe keep going forward?"

"Yeah, I don't think we passed it," said Gabby. "We haven't passed anything."

They rolled along and Danica felt the tension pulse. They were on a mountain after all, which meant they were, at the very least, above some kind of drop. And being on a shabby mountain road meant that the possibility of making a wrong turn had a non-zero sum chance of resulting in a deadly fall into a chasm.

Apparently, Danica, too, fabricated stories during times of stress. And they helped just as much as Gabby's.

"There it is!" Gabby pointed and turned right.

Like an optical illusion in new light, the house appeared from its hiding place. A split-level structure stood behind the oak trees. Its expanse made up for its modest height. A long porch trailed around the front and as far as Danica could tell, every light in the house was on.

A hedge rose higher and higher to a black gate, which opened as Gabby approached. From the driveway they could see into the house, through its enormous front windows. An inky figure moved inside from one window to the next, on and on, unstopped by even the idea of walls.

A cluster of cars huddled to the north side of the giant house. They parked next to a blue Kia.

"Don't worry: Lorena made it."

Gabby didn't respond to Danica's hilarious quip. She held her Garmin in one hand and pointed at the gate with the other. She mumbled something about turns and trees. After she grumbled, Danica inquired.

"Can't rely on this stupid thing. I'm trying to make a mental map for when I come pick you up."

The large dark-wood doors of the house opened, cutting their conversation. Music crept out from somewhere within the house, but nobody emerged. Not immediately. Footsteps clomped without an accompanying figure. Was she just supposed to take the open door for a welcome?

At last, a person appeared in the doorway. Danica recognized her orange jacket.

"Rough traffic again?" said Tori. "We were just about to start."

Gabby waved and leaned to Danica's ear. "Want me to hang around down the road?"

"No, that's OK. I'll text you."

"Remember: Find her or find something to help. Get the money."

"Avoid drama." Danica nodded, then hugged her. Withdrawing, she pulled her go bag on her shoulder and headed for the door. By the time she made it up the stairs, Tori had vanished.

CHAPTER TWELVE

8:26PM. THE STARR RESIDENCE, TARZANA, CA.

The term "open floor plan" did no justice to the front room, as that would imply a plan existed in the first place. It would imply a room with limitations. For this house, the foyer was the front room was the dining room was the living room and so on and so on until a wall finally interjected to call it quits. A sunken couch facing an indoor fire pit and the wall of windows signified a living *area* rather than a proper, compartmented room.

But that wasn't what Danica noticed first.

Nor was it the rows of chairs facing a whiteboard, set up like a mini conference area in the middle of this conference-hall-sized space. And it wasn't the sticky notes and markers, clips and tape next to the whiteboard, or even that the chairs appeared to be that good-quality-looking stuff, not some Walmart special.

No, what Danica had noticed first were the seven sets of

eyes staring at her. A sudden urge to check her zipper came to her, but she dared not move a muscle.

"Seat for you there." Tori pointed from the whiteboard area to a seat in the second row, the only seat not occupied. Danica shuffled toward it, trying hard not to scuff what she assumed to be a very nice hardwood floor. The sweat beading on the back of her neck put her back in tenth-grade science class, showing up tardy with half-completed homework as a bunch of cheerleaders acted like she didn't belong.

The only friendly face was Marty's, with enough wattage to illuminate the whole mountain. He sat in the front row next to a white dude with gray roots and gave a robust wave as Danica sat down.

"So great you made it, Danica."

He remembered her name. He leaned over his chair back and spoke in a polite whisper above the general chit-chat of the others. "Not sure you remember me. I'm Marty. I was at the shoot the other day."

They shook hands for two seconds, which — Danica admitted to herself — felt fantastic.

The fantasticness sprinted away when Marty said, "I knew you did make-up, but how long have you been working for Madame Lorena?"

In all the pressure of arriving late and entering a strange house full of strangers, Danica's vision must have blacked out for a couple seconds. The head in the seat next to Marty spun to face her, dragging a head scarf's train across Danica's knees. The look on Lorena's face reminded her of a cartoon cat with a tasty bird in its mouth.

As her mouth tried to create a response, her brain processed the words 'Worked for Lorena?' Through all the insanity of the day, she had somehow blocked out one of the more insulting bits of insanity.

With the question going unresolved for far too long, Danica decided to provide a safe, undescriptive lie.

"Oh, you know... off and on for a while, I guess." She wondered if there was a place where she could learn to lie more effectively. Perhaps a college course, something through the mail or online. At least an improv class. Anything to keep from yakking out the lamest tripe on Planet Earth.

"I believe you came under my wing last summer. Around July, was it not?" Lorena may have taken the lying courses Danica imagined. Perhaps she'd taught a few semesters, judging by her calm display of liesmanship.

The combo worked: Marty accepted it.

"Sorry you missed dinner, but I really appreciate you being part of this. It means a lot to me."

Danica gave a bow while she considered kicking the back of Lorena's chair. The whole tone of the house had thrown her off so much that she'd nearly forgotten the reason she was angry to begin with.

When Marty turned away, she gave a non-kicking tap on Lorena's shoulder. "I thought you were driving."

"I did."

"Both of us. I thought you were picking me up."

"I sent you the email with the information."

"Yes, but that was for...." Danica struggled to find that killer line to put Lorena in her place. All she came up with was: "Sharing. At the salon, we said you'd drive."

"I neither had nor gave that impression." Lorena's face held its ground and Danica retreated into her folding chair. She looked away from Lorena for fear of getting the punching sickness.

The guy next to Marty — the one with emerging roots — was getting an earful from Bobby, the oldest viral video crew member. He'd cleaned himself up. The beard retained its shag, but he wore a clean button-down shirt and equally clean jeans.

On the other side of Bobby sat a woman with black hair darker than her blouse and high-waist pants, and those things were both pretty damn black. If anyone in the house had cigarettes, it was her. She sat at the end of the row with an oozing desire to be left alone.

This vamp could not have been more different from the two women in Danica's row. Their sandals and tank-tops-under-sweaters look was so bright that they resembled parodies of surfers. They wore sweatpants with words written down the legs. The Black woman of the pair had her hair yanked back in a controlled-but-casual bun while the white woman's dusty blonde hair cracked from too much beach time. Danica placed their ages as "early college," judging mostly from the smartphones glued to their hands. They split their conversation between texting and speaking, stopping neither activity.

Though she felt bad for generalizing, Danica couldn't help thinking that the two surfer parodies and the vamp — in Danica's limited experience based on her absorbing years of phallocentric media and a so-so public education — did not strike her as 'detective types.' She threw in Bobby for equity's sake, but this inclusion did little to raise that measure.

"Is that all you brought?" said Lorena, pointing to Danica's go bag. "Did you get your gift?"

Danica slid her things under her chair, crunching something in the process: a canvas bag. A quick survey affirmed that every chair had one. Some even had names written on the sides; Bobby's read, 'BOBBY' while the young Black surfer's read, 'JOY.' Danica's was blank, as was the surfer's compatriot.

Inside the bag was a travel-size toothbrush set and a heavy plastic cup with a lid and straw. While she spotted a couple cups with names like "Marty" and "Lorena," Danica's cup simply read "Fun."

Tori tapped the whiteboard with her knuckle and the room hushed. Her other hand dove into her jacket pocket and emerged with a remote. One click and the lights dimmed — all but a few over Tori at the presentation area.

"Almost a year ago," she said, "Sofi began developing an elaborate, interconnected video series. A puzzle series, where she would mention or show off different bits of information to her fans. If the fans watched carefully enough, they'd solve the puzzle. One of those puzzle pieces was here."

A light snapped on from the back of the room, firing a beam onto the whiteboard and filling much of it with a map. Tori pointed at it.

"Six days ago, she went here. The desert, to shoot isolated footage for this puzzle series. She never came back."

Her hard English still allowed some warmth to slide by. Danica could see it in her eyes, too, when she said her sister's name.

"We spoke Monday, the twelfth. Her work was finishing. She said she would head home soon. It was the last time I heard from her directly."

She turned to the map. "Filming took place here. We used to camp near this area with Mother and Papa. Long ago. When we have gone in recent years, there's often a dead zone here for cellphones. Sofi knew this, I am certain, and would have made her call close to this location." Tori circled an area on the map away from the highway.

"When she did not return, I went looking. I found only her car. Here."Another circle, this time on the other side of the map, a few inches from the campsite circle.

"That was Wednesday. When I returned home, I searched for answers. Something hidden. Then I remembered a clip, a video, which Sofi made last month. A confessional. I talked her out of loading it."

Tori's remote returned and the light above her dimmed. At the same time, the projector light flashed. Its beam cut across the giant room as a large projection screen, lowering from the ceiling, fell into place and caught it.

The white woman with a no-name cup gasped as the video started. The Sofi on screen was not the lively girl trying to ride a bike or change a tire. She had little to no make-up and even less spark. She held the camera on her face and smiled as though it hurt. Even though the angle framed her face in the center, the camera wiggled. Danica realized she was on a bed, holding the camera up and out. A frilly something lay behind her shoulder.

"Hello hello," said on-screen Sofi, then looked away. "I tried writing this down first, but, you know, it never came out right so I'm gonna wing it. Lately, I have not felt safe. Around my home, working, traveling. It's been building up for a while now, but the last couple months..."

Sofi broke off and the video's dire spirit infected the house. The tears came, first on-screen then off. The women in Danica's row deteriorated. Marty's head sagged into his hands, earning a shoulder rub from Lorena.

"I wish I could say more," she continued. "I want to tell someone. If you, or anyone knows anyone who does not feel safe at work, or with fans or just with any people... you have to support them. Listen to them. Believe them."

Passion fired through the screen. The tears came again and Sofi let the camera fall to the side, a bright light blanking out most of the frame.

A few moments passed and the camera jostled back into position. Sofi's eyes were more red.

"A lot of people watch my stuff. I know that's great. I've

actually watched them watch, which is weird, but... that's me." She laughed.

So did the surfer parodies. They tickle-high-fived, then transitioned into a full holding of hands.

"But there's something else," said On-Screen Sofi. "Someone else. I know it's a He. It's all I've been thinking about lately. I've barely eaten and I can't sleep. Every little sound... I think it's him. Maybe it is him, sneaking around somehow, and he just hasn't found the nerve to do anything but sneak."

She looked away from the camera, but kept it on her face.

"I think someone's following me. Actually, I know they are. They tried to get in my house. Someone helped them or they knew somebody or something... They knew where to find things, how to get to certain places. And I've gotten letters. And gifts. I hid them. I didn't want to destroy them, for, you know, evidence and all that, but I couldn't be with them, you know? Out in the open? I just... I couldn't."

She wiped her nose, then smiled. Her teeth were the brightest things on screen, but their radiance dimmed. This was a different version of Sofi from the one Danica had researched. This girl was scared.

"I won't let him stop me," she said. "I'm gonna live my life the way I want to. Everyone should."

Blackout. The video stopped and the lights slowly returned. Sofi's words rang in Danica's ears.

Her eyes focused back on Tori, whose stiff upper lip quivered when she spoke. "I chose not to post this video. I convinced my sister it was not right for her. That it was private. She agreed. She, too, wanted to maintain her image. But now you see, clearly, she was scared someone was after her."

"So why not go to the police?" This came from the guy

with unnaturally darkened hair. The condescension in his voice was familiar.

"I understand it's controversial to keep this search quiet. But you must understand: her work is her passion. Her whole life! And her life depends on public perception, you see? Her dreams rely on presenting a good image, not a troubled one. I am positive my sister would want the search conducted this way. I know Sofi like I know myself."

After an uncomfortable amount of silence, the Black woman spoke up. "Can you tell us what that means and what-not? I mean, how do we help and all?"

"Sofi loved games. Puzzles and such. She has always loved them, even when we were children. It is why she worked Easter Eggs into her videos. And why she made that puzzle series. Teasing everyone with clues."

The words 'highlight the hidden tease' ran back into Danica's memory. That must have been what the crew meant; that or Danica *really* didn't understand video lighting jargon.

"In the video," said Tori, "she said she received a gift from this... person, and that she hid it. She filmed that video in the house, so it stands to reason the gift must be around here, too. Somewhere away, but safe. I believe it's here and it can help us find Sofi, along with other pieces of the puzzle."

Danica joined the rest of the audience in looking around the room for any treasure chests, secret passageways or anything that might have been labeled 'HIDDEN CLUES.'

Tori spoke to the front row. "You are Sofi's closest friends. Her collaborators. Partners. You helped build her and sustain her. You know her well. That is why I turn to you. To help find my sister. Save her and her good name."

The façade cracked again, as did Tori's voice. She pulled back and wiped her eyes. Some of the seated people squirmed, unsure how to respond. Marty's head did another droop and Bobby rolled his head back as if dazed. Even the vamp, who appeared to have a preternatural aversion to the emotions of day walkers, chewed on her blood red lips.

The young surfers both looked like they were on the brink. Well, one of them; the other, the white one with dusty blonde hair, raised her hand. "What's with the wifi situation in this place again?" Her friend swatted her leg.

"Yes, Kayleigh, that reminds me: some parameters. First, we have only three days time. After that — on Wednesday — if we have not made progress, I must involve the police.

"Second, we must be careful and thorough. I have developed a schedule and I insist we stick to it.

"Third, no arguing or fighting. We must be civil. Any fighting will result in expulsion from the investigation.

"Fourth: no videos or posting on Facebook or social media. This must be kept quiet."

The white surfer's hand shot up again, having learned nothing from the earlier swat.

"This means that while we normally have wireless internet," said Tori, "it has been shut down. I do not want word of our investigation leaking. Additionally, the mountain creates problems and sometimes we get a very poor phone signal. This may be to your benefit since anyone caught spreading information outside of this house will also be excused."

The group adjusted in their collective seats while Tori exuded a mix of emotions. On one hand, her clipped oration resembled gameshow host patter, introducing contestants to a new money-making challenge. On the other hand, her details arrived on a wavering voice, one of a woman in anguish.

The vamp raised her cup in the air. It read 'Alex,' and what her face lacked in complexion, it made up for in exasperation. Her lips parted from their perpetual pout and said, "What about the deal?"

"I have not forgotten," said Tori. "If we have not found

Sofi by Wednesday, then my hands are tied and we must call the police. However if one of you finds, or if you can help in a substantial manner by locating evidence, information, insight, clues... then I will pay you three-hundred thousand dollars."

Ever the professional, Madame Lorena released a sputtered chuckle. Most would have missed it, but Danica caught that shoulder shimmy. Also not missed was the memory of her saying 'one-hundred thousand' in the parking lot earlier that day.

The practicality of earning more money was not lost on Danica. A flurry of daydreams rushed before her. Being honest, some were wholly selfish, but a few centered around helping others. She looked around the room in search of similarly-excited faces.

She found none. True, most had their backs to her, but Alex the Vamp's face remained dour. Even the two surfers — curious about phone signals above all — knew enough not to cheer about money at a time like this. Only gross, self-serving opportunists would be happy in these circumstances. Danica slumped, unhappy with herself.

Then she unslumped. There remained one clear path to redeeming herself from this faux pas: hunkering down and helping find the missing woman. And she had experience in that realm. Some. More than most, she guessed. How many cases had that Goth girl solved? One, tops?

Danica's energy rebounded. She had a fresh notebook, a couple working pens. And a spirit ready to find some information. To save a life. To protect that life's dreams. She was ready to get to it.

Tori tucked the remote into her jacket pocket. "Thank you for coming. I know with your help, we will find Sofi."

Danica nodded, to herself and the room.

"Working together, I am certain we will succeed."

Damn right we will, thought Danica.

"The official investigation will begin in the morning. Help yourselves to snacks and adjourn to your rooms. Goodnight."

...Wait...

'Begin in the morning?'

'Adjourn to our rooms?'

'*Snacks?*'

Wait...*what?*

Neither the email nor Danica's 'partner' mention anything about staying the night. The faces of every other person did not appear concerned with this, and with good reason; beyond Alex stood a stack of mismatched luggage.

She took a moment to remind herself that this was not her house, her sister or her show. It was Tori's — clearly. If she wanted it handled this way, nobody would argue with her, least of all Danica. This could be fine. It would have to be.

Still, Danica had questions and wanted to raise her hand. Marty beat her to it.

Unfortunately he asked a different question, unrelated to the newly-revealed-to-her notion that they would be spending the night.

"So we know where she went. Out in the desert and stuff. Did anyone else know Sofi was going to that campsite?"

Tori set her shoulders. "Yes. And they're all in this room."

Another three years of silence cooked the room, house and most of the mountain.

CHAPTER THIRTEEN

10:49PM. THE STARR RESIDENCE.

Growing up where she had (central Illinois) and when she had (central 1990's), Danica's musical tastes were dictated by access. The radio played music, she responded to that music depending on her mood at the time, nudged this way or that by her feelings, the weather and those around her. In her step-father's truck, they listed to the oldies station. While she enjoyed a lot of it, the music of the past provided a distance from her own self. On the few occasions when she hung out with friends (and when those friends actually had cars), they listened exclusively to Top 40 radio. This managed to plug her into a time of her own, yet a distance still remained; how personally connected could one get to Mariah Carey when the woman sold ten zillion records to three zillion people? As a yearning, young teen, she wanted something contemporary, fun, but a little more accessible than Mariah. She chose En Vogue for a while (she liked their two big hits, taped their appearance on *In Living Color*, etc.), but their well soon dried up and Danica needed a new thing to cling to. To claim.

Rock radio transformed a few times in this era, with Green Day wearing the crown at this moment in history. Somehow, despite all circumstances around growing up a pre-internet-era teen in Central Illinois, she had jumped on their wagon quick (only their third and biggest album!). Again, she decided: this was *hers*. She was part of the group around the group. When she caught clips from their concerts, she saw more shaved heads than cowboy hats and barrettes.

She felt like she could be part of that club; a club for people who hated clubs.

So she bought a *Dookie* shirt.

For central Illinois in 1996, wearing a shirt of a super successful pop punk band counted as rebellious.

For Los Angeles in the early 2000's, Danica's shirt elicited other reactions. At first, she told herself the shirt helped to weed out snobs. Anyone who sneered at a *Dookie* shirt either thought they were immune to popular things (like they hadn't screamed along to "Basket Case?") and were lying to themselves since they likely owned the album, too.

Nevertheless, she stopped wearing the shirt to work, opting for one of her shirts nurtured by her new big-city tastes. She found a kind of warped Liz Phair shirt, with her "Exile in Guyville" face wrapped around her entire body. A fruitful yard sale provided a cedar chest full of shirts that would make any poseur blush (Bad Brains' first album cover shirt, a couple horror movie poster shirts, and one of Keith Richards himself wearing a shirt asking 'Who the F is Mick Jagger?'). She made it a particular quest to seek out more shirts with women (without featuring Marilyn Monroe's cleavage). And in a period of 'retro re-issues," her search finally yielded a 'Funky Divas' tour shirt from her beloved En

Vogue. Finally, after years of truly believing she was never gonna get it, she did!

Sadly, Laundry ate that shirt, yet the *Dookie* shirt — like the album of the same name — lived on, forever and ever, persisting and insisting that it never cede its spot in the public consciousness or Danica's dresser. She wore it thinking of En Vogue, wore it with irony and wore it on desperate days. But if she was being completely honest with herself, she loved that shirt.

She was wearing it in the living area of the Starr Residence. She'd worn it all day and now, having learned that she would be spending the night there and having packed no change of clothes, the shirt's inappropriateness had never been more fully realized. Maybe if the Funky Divas shirt had survived, she might have been saved a modicum of her dignity, but it was not to be. She pulled her sweatshirt around those huge, puke-green letters. Her credibility as a functioning adult had little support from her wardrobe.

The group began to disperse, grabbing their bags from the pile near the back. Lorena didn't hesitate, swooping out of her chair and through an exit in the rear of the living area. Alex the Vamp also moved quickly, but headed for the stairs near the back hall. Others followed while Danica hung back, catching Marty's attention at the door.

"You all set?" he said.

Not at all, she thought. Farthest thing from it.

"I was hoping to get a few things straight. Or maybe we could go over the evidence?"

"No," said Joy. "Uh-uh. That one right there wants to start now, when we're not starting. To, like, cheat and whatnot."

Tori returned to the living area and stopped the world with her stare. "We have a schedule and we are going to rest now. Investigating will start in the morning."

"Sure, but..."

Ice dripped from Tori's lashes. "In the morning. Per the schedule."

Danica got the message and clammed up. She didn't understand why they wouldn't be rushing through the investigation process, but Tori's deep stare informed her that she didn't have to understand. She just had to comply.

The woman turned and left her guests, disappearing down the dark hallway.

"Sorry," said Marty. "We went over it earlier, before you got here. We're all supposed to work as a team, on the schedule. It's what Tori knows."

He looked toward the hallway as though remembering something he'd forgotten. Marty excused himself, promised he'd come back, then jogged up the stairs.

To avoid small talk, Danica pulled her notebook and pen from her bag and jotted down a few notes from the presentation. Mostly she rationalized. Gathering Sofi's closest friends and co-workers instead of going to the police *could have* made sense. In fact, it showed even more faith that she wasn't in true danger if Tori would steer the operation in this manner.

On the stairway, Joy and her friend Kayleigh clumped their clunky shoes up each step, phones still in hand.

"This is supposed to be, like, a mansion and whatnot, then why can't we get a signal?"

"I know right?" said Kayleigh. Danica presumed their commiseration would continue for the totality of the stay.

God, 'the stay.' Did Lorena know this coming in? Had it been some subtle bit of sabotage, or was she just inept — which was worse? She scribbled Lorena's initials along with these questions, then considered adding some nasty commentary.

Movement pulled her eyes from her page. They landed square on the man next to Bobby. Not just his eyes, but to his roots. Just as she'd done upon arrival, spotting their lightness contrasting against his unnatural, unbelievable darkness on top; a still-growing toupee. Her experience as a hair stylist allowed her to notice such casualties, but the man himself seemed strangely familiar, too. He'd avoided eye contact when Danica had arrived, all but hiding in the seats. And now, there he stood, his face contorted into a forced smile. It was James Van Owen, one of LAPD's 'finest.'

He wore the same Polo-shirt-tucked-into-jeans look as he did the first day he came into Earl's, the day he accidentally shared his vision of a dead Drake Alberts III on a grassy lawn with Danica. Wherever he was getting his hair done since, they owed him a refund.

The more she stared, the more panic consumed her. James was a cop. Was he undercover? Would she blow his cover? Would he blow hers? Did she even have a cover to blow?

As though in answer to her questions, a creepy focus erupted across his own face. He made a motion for Bobby to go ahead, then nudged closer to Danica.

"Well... we should probably talk real quick." His eyebrows scrunched as he nodded toward the go bag on her shoulder. "That all you brought?"

His cop essence came at her in full splendor. His legs spread, with the right slightly in front of the left, creating a power stance. He asked, "What are you doing here, Danica?"

In all the weird of the last ten minutes, answering such a simple question felt intimidating. "I was gonna ask you the same thing."

"I'm part of this. Saw you show up. I mean, we all did. Don't think you noticed me though."

"You were hiding."

"Sh'yeah, right. You had eyes for Brad Pitt over there. Is Marty your ticket inside?"

A compulsion to make up excuses sprouted in Danica's

mouth. She grabbed her canvas guest bag from under her chair. "I am a guest."

"I can see that. You with that Lorena lady, too?"

Danica nodded.

"Did you know anybody else prior to arrival at the premises?"

"I didn't think I would. But then you're here, so I guess that counts."

She wanted to keep talking so that he could not speak, not ask another question. He was pumping her for information, the way the force had trained him. But in her pause, she considered the questions he had asked. James was only asking certain questions and none about the case itself. She cocked her head back.

James hung his hands on his belt, then changed course and put them in his pockets. Danica recognized the discomfort. Of struggling (and failing) to look cool.

And he wasn't even wearing an outdated Green Day shirt.

Her urge to make up excuses disappeared, replaced by a pressing curiosity. The kind she'd been trying to stamp out.

Just this once, she'd give in to her investigative tendencies.

"How is it that *you're* here, James?"

His mouth opened, but nothing emerged. The confidence of James' earlier expression departed, throwing his 'I've-seen-it-all,-girl' stance to the curb. It reminded her of their first encounter. At Earl's when he asked for secrecy around his requested hair coloration.

Danica put it together.

"Jeez... you just want me to stay quiet about you. Again!"

"Please keep your voice down."

"Really, man, why *are* you here? Aren't police supposed to... they're not... what are you doing here?"

"I'm not here as a cop in the strictest sense. No badge, see? I was hired independent of the force."

"You can do that?"

"Sure."

"You can do that and not be tied to mobsters? Unless you *were* hired by mobsters? Not good either way."

"All right, calm down—"

"Has that ever worked? Telling people to calm down? 'Cause if so, I'm about to break your winning streak."

Danica watched his training kick in. His face clicked into memory mode, recalling all those mandatory classes and exercises the LAPD had put him through on how to de-escalate situations with upset people. Yet he somehow ignored that training, instead taking a breath and speaking to her like a human being.

"I had time off, got contacted, liked the opportunity. So... now here I am."

"With who? Who hired you?"

"I'm not sure I can divulge the—"

Man, more of this confidentiality crap. Danica had lived only part of her life in the world social media had created, but she knew enough to understand that privacy meant jack. "It's fine. I saw you chumming it up with Bobby anyway."

"He knows my dad," said James. "Well, they did, a while ago. Look, I just want us to be cool. We have a delicate situation between us and we should handle it..." he scavenged his tremendous vocabulary for the perfect convincing phrase, finally deciding on, "good."

His pause allowed Danica ample time to think and scheme for herself. The opportunity had walked right up to her, pulled on her pant leg and begged to be taken.

"I'll keep your secret. For a fee."

"Like what?"

"Just share what you find. About anyone else in the house, or anything you learn. Two heads are better than one." Even if it is his head, she did not add out loud.

"What type of information are you thinking of... like, personal stuff?"

"Anything that relates to the mission, dude."

After half a second of deep consideration, James said, "Sure. But like what?"

"We're supposed to be finding a...." Danica pulled her anger back from the edge. Insulting him would get her nowhere closer to the cash. "You're the most qualified detective person here. You are a professional. So snoop around and try to find out some stuff, then share it with me. That'll be enough."

"So you're not going to... you won't..."

She sighed. "No, James. I won't. Your secrets, plural, are safe with me."

He grinned like Maury had told him he was not the father. "Great. Thanks. But I don't know what we're gonna find. Any of us. Between you and me, I think this girl just up and ran away."

This information had been offered so freely and made enough sense that Danica questioned whether it had come from James' mouth.

He continued, "You know, you see this environment. Kinda up-tight, right? She's got lots of responsibilities, a young woman, got money... If I were her, I would've at least considered bolting."

Danica admitted to herself that she had yet to consider it at all. But didn't want to tell him that. "OK. Thanks."

She excused herself to go grab snacks she didn't know about before going to a bedroom she had only just learned existed.

"Good to see you," he said. He had that cheerfulness in his voice, as learned through forty years of being a white man in America, relieved things were yet again working out for him.

Danica ignored him.

White light blasted the kitchen, a shimmering testament to home appliance acquisition. Everything was white or light grey and appeared to never have been used.

Everything except the bar, which was presently very much in use. Joy and her friend huddled together facing an enormous man behind the bar. Towering over everything, he resembled The Rock — not approachable-and-marketable movie star Dwayne Johnson, but *The Rock,* packed into a shirt and tie. He did not smile as he filled their plastic guest cups with some mix of booze.

The large island in the center of the kitchen held food. It carried a leftovers vibe. The dips held deep trenches, and many of the items to be dipped had vanished.

As she made a plate, Danica ran the last hour back in her mind. Sofi was missing. Tori was controlling. The group of friends to find Sofi possessed only one confirmed expert (James) and he sucked. Lorena had ditched her (accidentally it seemed, but that didn't make it any better). And they were all spending the night in the house.

All the suspects. Together.

No. Despite her naturally foreboding tone, Tori had not used the word 'suspects.' She must not have believed that to be a possibility. Otherwise, why would she invite the likely suspects to aid in the search?

Danica reached for a bagel but a hand grabbed it first. It was Kayleigh. In a flash, Danica finally recognized her. She and Joy were the young women hanging around at the shoot in the storage unit. The ones Tori scolded and kept at the door.

"You're Sofi's friends, right?" said Danica.

Kayleigh flipped her blonde hair back to her friend at the bar. She giggled, just as she had at the set and said, "Yeah?"

"We saw each other. At the set this week. I was doing makeup."

"OK?" More giggles.

In Danica's limited experience with groupies and fake friends, she had come to understand that they normally hung around the famous person; this was the second time seeing these particular ones hanging around the famous person's interests and property.

Also in her experience dealing with judgy people who laughed at the very idea of being spoken to, dropping the conversation where it stood sometimes made for a better night than fighting to keep it alive. Danica put her eyes back on the food and let the young woman scurry back to the bar. There were more giggles, a big time laugh, then they left.

She hadn't realized how hungry she was until she saw her plate, a tiny thing now overflowing with starches. Danica placed a bagel in her teeth and a napkin on top to steady it. Then Marty entered, catching her at her most ladylike.

"Good, you're still here. I wanted to take you to your bed."

Danica choked on a bit of bagel as she doubled checked that Marty had, indeed, said 'your' between 'I wanted to take you to' and 'bed.'

"Fine. Fine and dandy," she said, trying to forget saying such a stupid thing.

He took her go bag for her. "Do you want another plate to carry that stuff?"

Danica insisted she did not.

They wound back through the living area and toward the stairs in the hallway where Tori had gone. The stairs were carpeted with no backing, so Danica could watch the darkness below disappear as she followed Marty up.

More carpet at the upstairs hallway, but somehow older, with thicker matted tufts. Down the hall were several brown doors. While not a traditional mansion, the Starr Residence still exceeded the needs of anyone who could not already afford a palace. The building's expanse drew far beyond what Danica imagined when she'd arrived.

She covered her T-shirt with her food tower. "How long's Sofi lived here?"

"Couple years I think. I heard Warren Beatty lived here back in the day. Or Warren Buffet? I can't remember. One of the Warrens."

"It's cool. I mean it's actually chilly."

"Yeah, we're kinda in the mountain. Probably saves on AC in the summer." He stopped at a door near the end of the hallway. "This is you."

She found it strange that he knocked before opening the door. Stranger still that someone inside said, "Come in."

The door opened to two beds with enough room for two more. On the nearest bed sat Madame Lorena, posed by leaning on her right arm and hanging her left on her knee.

"Oh, I'm sorry," said Danica.

"Whatever for, my dear?"

If Lorena didn't understand how intrusion worked, then Danica wouldn't explain it to her. She recounted the beds and put it together.

Then Marty spelled it out. "You're bunking together. We thought... I mean, I suggested it. Since you are partners and all that."

Danica fake-smiled and entered, stepping onto a lush rug. She moved toward the inner-most bed and set her plate next to the pillow, claiming it like she wanted it. Working with Madame Lorena had never been at the top of her life's to-do list. Sleeping next to her hadn't even entered her imagination.

Her bed sprawled next to the window. At first, she

thought the darkness in the window related to the wilderness evening. But as she examined closer, the kind of darkness through the glass had no life to it. It was motionless.

"Is that... dirt?"

"Yeah. You're in the mountain here, like I said. When the sun comes up I think you can see a little light, but... yeah."

"I understand it is a cost-saving measure."

Shut up, Lorena.

A bottle of Jack Daniels sat on the dresser, next to a clean tumbler glass. Marty added Danica's no-name guest bag and plastic cup to complete the set.

"I think I'll turn in, too," said Marty. "Big day tomorrow. Starting early. I'm in the first room if you need anything."

An explosion of needs came to Danica all at once, all in the form of questions. Why weren't we investigating right now and all through the night? Why didn't Tori invite more professionals than freakin' James Van Owen? Does she know she invited one of the dumbest cops in town? Why would a room enclosed in a mountain have a window at all? Why was she staying with her fake boss who was actively tormenting her actual boss? How did he get his hair to dance in the light as though God herself kissed it with the wind?

Not all of these questions qualified as top priority, so all she managed to say out loud was, "Bathroom?"

"Right there." He gestured to the door next to Lorena's bed. "All yours. There's another one down the hall if you need it."

His smile acted as a period, the clear indication that he was finished speaking, having satisfied all inquiries. He closed the door upon exit, taking all the handsome with him.

"Well," said Lorena, spinning to face her. "What shall we do now? I see you got your own snack plate. Good thinking. Truth be told, I hadn't planned on sharing, so this makes it easier."

Two plates full of food somehow appeared on Lorena's bed. Danica wondered how she'd missed them, realizing slowly that Lorena had hidden them under her considerable wizard sleeves.

"What's the plan though, Lorena?"

"I figured, that is, if it's all the same to you, that I shall shower tonight. I prefer that to mornings..."

"I mean our mission. Do you want to compare notes? I tried to write down all I could from that presentation. I mean, Tori's organization is off the charts. I think, with all this control that Tori has over her, there's a possibility that Sofi might have—"

Lorena held up her hand. "I apologize, but can this wait until after the shower? They have scented oils here."

Scented oils? While Danica would have never said their partnership was off to a great start, she also never would have prioritized the accouterment of their guest bathroom over debriefing from their first meeting.

Lorena unzipped her suitcase, then glanced at Danica's bag. "I'm sure they could run to your car and get your bags."

"I don't have any bags or a car. You didn't tell me this was a sleepover."

"Oh, I'm certain I wouldn't have forgotten a thing like that. And I didn't. See?" She motioned to her luggage.

"Yeah, you just forgot to tell me. Now I'm stuck here wearing the same clothes for who knows how long."

"Three days max."

This didn't help, but neither would screaming at an older woman. Danica took a deep breath, scratching at anything resembling a solid thought.

"You want to earn the money for solving this thing, right?"

"Yes."

"Then... help me to solve this thing!"

"I will. I am. I believe in us, just as I believe that the work

will come in good time. I know myself and where my exper-
tise lies. And where yours lies as well. Certainly we both agree
this is more your field than mine."

It was the kind of compliment usually exercised by car
salesmen. Danica couldn't disagree with any of it on basis of
facts, but its implications pissed her off. As much as Lorena
wanted the money from the reward, she was in the cat bird
seat: if they found Sofi or not, Lorena would be fine. She had
nothing at stake. Nothing to lose.

"I recognize I have no notes to offer at the moment, but
I'm sure to have some tomorrow." Lorena moved to the bathroom, pulling off her head scarf and revealing a mess of gray
hair.

"This isn't a vacation."

"Of course not," said Lorena. Then she pulled on a shower
cap and closed bathroom the door.

In search of another sink or an excuse to put distance
between her and Lorena, Danica slipped back into the
hallway.

She wandered deeper into the hall, away from the stairway. The cool night had swallowed this portion of the house
and she regretted leaving her sweatshirt in her room.

Giggles crept from the doors at the end, both of which
were open. Joy crossed the hall from one door to the other —
right to the left — her face on phone and wearing jammie
pants worth a car payment. More giggles, then Kayleigh
crossed from left to right, barefoot and phone equally in face.

Then Joy crossed back again. "Biz-arre," she said as she
disappeared.

Danica snuck around to the door's edge and peeked
inside. The room on the right was another guest room, much
like her and Lorena's. The other room was a small bathroom
with blue walls and a white tile floor.

"You need something?" It was Kayleigh, staring at her from the doorway of the other room.

"I was looking for a bathroom," said Danica.

"Oh," said Kayleigh, almost shocked by such a request.

"There isn't a bathroom in your room and whatnot?" said Joy from behind. Her resting prosecutor face set, ready to jump down Danica's throat at any response.

"It does... my roommate is... can I just use that one?"

Kayleigh folded her arms. "But... for what?"

The question halted Danica's brain in its asininity. She tried to gauge how detailed or rudimentary she would need to be for Kayleigh's satisfaction.

Fortunately, Joy jumped in to command them all.

"Just give us a minute. We're finishing up." The Black woman pulled her white friend into the guest bathroom and closed the door. A sharp explosion of laughter followed.

Danica gave up and headed back to her room, ready to climb under the covers and hide.

CHAPTER FOURTEEN

Monday, January 19, 2009. 7:36AM. The Starr Residence. Danica and Lorena's Room.

Danica lay in bed all night wearing strange clothes and listening to Lorena snore while details swarmed through her mind, mixing around with each other.

All night, she'd heard noises and thought thoughts. The noises ranged from typical Different House Stuff (creaking walls, running pipes) to voices and footsteps. Joy and Kayleigh were dead set on enjoying their youth; they tried to sneak out of their room to do something they deemed fun. A booming voice scolded them and sent them back to their rooms, which they presumably did.

When Danica snuck a look out the hall, she saw a large figure sitting at the stairs. He had a masculine shape and wore a yellow shirt, tight against this body, like the bartender from the night before. Some kind of security guard inside the house.

'Maybe Sofi ran away,' thought Danica as she tossed and

turned. If a security presence inside your own house was the norm, then a runaway scenario felt more and more likely.

At some point she fell asleep; the last time she checked the clock, it had been 4:34AM. Now, in the morning, the smallest crack of light penetrated the mountain and slid through the window to land directly in Danica's eyes.

Lorena's bed lay vacant and remade with military-grade corners. Danica contemplated a shower, instead opting to check her phone. A litany of messages greeted her, all from Gabby. She cursed herself for not remembering to call her back; according to the messages, her roommate was not handling things well.

She tried to call, but got the CANNOT CONNECT message. Her phone had no bars; the thing had enough to receive all the frightened messages, but not enough to send anything back. A nicer person might have pitied Joy and Kayleigh, the suffering addicts of screen fascination.

In the dresser facing her bed, Danica found two sets of flannel pajamas, three sets of socks, toiletries and snacks. Good thing, since she'd had packed none of those things, but would have been great to know ahead of the night spent in her already-sweaty clothes.

The door opened and Lorena emerged. Good. It was time to get as many facts straight as possible. The woman had fallen asleep as soon as Danica went to brush her teeth the night before and this might be their only chance to get on the same page.

"Breakfast is ready," said Lorena.

"We gotta get our stories lined up. In case anyone asks questions or—"

"But... breakfast is ready. There's a schedule," said Lorena. She leaned down and picked up a sheet of paper and handed it over:

MORNING SCHEDULE:
7:30 - 8:15 — Breakfast
8:16 - 8:30 — Post-Breakfast Prep
8:31 - 9:29 — First Room (Invest.)
9:30 - 10:29 — Second Room (Invest.)
10:30 - 10:44 — Snack
10:45 - 11:44 — Third Room (Invest.)

"And you heard the woman," said Lorena. "We must stick to the schedule."

"We have to get our story straight."

"You'll be late."

Danica checked the clock.

"That's slow," said Lorena.

Danica looked closer at the second hand, perfectly motionless. She looked at her phone in time to see 8:09 turn to 8:10.

"Why didn't you wake me up?" She grabbed pulled her day-old socks back on and ran to the bathroom to dress. "You obviously got up early enough."

She heard no response. By the time Danica had washed and returned to the main room, the older woman had left again.

Unsurprising even to herself, Danica appeared to be the last to attend breakfast. Every other guest had either food or an empty plate in front of them. This, on top of their changes of clothes placed Danica firmly into the category of House Bum Wad. She zipped her sweatshirt and calculated the feasibility of creating multiple looks with her limited clothing (Zipped sweatshirt for one, unzipped for two, t-shirt without sweatshirt, sweatshirt without t-shirt...). The pajamas upstairs might have to jump in, too. Either way, her bra was looking at a rough couple days.

The hotel vibe of the house continued with its breakfast spread. Though picked over, Danica could still marvel at the ruins of what must have been a lovely smorgasbord. She grabbed the last bagel, scraped the bottom of the cream cheese and searched for an unoccupied seat. If she could chat someone up, maybe they'd clue her in to their situation, Sofi's, Tori's, or anything. Or maybe she could just eavesdrop.

Bobby, James, Joy and Kayleigh occupied the main table, though absolutely not in a together fashion. The two women gave the men full view of their backs, with the only empty seats being directly between the two parties. Danica didn't have the guts for that yet.

The two women wore designer sweats and picked off each other's plates. They were whispering, as always, and a quick observation told Danica their subject of conversation sat across the room.

There, Alex leaned against the refrigerator and scowled at every thought in her mind.

Danica had done some traveling. A little; not around the world, but considering that she came from a small town in rural Illinois, where most people were born, raised and died in the same zip code, she was, by comparison, cosmopolitan. She had visited the East Coast, lived on the West, and in her time she had learned about herself and the differences between the people in those places.

One difference: in the Midwest, people waved at every passing car and smiled in the grocery store. Such smiles and waves did not occur on the East Coast, where people moved as though every person they encountered represented a speed bump to conquer. The West Coast, while uniformly more friendly than the East, was still not as open to displays of friendly behavior as the Midwest; not unwelcome, but more often you received a smile until they realized you were not a celebrity.

So the score went:

Midwest: most outwardly friendly displays.

West Coast: less outwardly friendly displays.

East Coast: least friendly period.

The Midwest levels never agreed with Danica. There, her temperament qualified her as "unfriendly." Yet, through the sheer experience of existing in that region for so much of her life, the Midwest's patented and league-leading Displays of Friendliness osmosisized itself into her system.

This was the only way she could explain what in the world compelled her to say "Hi" to Alex, the most East Coast person in the house. The woman was practically European (a whole different scoring system).

To the surprise of both of them, Alex nodded back. A few more moments of awkward bagel chewing later, she even spoke.

"You came with the great and powerful Madame Lorena, huh?" said Alex.

Danica nodded, trying not to spit cream cheese. "We came with Marty. Sorta."

"Oh, I know. He wouldn't stop talking about her at dinner. The dumbass is a believer."

"Was this something everyone talked about, or, like, were you talking to him or—"

"Don't try to read me," said Alex. The anger in her eyes flared. "If I wanna get ripped off, I'll make an appointment."

"I wasn't."

"And you have crap on your shirt."

Danica looked down. A dime-sized glob of white cream cheese sat right on the big green Green-Day "G."

Alex turned away. She reached for a cabinet, opened it, grabbed a roll of paper towels. Danica was ready to thank her, but Alex put the roll under her arm and left the kitchen. She moved with purpose, certain of her surroundings and in her opinions of everyone around her.

Danica ignored her first failed attempt to get to know anyone else. She also ignored the fact that this first attempt had failed before it even started thanks to her association with Lorena. She ran some water and dabbed a thin napkin at her shirt. As Danica looked away, Alex thumped up the stairs.

Alex's exit started a trend, with Joy and Kayleigh following a bit later. After another moment, Bobby cleared his spot, too. He nodded to Danica, saying nothing. Same, thankfully, for James Van Owen.

Alone again, she chewed. The refrigerator gurgled and she had no answers for that either. She'd never been much of a team member, but the overwhelming sensation of isolation sat on her chest. Totally not related to this sensation, she checked her phone's service and — once she confirmed there *was* service— called Gabby.

"Phew!" was the immediate answer. "Wait. Say something so I know you're OK."

"I'm fine. We're staying the night. Apparently. Sorry I didn't tell you."

"For how long?"

Danica explained the situation, as much as she could anyway, all to a variety of reactions from Gabby. About adherence to the schedule ("Whaaaaaa?"), the others in the house ("Weirdsville") and rooming with Lorena ("WHAAAAAA?!").

"At least you're getting fed."

A hidden loudspeaker snapped on, filling the air with a pop. Then a bell chimed and Tori spoke.

"All attendants to the hallway for the first investigation."

"What was that?" said Gabby.

Danica stuffed the rest of her bagel in her mouth. "The end of breakfast."

CHAPTER FIFTEEN

8:31AM. The End of the Hallway.

The name of the bartender-turned-security force was Huelo, and he stood in front of the last door on the ground-floor hallway. Danica overheard Joy say his name to Kayleigh, who responded with something like, "Yum." If Huelo heard this, he didn't let on, as his expression did not change. He just stared ahead, arms folded, biceps resembling horse legs. His triangular shape reminded her of the security guy who sat outside their bedrooms the night before. Glued to his side was a black holster with three security straps.

The search party gathered near Huelo, keeping Danica near the back of the hall. Everyone appeared — in Danica's opinion — showered, dressed and properly fed. How many of them had stayed up replaying that confessional video in their memories? Were any of them losing sleep over this? She realized how much her detective work relied on assumption and catty judgment.

Through the general murmur of the group, Madame

Lorena pushed her way by the crowd to rejoin Danica in the back. She tapped Danica's notebook with her finger.

"Very good," she said. "Prepared."

Lorena had changed into what Danica assumed to be her 'investigation robes.' A twisty green pattern twirled around her chest, arms and waist, with a headscarf complementing the color scheme. She possessed no notepad of her own. Neither did anyone else, but that didn't piss off Danica as much.

"We have to collect information about everything, including people."

Lorena nodded. "His name is Huelo, the big guy. Marty you know already... That's all I have at the moment. Oh, and Tori, too."

A tremendous help. "When you're making your rounds and disappearing for long stretches at a time to do God knows what, if you could chip in with useful information, too, that would be great."

Lorena made another bow. "We will get them."

"Not just names."

"Oh, of course."

"We need to know why they're here, how they fit in here, stuff like that."

"Yes, yes," said Lorena, that classic line of the focused professional. She smiled wide as she found Marty, who pulled her into a hug.

"What kind of psychic are you?"

Danica snapped out of her building anger to see the faces of Joy and Kayleigh studying her. It took another couple moments for Danica to realize they actually wanted a response, through she couldn't tell which of them had spoken.

"I'm her assistant," she said, pointing at Lorena.

"But you're, like, a psychic and whatnot?" This was Joy. "So, y'know, what kind are you?"

Marty's habit of finding Danica's eye line at the exact moments when she preferred to disappear had become quite irritating. He broke off his heart-to-heart with Lorena just in time to catch her latest point of vulnerability.

She stared back at him a moment, searching for a suitable lie, but any of her usual deflections vanished, intimidated away by Marty's good-look lasers.

"I'm a telepath," she said.

"That's not psychic."

"It is, Kay, but it's just a different kind or whatnot."

"Actually," said Danica, "a psychic can predict things. Predict the future I mean. And a telepath can see what has happened, get visions from people's minds. Channel their thoughts."

Honesty had come so naturally. Danica couldn't recall a time when she had ever said those words to anyone before, in such a clear cut manner. Not even to Carla or Gabby or her mom. The facts dangled in the air and Danica watched as they cracked the mean girl masks of Joy and Kayleigh.

"Plus tea leaf stuff," she added.

Kayleigh gave a nod-shrug and turned back to her friend and phone, accepting Danica's deepest secret as an answer. "Nothing, right?"

"Nothing," said Joy. "It blows so hard."

"Iknowright?" Like one word. They acted like sisters. Sorority sisters, at least.

"I mean, I get it. I literally heard her say, y'know, we cannot post things. I get it. But without a signal and whatnot, what're we supposed to, like, do and all? Read books and stuff?"

From a neighboring doorway, Alex spoke without turning her head. "Nobody's expecting that."

This insult cut deep, and as such could not stand without proper retort. Kayleigh turned her body fully to face her opponent. "I guess we could just sit around and pout and smoke like you."

This insult cut less deep, and Alex returned to her solitude in the doorway. Nobody else said anything, but Joy and Kayleigh laughed and "Oooooooo'd" as if they'd landed the knock-out blow.

"You smoke?" said Danica. Her brain kicked into overdrive, rationalizing the question. This was part of the job. Her mission. Learning about the people who knew Sofi. That could only be achieved by asking questions. She wasn't desperate for clues *or* cigarettes, of which she had not enjoyed for who knew how long (one year and two-hundred-thirty-eight days).

"Yeah she does," said Joy. "You can smell it."

Danica hadn't wanted to admit it to herself, but once Joy committed the thought, she had to agree that a nicotine scent had been lingering in the background of the house. She hadn't gotten close enough to smell anyone's clothes to confirm it, though part of her desperately wanted to.

Alex did not confirm any of these accusations. Neither confirmed nor denied.

"So stupid. It'll kill you and whatnot, you know that, right? Smoking? It'll totally kill you."

"Not soon enough."

Joy clutched at invisible pearls. "Tori! Did you hear her? She's suicidal! This girl's suicidal and has a death wish and I don't think she should be here when she has a suicidal death wish!"

Tori was already walking toward them when Joy had started yelling for her. She held up a hand and said, "No more."

"But she's sick and mean."

Tori sighed at the whining. For the first time since talking to Bobby on the set, Danica saw her offer some kind of compromise. "Alexandra, leave them alone."

Alex waved a hand by way of accepting the order. Kayleigh clucked her tongue, earning another scolding look from Tori. Then Joy pulled her friend close and held her fist with a little shake. They both giggled and moved on, sorority sister mode activated.

Tori reached Huelo and the doorway, where she pulled a little bell from her orange pocket. Like a school bell, one from *Little House on the Prairie*. She rang it with crisp peels and all chatter ceased.

"Behind me is Sofi's bedroom. We keep most of the house free of personal things. Makes it easy to clean and use for filming. But this room." She tapped the door with her open hand. "This room is all her."

Danica seized on a plan for herself: the others would probably go for the biggest targets like the bed, the dresser, or any kind of shiny thing Sofi had inside. Meanwhile, Danica could use her time to search for small identifiers. Receipts, tags, bits of paper stuck to pockets — anything tying Sofi to certain places at certain times. Search for patterns, she told herself. She would mark down everything she could find and opened her notebook to be ready to do just that.

"No notes, please," said Tori. "Just observation."

Danica struggled for a suitable argument, with all eyes on her. She wanted some way to reason with Tori, beyond the obvious, and even the obvious evaded her. No notes? What did that even mean? Was Tori afraid of stray pen marks on her sister's things?

As words failed her, the load of Tori's gaze rested a verdict which she could not fight. Danica put her pen in her pocket and closed her notebook.

Tori held out her hand. "Please. To be certain."

It was not a request, but another order. Danica locked eyes with Marty, who responded with chagrin. She handed the notebook to him, who passed it to the front of the group, to Tori, who passed it to Huelo, where it disappeared in his muscular gravity.

"Pen or pencil as well. Please."

She complied.

Okay. New plan: Gather items that may be connected to Sofi. Grab as many as possible and bring them back to the room to look for patterns. Then write them down in private.

"You may look around the room, you may touch, but you may not take items from this room unless you have permission. Anything you find of value, bring it to me."

Okay... *New* new plan: (file not found)

Tori made an infinitesimal nod to Huelo the bartender-bouncer-butler, who removed a key ring from his pocket. The ring held enough keys to tip over a bear, but Huelo Horse-Legs-For-Arms didn't sweat it. He picked one out and unlocked the door. The light behind the door drowned the entire hallway.

"You have one hour. Please see what can be found. Whatever can help find Sofi."

Danica took her first step with the rest of the group, prepared to storm the bedroom like five golden-ticket holders in Willy Wonka's chocolate room. But at her second step, Lorena held out her arm, a crossing-guard stopping a first grader.

"Wait." Lorena spoke with closed eyes. She rubbed her free hand on her temple and let out a slow, low moan.

"For what?"

"Forgive us, spirits, for my assistant is still learning," said Lorena, followed by grunting noise.

One might find it admirable, Lorena's commitment to character and to the ruse she and Danica were playing. But that one might be a moron, because Lorena knew Danica was not her assistant and that dressing her down in front of others was (at best) insulting and (at worst) an unnecessary delay to their clue search.

Again, Danica looked to Marty for help. Also again, he gave very little. In fact, the man was beaming at Lorena, basking in her ethereal connection to the spirit world.

Danica searched for someone who shared her opinion, but the hallway had been vacated. Only Huelo remained and his face had reached full club bouncer level, locked in passivity.

Embarrassment burned Danica's cheeks. Everyone else was in the bedroom — even the two women who seemed more concerned with Facebook status than status of their friend. Everyone except them. The longer they stayed outside, the longer they separated themselves from any true connections to tangible evidence. To reality.

After an excruciating couple of minutes — *minutes!* — doing nothing but stand, breathe and be idiotic, Lorena opened her eyes as though awakened from a nap and said, "Now."

She stretched her fingers and walked to the bedroom door. Stripped of her notebook, forever connected to this circus act, Danica followed in Lorena's shameful wake, certain that the room would be picked clean of anything useful.

If Sofi had a hobby, and if said hobby occupied her bedroom, then her hobby was possessing one of everything in the world. The clutter sprawled off dressers and bedside tables to create a floor of its own. And yet, the room still held its ground to some kind of order. Books were in the book pile, perfumes were in the perfume heap, earrings and jewelry owned dresser tops, and so on. Light came from both the window letting in an impossible amount of sunlight and the recessed lights above.

Madame Lorena took the room in full regalia and actualization. She smelled the air. She moved in long, odd strides, dipping her knees a bit with each step. One hand held out toward her front, the other raised toward the back as if holding a wire for support. She closed her eyes once more. As she strode by the dresser, her fingers slid along the drawer handles. Her every move begged for attention, and as far as Danica could tell, she got it. James and Bobby gawked from the nightstand. Joy and Kayleigh exchanged glances from the closet area. Even Alex, jaded as all get out, recognized the display before them.

The one who noticed the most was Marty, who stood in the doorway, too transfixed to completely enter the room. Lorena's performance nearly washed away that hurt look from his eyebrows, replacing it with something else. Hope, maybe. Marty not only believed Madame Lorena, but believed *in* her. It reminded Danica that she was actually supposed to be doing some of the same things as well.

She walked toward the closet with deep-knee strides. When she met Kayleigh standing guard while Joy rummaged through the hanging clothes, Danica bend-walked to the bed instead. She felt the pink bedspread and the satin pillowcases, twinkling her fingers like Lorena. For good measure, she added some deep exhales and occasional "Mmm's," just so anyone watching could tell that her 'gifts' were working properly. It almost didn't feel moronic. Almost.

In all her mimicry she'd almost missed the fact that before her was the same bed from Sofi's confessional video. She recognized the frill on the pillow.

As she drifted around psychic-ing up the bed area, James Van Owen backed away from the nightstand. It was a simple wood top with barely enough leg to support the clutter upon it. Among the phone chargers, headphones and paperback novels sat several pens and pencils. None of them fancy, with most of the pens missing their caps. The ones with caps were chewed up. Some appeared to be dried up while others fell to the floor, lost to the dusty underbelly of the bed.

She shuffled around in the pile of books on the floor, letting out a legitimate "Mmm."

As if summoned by this siren song, Lorena sidled up next to her. "What have you found, dear?"

"Lots of pens, but nothing to write on." Danica leafed through the paperbacks, on the off chance that Sofi was a notes-in-the-margins kind of reader. No such luck.

Her hand felt around under the bed, at the edge of the book pile. Her fingers hit something metal and springy. A simple red Mead notebook. Its corners were still pointy and inside held no writing. Like Sofi had been saving this for later. Whatever the reason for its untouched status, the book represented a dead end for Danica.

Without asking, Lorena swiped the book and held it over her head. She smelled it and wiped her fingers across its cover.

The other guests moved in Danica's peripheral. Most of them moved away, with varying degrees of scoffing and eye-rolling.

She lowered her voice, "Do you have to make such a performance of everything?"

"I do not know what you mean!" said Lorena. Danica believed her.

The pens on the floor and nightstand were Bics. They weren't Danica's preferred brand, but the instinct to jot notes went unfed since her things had been confiscated. Who would miss a pen from a bedroom? To play it safe, she waited for Lorena to deliver another patented twirl, which —

coming a mere three seconds later — offered the perfect distraction for Danica's low-grade theft.

Lorena spun near the window, all eyes went to her and Danica pocketed the Bic. She'd find some paper somewhere. For the moment, it just felt good to have a totem.

"Oh!"

A flash of fear sprinted through Danica's spine as she assumed the scream was a response to her stealing. It faded as she looked to the closet. For the first time since entering the bedroom, everyone turned to see a spectacle other than Lorena. The shout had come from Joy, who stood in the closet doorway, looking at something small in her hand.

Kayleigh got closer and said, "What is it?"

"Shh."

"But I wanna—"

"Kayleigh!" Joy said her name with three syllables. "Kay-leigh-UH!"

The message set in Kayleigh's sun-bleached head. Both women looked at Tori, who motioned them to come nearer.

Danica skulked over to Lorena, who stretched her fingers toward the closet. "Thissssss way," she said, pulling Danica along.

"Did you see what they found?" said Danica. "Or where they found it?"

"Who?"

Never mind. Danica dug her fingernails into her palm and tried to use her time wisely. The closet had finally become available.

The enormous closet offered enough space for a small family to live in comfort. It contained more shoes than oxygen, all in excellent condition. Both sides held hanging areas, and both hanging areas were full.

"Those two girls shouted about something in here," said Lorena, almost helpful.

Danica kept her angry sighs to herself. "Look for receipts or tags or stickers — anything with a location or a date on them."

"She wouldn't have brought back a receipt after disappearing."

"No, but if we get some ideas on where she goes, maybe we'll find someone who can tell us more."

She started rifling through the pockets and Lorena joined her. The older woman brushed her hands along the left side, going through her deep-breath-and-moaning routine. When she thought Danica wasn't looking, Lorena opened one eye toward the door. Seeing no audience, her posture and voice changed.

"These look new," she said.

Snapped awake by logical engagement, Danica examined the carefully displayed wardrobe. "Your side does," she said to the clothes on the left. A pink ski jacket on her side showed fraying at the sleeves, along with some broken threads inside. "These have seen some use though."

"The poor dear is organized. Fancy things on one side, every-day clothes on the other." Lorena moved to the right side and pulled a pink boa and shiny boots from the back. "Or perhaps fancy on both sides."

They resumed digging in pockets. The crunch of plastic pants and rubber jackets bounced off the low ceiling. Danica moved quickly down the right side to the wall. Gabby would have called the right side 'Cores'; occasional boas aside, it held the stuff worn to do grocery shopping or go any place where one did not have to be 'on.' The cores appeared clean, but loved. Danica found some jeans with non-designer holes in the knees. Even the hangers seemed older. And the whole while, going through those pockets, she collected all of nothing.

Lorena paused, as she'd reached the end of the left side.

Her side was less stuffed while Danica could barely pull the shirts free from her right side. Some of the shirts in the back were on hangers floating above the line, held up by the pressure of the surrounding clothing.

The left side had a few empty hangers near the middle. It also had style and uniformity: all shades of white and red.

"They're costumes," she said. "She probably wears them for shoots."

The fancy clothing river rolled all the way to the back, where one color exception hung so uniquely to itself that Danica scolded herself for missing it earlier. There, a puffy gold vest with a fuzzy collar hung in relative isolation. The light above it transformed it into a wearable disco ball.

"We're moving on," said Tori to the whole room.

"But... Tori, we just got in here." Danica refused to leave the closet, her hands just shy of the golden vest.

"We have found a valuable artifact — a clue — and we must capitalize on this momentum."

Marty joined them at the closet door. "Any luck from my team?"

"Indeed," said Lorena, changing course completely. She snagged a white denim jacket from among the basics. "She likes this, doesn't she?"

"Yes!" Marty beamed, marveling at Lorena's awesome power. "It was one of her favorites."

Tears arrived in his incredible eyes, then he added "*Is*. It *is* one of her favorites. She's worn it lots of times."

Never one to miss a hot opportunity, Lorena grabbed another jacket from the fancy side. "But this one... I can hear her saying it is 'cool.'"

After a few more empowering, thrilling moments in the presence of unmatched greatness, Marty came out of his trance and looked back at Tori. "We should probably get going, huh?"

Danica stared at the disco-ball vest. It didn't appear to have any scuffs or tears, retaining an immaculate quality even above the rest of the fancy side (which was saying something). Joy and Kayleigh must have noticed this vest, too. The thing was practically on stage.

The bell rang at the door. "Time has ended. Please return to the hallway."

That was not a request. Lorena remounted her performance beyond the closet and toward the exit, while Marty joined her like an excited golden retriever.

"We got some good stuff in here, Tori," he said at the door to the hallway. "Lorena sensed a ton of stuff from the bed and her clothes."

Tori nodded. Danica recognized the move from grade school, when a student scribbled three lines on a page and the teacher acknowledged it, but nothing more.

As they left, Danica snuck one more glance at the piles near the bed. The chewed pens were out of sight. Knocked over, perhaps. That or the untidy tide of bedside books had claimed them.

She could come back later to dig through the piles properly. With more house to pick through, time was of the essence. They hustled out of the bedroom and toward another door down the hall. Danica looked back.

Beyond Marty's shoulders, she caught the last glimpse of Huelo re-locking the bedroom door. So much for going back later.

CHAPTER SIXTEEN

Once again, Horse-Legs Huelo stood guard, offering little conversation or eye contact to the huddle group before him.

Tori joined him, but still stood apart. She put her hand on the door and paused for a moment, staring at it. From what Danica could see of the side of her face, Tori's expression showed something different from her standard angry principal look. A mix of frustration and fear, or perhaps just confusion, dashed across her cheek as it flexed, almost in a spasm.

'She's gotta be lonely,' thought Danica, remembering the drive to the house. Up the hill, through the forest, surrounded by nothing. Stranded away from people, with a personality not designed to attract, it was easy to see how Tori could distance herself from others and get lost in her anxieties. Or how she could fall back on her organizational habits to inflict sense upon the world.

Yet something in her eyes was alluring. It drew Danica in, and must have drawn others, too; that and the money. She wanted to talk to her and assure her that they would solve this problem and bring her sister home safe. Give that uneasy cheek spasm a rest.

"Kayleigh and Joy," said Tori, "did good work in the bedroom. Very good work. And they found something intriguing."

Tori held up a brown key, longer than an apartment key, but shorter than a pencil. In the low light of the hallway, with the lamp behind it, the key turned black.

"We will inspect the game room next. It was a place where we frequently relaxed with friends and family." Danica heard Tori choke a bit on that last word. "Let us search for any connections to this first item. Two at a time in this room as it is smaller."

She nodded to Huelo and he unlocked the door. Then she handed the brown key to Joy. She took it, then walked arm in arm with Kayleigh into the room.

The message of Joy's smile was crystal clear: We Are Winning. As though this procedure could be measured by points. But what if it was? Tori's instructions had stated 'whoever helped find Sofi *or helped find clues to find her*.' Finding Sofi was not the only requirement for reward. Therefore notable bits and pieces discovered around the house could be counted for their individual weights. Points.

If Joy and Kayleigh were winning, then Danica was losing.

She looked at Marty, her week-old hobby, as he engaged in another low-voiced heart-to-heart with Lorena. He was smiling and it looked kind of sincere. She wondered if he was putting it on for Madame Lorena, if he had to put on a good face to hide his own fear and disappointment. Was Lorena telling him about all the progress they'd almost made in Sofi's bedroom? 'We found some clothes in the closet and some chewed pens, which are super uncommon for this hemisphere, so we totally have a great lead.'

His smile didn't waiver though, somehow making Danica feel worse. His hopes were likely being lifted by Lorena, setting him up for a harder fall when — surprise, surprise — two fortune tellers hadn't come through for him.

From across the hall, James tapped his nose then drifted back toward the stairs. After a moment, he came back and looked Danica straight in the eye, tapping his nose again. This time she got the signal and joined him.

"I'm not a spy, man. And neither are you."

James lowered his voice. "I was being subtle. And I found out something, but if you don't want to hear it...."

Danica urged him on.

"Alex and Marty are exes."

It was the kind of statement so sudden, strange and improbable that Danica felt its truth. She reeled a little, shaking her head, then lowered her own voice. "Come again?"

"I found out your boy used to date Alex. You know, that woman with the dark hair—"

"Yeah, I know." She scrunched her face.

"You wanted me to share what I learn. This is what I've learned."

She shook her head again. "Alex the Grumpy Mistress of the Night and... and *Marty?*"

"Yep."

"When was this?"

"I think about a year or so ago."

"How do you know this?"

"I know things." There was that cocky attitude, back in the swing. "I've had training and years of experience at this sort of thing, remember?"

Bobby had told him. They were rooming together and Bobby didn't seem shy for sharing his thoughts. Danica let James have his secret moment, but pressed for some more. "OK, so she's his ex. That's interesting. What about the bedroom? Did you find anything there?"

His eyes crossed. "The bedroom? No. Nothing you didn't see, too."

"So you just have gossip then."

"We're trading information, right? I did mine. Now you go."

"I'm not sharing with you."

"Oh, come on. Please?"

She put her hands in her pockets and shrugged. Something stabbed her finger — the pen she'd 'borrowed.' "Alright, James: I found some chewed pens and a closet full of clothes, organized by usage. Everyday stuff on one side, fancy stuff on the other, with a really shiny vest at the end under the light."

"You seriously gonna talk about clothes? Now? I mean, I don't wanna be sexist, but...."

Why stop now? "It would be sexist to ignore the clothes. And the chewed pen. It's what I found, so I'm sharing, right?"

James chewed on his lip, really working this one out. "Hmm... OK. Fine. Nice work. This make us square?"

"For now. But keep it coming."

Danica returned to her place in the hallway, keeping her eyes away from Marty, then keeping them away from Alex. While still technically gossip, their former relationship certainly had juice to it. Danica struggled to imagine a planet where she would help any of her exes to do *anything*, let alone find their current paramours. She tried and failed to imagine it.

Yet, there was Alex, leaning in her ex-boyfriend's girl-friend's hallway, ready to help out.

Joy and Kayleigh bounced back out of the room. "Next," said Kayleigh.

"Hold on," said Tori, pausing the entire hallway. She spoke with the young women in a hushed voice and slumped shoulders. Joy and Kayleigh shook their heads and after a brief thought, a resigned Tori turned back to the group.

"You, please," she said to Danica and Lorena. "And Alex."

The game room was not much smaller than the bedroom, only filled with more things. Two matching leather couches claimed a wall and corner and an old-looking drink cart collected dust between them. A foosball table inhabited the center of the room, while a television the size of the living area's whiteboard rested on a shelf. Underneath it were several gaming systems.

Given the limited time they had before this room got locked off, too, Danica set to work scanning around. She ran her fingers along the shelf, tripping on the remotes and controllers. She moved to the couches and dug between the cushions. Gum wrappers, loose pennies and a busted paper-clip were all she found there. On the floor she found phone chargers plugged into the wall: one for a phone, the other for a first-generation iPod. The phone charger was tattered, its wires fraying at the block.

If anything in here was worth finding, surely Joy and Kayleigh had found it already. Probably even snatched it. But they'd only been inside for a few minutes.

Alex and Lorena hovered around the foosball game.

"My apprentice," said Lorena. "See here. This table of men."

Danica complied, noticing the audience at the door. As always, Marty beamed, but Tori was whispering in his ear. Probably about how poorly he had chosen his help. But drawn in by his belief, Marty broke away from Tori and broke protocol to be a *fourth person* in the room. He, too, joined Lorena at the table.

A show was required and Lorena delivered. "No ball. No ball, and so... no game."

Danica closed her eyes; partly to appear the slightest bit connected to the spirits, but mostly to mask how they crossed themselves twice. If the ball was, in fact, not on the table, it didn't warrant a whispery fortune-cookie voice announcing it to the world.

Alex had enough eye rolls to cover for her. The vamp moved around the table, like she was unable to step away from it.

However, the devotee next to Lorena ate the performance up. In that instant Danica understood a little more of Lorena's methods: find something odd, something out of place, and explain it without explaining anything.

Taking that cue, she turned toward the chargers on the floor. "And here: two chargers. Similar in purpose, but not compliant."

"Mmmm." Lorena moved to the game shelf.

Danica thought her psychic BS deserved more accolades, but took Lorena leaving her alone as prize enough. From her knees, she looked again at the foosball table. She'd seen a couple of them in her youth, but not quite like this one. Hard wood frame, with steel legs bolted to the corners and a glossy coat around the sides. It appeared to be tailor made; either that or someone had removed all markings of the manufacturer. Under the base appeared to be some kind of switch. A panel at least. It felt metallic, with curlicues around it.

She didn't have the most robust experience in furniture design, but something about this foosball table stood out as Danica looked back to the shelf with the game consoles. The shelf held many things, but compared to the foosball table, it looked positively flimsy. The table had heft and weight, as she confirmed when she tried to lift it.

She lifted it just above her toes. Someone grumbled behind her, then Marty actually lended a hand. The table tipped with ease once his arms got involved. Once on its side, someone behind them gasped.

It was, of all people, Alex.

The vamp stared at the tipped table's underbelly and ran her fingers over the switch cover. Just as Danica had thought, it was a plate like one would see over a light switch, with ornamental curls creating a frame within its frame. They circled the center hole, making it look like a key hole. It had been painted to match the rest of the table, but the curlicues gave the panel a rustic quality, like it had been stolen from a turn-of-the-century farm house.

"Gimme the key," said Alex, hand already out to Joy.

Danica examined the spot. "There's nowhere to put it. Look." She wiggled her finger in the center space — where a key might have gone — and hit paneling. "It's a closed keyhole."

Alex's finger confirmed as much. She remained silent.

As Danica stood back, she found Lorena had not only returned to the table, but had reached elbow-deep into the goals near the floor.

"There's something in here."

As Lorena rattled her arm, a strange noise shucked around the table's outside walls. Whatever it was, it made a rattle distinct from that of the wooden men on metal rods. Lorena shook the table to elicit the noise again.

A crunch.

Danica snatched one of the charger cords and returned to the table, to the ball-return hole. She slid the cord inside, its flexible firmness snaking around the inner workings. After a few seconds, the crunch came again, as did some mild resistance in the tube.

"A little more," said Lorena.

Danica fed more cord until she got to the USB connection, then stuffed her hand inside. With a final push, the crunch turned into a crinkle. Lorena extricated her own arm, bringing with it her treasure: a plastic Easter Egg.

"Nice work, ladies," said Kayleigh, looking for a high-five for her sarcastic quip.

"A moment, please," said Lorena. She held the ball aloft to the window's sunlight, then put it to her ear. She shook it, like a kid with present, then cracked it open, spilling its contents into her palm.

A scrap of paper. Roughly the shape of a triangle, it had lines and a hole, as though it had been torn from one of those Mead notebooks.

Lorena unfolded it and read, "'Caged.'" She turned the paper around for Danica to see.

On the lined scrap of paper were the words "CAGED CAGE," written in ink and in large letters.

Danica's toes were electric. It had all happened so fast, her head swirled. Sofi's words — her *vision words* — had come to life, as it were, right before her eyes. Had she predicted her feelings? Or Marty's? Did Sofi often talk about this sort of thing with him, or with anyone else?

Tears streamed down Marty's face, as did a look of recognition. He'd seen these words before. For sure.

All this was processed in under three seconds. At second four, Tori swooped in and claimed the paper from Lorena's hand.

"This is very useful. Remarkable even. Everyone! I feel we have found a major clue!"

"We still get some credit, right?" said Joy. "Because this key was all, you know, important, too, and whatnot?"

Kayleigh agreed while Tori charged out of the game room, the others following in her wake. All but Danica and Alex.

Danica stared at the empty egg shell. The image of the paper — the words — lingered with her, burned from her memory.

Alex's fascination with the foosball table continued without sign of stopping. After another moment of studying the keyhole without a keyhole, she finally looked toward Danica. And when she did, the look on her face almost supplanted Danica's memory of the paper. The pale woman's dark eyebrows crushed together above her nose. Her eyes stared at Danica yet beyond her, beyond the walls. Somehow, Alex had seen a ghost.

In a foosball table.

"You OK?" said Danica, trying for the tenth time to be nice to this woman.

"I think it's snack time," said Alex, forcing herself out the door.

Danica followed her and bumped right into Lorena, who stopped hopping around long enough to speak. "We have made real headway. Did you see it? Wasn't it thrilling?"

"I've seen those words before."

"The words, from the paper?"

Danica nodded.

"You've... *seen* them? Are you certain?"

Danica heard her exposure quoted back to her and almost didn't care. She hadn't actually *seen* them. She'd *heard* them in Marty's vision. Which, sure, she had technically seen, but Lorena didn't have to know all that.

"They must mean something."

"Most certainly," said Lorena. "But where did you *see* them prior to today? That could help us with this hunt."

Smelling the trap, Danica retreated from opening up too

much. "I think I need some water. And some sugar. I stood up too fast from under that thing."

Lorena nodded, saying nothing. She left her alone, off to raid more snacks.

Marty's vision ran on a loop before her eyes. She realized that she knew more than anyone else in the house, about the missing woman and puzzles and everything, yet could not get past the overwhelming sense of drowning in confusion.

She took a deep breath to wash the feeling away.

It didn't work.

CHAPTER SEVENTEEN

Tori took her snack to go, exiting quickly. Even without her presence, the kitchen still felt as cheerful as a prison yard, with everyone eyeballing their stuff and keeping others away. Danica grabbed a granola bar and a seat at the window.

Risking whatever punishment accompanied writing things down, she retrieved the stolen pen and slid a napkin close to her chest. Her jaw clenched as she tried to keep details she'd seen in the bedroom and game room inside her head.

The first thing she wrote was 'Chewed pens,' and immediately recognized it as a warm-up thought. This was followed by 'Book and clothes piles,' 'super closet,' 'brown key??,' 'magic secret foosball messages???,' question marks included. Usually, writing down chaos helped her think. Not so much this time.

Those words returned. She dared not write 'CAGED' anywhere for fear of outing herself. She thought of Marty, of invading his privacy but having that invasion become reality in an Easter egg shell. Best to keep that to herself.

Instead, she wrote 'Is instead of was.' Besides the obvious trauma the man was going through, Marty's grammatical slip had implanted an idea and Danica was ready to let it fester. She'd always tried to resist darker impulses, trying not to be a Negative Nancy who only saw the bad side of things, who expected only the worst.

However, in her head, the worst had found a home. It seemed so obvious that she became fearful of the facts that fit an alarming pattern:

Sofi had disappeared from a place that she knew very well.

Sofi was a celebrity who attracted a lot of attention.

Sofi had also admitted a fear of being stalked.

Sofi's boyfriend had used the past tense. it all fit into an alarming pattern.

Faced with these facts, Tori could have been in denial for her own mental protection. Protection which — while manifesting as organization — might cost her sister's life. Marty had to be thinking it already; that's why he used "was" instead of "is" in the game room; was he really the best one to bring Tori the truth?

Was Danica?

As if on cue, she spilled granola crumbs down her shirt to put her ego properly in check. The circumstances of recent events did feel suspicious, but how would a message stuffed in a foosball Easter egg fit in? Why would a kidnapper allow that to happen? Why would someone place it in there at all? The fact that the message shared words with Marty's vision might only prove that, well, Sofi used the word 'Cage' a lot.

Besides, Danica had only just heard of Sofi Starr earlier that week. She was no expert on the woman. Most of the people in the house knew her much longer.

She'd assumed.

Across the room, Joy and Kayleigh refilled their plastic cups with bright drinks, sighing and giggling out of the room. Gauging their ages for early twenties, it didn't seem possible to Danica that those two had done much of anything for very long. They didn't seem very worried about Sofi, the world, or anything. Why should they?

And why should that stand out?

Because of the Solving-Stuff Buzz. That part of Danica's deep-down self she had been denying since returning to town, even before Gabby gave it a name. Maybe Danica really did seek drama where there wasn't any. Or maybe her eyes were open to that drama and the Buzz was her reward for paying attention.

Lorena, finally finished with filling her plate, floated toward her table. Danica expected someone in Lorena's profession to be adept at reading people, to know when they didn't want to be bothered.

If Lorena was good at reading people, she was ignoring that read at present; she sat down in the opposite seat with a wide smile.

"I don't know where they find their fruit, but it's very fresh. Practically right off the tree." Lorena sucked down an orange.

Danica kept her head down, sensing Lorena looking at her notes and breaking the prison yard rules. The pen chose this precise moment to dry up, but Danica pretended it still worked in an effort to avoid the older woman's engagement.

This did not work.

Lorena said, "You should write down 'hangers.'"

"Why?"

"Those are your observations, are they not? Write down 'hangers.' Like from the closet we inspected."

"I'm actually working on some things here. Important things for this case."

"Someone's in a mood."

"Look around, Lorena. *Everyone* is in a mood."

"What did you expect? This is a competition. They are our competition. They're not going to be our buddies. This crowd has been poised against one another." Lorena had a mouthful of banana, Nutella and (apparently) opinions. "We just scored a major point or however you want to say it. Another notch for our team. Don't cloud the truth with ideals."

"I'm trying to see things as unclouded and truthfully as possible. It's all these other people who are getting in the way."

Lorena peered at Danica's notes. "'The key?' Those two young ladies found it."

"I know."

"It failed to work on that table. What else would you like to know?"

"It's not like that. This is just a list."

"Well, we shall ask them. Excuse me."

Joy re-entered the kitchen and Lorena sprung to meet her. The older woman began asking a question of the younger, but stopped after a few words when the glare from Joy's face shut her up.

Joy grabbed a granola bar and returned to the living area, saying nothing.

Lorena sat again, quite shocked. "That was aggressive. Whatever has her so annoyed?"

"Gee," said Danica, looking right at Lorena, "I wonder."

Lorena opened a bag of chips. "Perhaps your haircut."

"It's you, *Madame*. You just said this is a competition, sure, but then there's the way you go about 'competing.' You're making a scene of everything."

Lorena shrugged her off. "Me? Me, they like. I am harmless. The non-believers do not take me seriously, so I am no threat at all. I put on a show. The theatricality gives me distance.

"To others, the believers, I am a true mystic with powers beyond this world, so the performance is a necessity. It explains my behavior. You, on the other hand, just seem pouty and angry."

Danica stood, tossed the dead pen in the trash and walked to the door, mumbling something about wanting to get some air before they resumed the investigation. She walked straight to the front door.

What did Lorena know? She was the annoying one. Danica wasn't the one making a spectacle of herself, trying to distract people from actually finding helpful information.

Then again, Danica's arrival didn't receive the warmest reception. She'd often considered her shaved head to be a litmus test for weeding out unfriendly, uncool people. But she also had to allow for the possibility that these people didn't dislike her *just* for her hairstyle. They might have disliked her personality, too.

Outside, she wandered down the long porch running the length of the house. It headed toward a barn the size of a small airplane hangar. Beyond that, the hill dropped into nothingness. Logic told her that there had to be something beyond the crest, but at the moment her eyes were in charge and logic took a backseat. The encompassing isolation overwhelmed her, the sensation of complete removal from any other humans became so total that she hoped to hear Tori's bell. Just to remind her other people existed.

Instead, her prayers were answered by Joy and Kayleigh slinking out from behind the barn garage, phones glued to their faces. Their chatter only stopped when the noticed her.

They'd held that brown key for a while. Maybe they'd noticed other things, about it or anything. They were part of Sofi's world. They seemed like friends, or at least friend adjacent. As such, they might possess certain insights. Maybe they could tell if Sofi had been thinking about running away, leaving it all behind. Maybe they knew more than even they realized.

But they weren't going to share any information with people they actively disliked.

Why did it matter to be liked? Danica had felt a general distaste from most people around her for her entire adult life.

That wasn't true, she admitted to herself. She'd felt comfortable and trusted and warm in the salon. While working.

In a role.

Playing a part.

...She hated when Lorena was right.

Danica followed the two younger women to the porch. To weasel out some information, Danica would need a solid 'in.' Something those two co-cheer captains would enjoy and would not resist.

She zipped up her hoodie and her courage, forced a spring into her strides and stepped onto the porch. Her imitation Docs clunked onto the wood and a cloud of tension rose as she approached.

"You guys want a free reading?"

The cloud of tension partially evaporated. The two younger people shifted their shoulders. Kayleigh even put her phone down. Joy looked less hardened, but retained her sneer.

Danica thought positive thoughts, even as she realized that she had never done anything like a psychic reading or a sitting or whatever they were called. Was she underdressed? Overdressed? The daylight bounced off the windows making it seem way too bright to set a mood similar to that of Lorena's parlor. Danica made Kayleigh as the easier mark of the two. As a pure defense tactic, she tried her best to match Kayleigh's enthusiastic posture, moving onto their bench.

Kayleigh slid her purse over to make room on the bench for Danica, the totally legit and knowledgable communicator with the spirit world.

With no plan — but also with no *better* plan — improvising appeared to be Danica's only option to learn anything from these two. She flourished her wrists, ignoring the sting in her right wrist for the sake of the show.

"May I see?" she said.

"Is this really how it's done?" said Joy. She must have noticed the hesitation in Danica's manner.

"Usually I do it in the parlor, but yeah, this'll work. There are many paths to…" another microsecond of hesitation, only this time on purpose, for effect, before she added, "…the unknown."

Danica took Kayleigh's hand and ran her fingers around the palm. They were some of the softest non-baby hands she'd ever held.

She kept her eyes down, her eyelids low and her voice calm. "You have a bright spirit. You have lived well."

"Yeah she has," said Joy.

"Shut up."

"Too well, some days," said Danica. "And nights. And mornings."

This drew giggles.

"Your fingers are long and could bring good fortune."

"Concert piano," said Kayleigh. "Mom made me."

Danica continued, "You have a good heart. Here. Your life line shows you will make many turns, but always find your way back." The BS was coming easier, as long as she turned off her personal vomit meter.

Reading Kayleigh's reaction came less easy. She probably only considered her future in weekend increments.

Danica took a big swing. "Yet you are troubled it seems. You have seen some difficulties."

"Why? Do you see something, like, disturbing?" Kayleigh's voice had urgency, but not from refuting Danica's stab in the dark.

"Something recent. It has... has made things challenging."

"Hm." Joy spat out the sound, not buying it.

Danica pressed on. "You are worried about your friend. You have not spoken to her in... in..."

She stalled, hoping Kayleigh — pressed by that deep-rooted societal norm that silence needed to be filled with words — would take the bait.

Kayleigh, it seemed, had more patience than Danica had hoped. Her blue eyes judged Danica with focus. Sweat broke out from Danica's arms; she thought silent curses at herself on behalf of her already dirty shirt and her lack of deodorant. And here she'd backed herself into a corner. Guess the wrong time they'd last seen Sofi and lose what little ground she'd made.

"Well...?" said Joy. She wasn't letting her off the hook.

Desperate, Danica's eyes darted around the porch for any sign of, well, anything. She kept her eyelids low and moved her head side to side in an attempt to look for an answer while also appearing vaguely connected to another world. Her eyes landed on Kayleigh's purse, where Danica hoped a.) she kept a diary, and b.) said diary would be lying face up and open, with secrets written in big, bold letters.

The purse held no such fortune. It was just a little handbag of a thing, capable of holding next to nothing. A few scratches on the strap were all that counted for writing.

The scratches were in threes, all on one side.

"No. It's not a person you're missing," said Danica, shifting gears. "It's an animal."

Kayleigh's hand went tight as Joy sucked in a rapid breath.

Danica pushed. "A pet. Someone special. And you miss them." If she had enrolled in a proper palm reading school (such as Psychic Reading Technical Institute or something), Danica doubted her teachers would have encouraged such a brazen tactic. Scratches on a purse meant only that the purse had been scratched. The P.R.T.I. instructors would probably mark her down for recklessness, adding demerits for bad setting of mood and spelling errors (just being honest with herself).

But those instructors would be badly dressed and dead wrong. Kayleigh rubbed her eyes with her free hand as Joy hugged her shoulder. There was hurt in there. Danica had guessed weird yet guessed right.

"My family's dog. Moxie. I miss him a lot."

Joy added, "He was crazy sweet."

Kayleigh's palm transformed from a limp leaf to a strong oak tree. Her face steeled, steadying itself for waves of emotion in another dogless day.

"He's better now." Danica felt a little guilty saying it. But Moxie probably was OK. None of them knew for sure, so she might as well act like the fake expert with good news to share.

Their grip got tight, becoming a full hand hold. They looked at each other for an intimate ten seconds; deeper than Danica thought she'd ever do with Kayleigh.

The young white woman broke the hold, pulling her hand back to wipe her eyes again. "That was totally powerful. At first I thought... but then... oh my gawd, that was a-mazing."

"Yeah, no, it was. Your feelings were powerful and... and all." Danica bit her tongue a bit too late to keep the stupid from creeping out. "How long's it been?"

"Just a few days. He was old. About fifteen."

"It all happened around the same time," offered Joy. She kept rubbing her friend's shoulder. "It's been a tough week.

It's not, like, the same-same and whatnot. But it all felt like about the same, you know? First one, then the other."

The "same" in question lined up with Sofi's disappearance.

"Moxie was part of your life for a long time," said Danica. "And sometimes, that's even more meaningful than relationships we have with people. But when your good friend disappears, too... yeah, that's gotta be double hard."

"Oh, way good friends," said Kayleigh.

"I figured. I mean, I don't know her, but you two gotta be close. Closer than some others."

"Totally. A long time. Since at least last summer."

Yeah, a real long time. "How'd you meet her and all?"

"Just around. Parties and stuff."

"Oh, sure." Danica stretched her arms, wondering how she could turn this back to a discussion of hidden keys and their hiding places.

"You know," said Joy, "have you ever thought about putting that stuff online? The psychic reading stuff?"

"What? *This?*" The words flopped from her mouth like a crippled frog. "I can honestly say I have never considered it."

"You should think about it," said Joy. "You're good. And your look is interesting, too. You might have to work on it a little. I mean, I thought you were a lesbian at first."

"Joy, you can't say that word," said Kayleigh.

"What? I mean, I guess you could still be. Are you?"

Danica saw no path toward a suitable answer to these questions and did not enjoy being put in such a position.

"Doesn't matter," said Joy. "You do you and do whoever and whatnot, right? Point is, you should monetize all this. At least use it to get some customers." Her fingers danced on her knees, waiting for Danica to come up with a clever response.

"Um..." was all Danica managed.

"Just film something. Anything. You don't have to put it

all up. Sofi filmed a bunch of stuff a while back and I swear she just trashed it all."

"That limo thing?" said Kayleigh.

"I was thinking of the library thing, but that, too."

"Oh, yeah. I think she just, like, enjoyed doing that stuff. She filmed those things for a month."

"Girl's a pro," said Joy.

Danica held her hands still and wondered at the footage of Sofi playing in limousines and libraries.

"So," Joy turned back to Danica. "Are you on Facebook or anything?"

Danica hesitated so Kayleigh jumped in.

"She's so good. Joy's got major planning skills. She can totally help you out. She even helped Sofi."

"Truth," said Joy.

Danica was impressed. "Like how? I thought she was pretty well hooked up."

"I mean, sort of. But her socials were all, like, jacked up and whatnot. I got them in line with her brand. Streamlined things."

"Recently?"

"It was around the time we met. So way back. Like six months ago."

"It was in the summer," said Kayleigh. "We were wearing shorts for sure."

"Anyway, I can totally help you, too. What's your email?"

Danica offered her embarrassing email address and Joy happily typed it into her phone. "Just accept what I send you. You'll probably get a couple things from me and whatnot, but accept them, too, and we'll be good."

"Oh... OK." The image of that dark key launched itself back into Danica's mind. It teased her, letting her know she'd never get anywhere without being bold. Just like she'd done with Moxie.

"This is so random," she said, "but how'd you find that key? The one from Sofi's room."

"Well…" Joy paused. Danica could see her weighing her options of sharing information.

Kayleigh had no such problems. "We found it in this gold vest — super cute — in the closet."

"I found it," said Joy.

"Yeah, but we're a team, right?"

"Oh, yeah, for sure."

The bell rang from inside the house. Joy stood, mumbled something that sounded a little like 'thanks,' and grabbed her purse. Kayleigh followed along, promising to come back for another reading. The recent friends of Sofi shuffled off the porch, taking the last remnants of the Cool Kids Table with them.

Danica watched them leave, considering the flurry of information thrown at her. The key was in that gold vest — the one lit like the Vegas strip? If she had gone in when she wanted to, then she might have found that key first. And Joy and Kayleigh had only known Sofi for six months?

None of these discoveries explained the tie between the vision 'cage' and secret-egg-message "CAGE." They didn't explain anything.

It was all just list making.

CHAPTER EIGHTEEN

10:45AM. THE HALLWAY OUTSIDE THE MUSIC ROOM.

Tori changed the setting for the meeting a bit, but the tone remained the same: she commanded attention and everyone gave it. The house field general delivered orders with a sharp tongue, demanding attention from all in her presence.

Despite those demands, Danica's mind managed to float around. Even as Tori spoke about the key and the secret message and invited theories as to what they could possibly mean (the idea that Sofi belonged to an underground frat-house game network caught some heat), Danica still drifted into herself. Worrying.

Why, one might ask, would the connection between the scrap of paper and the visions of a handsome bohunk make a hairdresser-turned-detective-with-secret-psychic-abilities worry so much? Why, one might also ask, would those connections arrest her imagination so completely?

Excellent questions, One.

As she stared at the tan floor, Danica formulated explanations. These explanations relied on hard facts as she, and only she, understood them to be.

They all boiled down to: just had ta' be.

There had to be a reason for hearing those words only to see them later on a hidden scrap of paper. There had to be a connection between Sofi's propensity for puzzles, the vision version of herself and the message hidden in a literal Easter egg.

Danica's authority on the subject was assisted by her seclusion. She was, to her knowledge (but felt pretty confident in that knowledge) the only person capable of reading anyone's mind, in the house or anywhere else. She had done it many times prior; successfully, even, to Marty the concerned boyfriend and wannabe viral internet sensation. In that vision, she had seen the missing woman saying something about being caged, among other troubling details and non sequiturs.

Her singular position meant that Danica was the only person who knew the truest level of significance held by those words. She let her mind meander, kicking the details around like a storm had gone through an old house.

A key. To a foosball table, but not.

A plastic egg posing as a foosball and holding a message. One that tied to her vision of Sofi.

A group of inexperienced, improperly-motivated people in charge of finding the missing girl.

A missing girl with troubles.

A controlling and worried sister.

After considering the facts along with the 'facts,' Danica settled more comfortably into herself. She watched the room with a kind of twisted humor. It was a familiar feeling, one she had developed during her teen years and honed while living with her ex-boyfriend.

That feeling was snobbery.

Sure, she didn't know what all these clues meant, but she felt certain that she knew better than any of *these people*. And yet, with these people she remained, tied tight to the boss' schedule.

"I just don't get why we can't look at her car," said James, managing to sound reasonable for once.

Tori explained, "We will get to the car in the afternoon."

"And there still might be something valuable in the bedroom," said Bobby. "We should spread out. This crime could've been a massive effort."

"Yeah, lots of people could be involved," said Kayleigh. "The government even."

Tori slapped her clipboard against the wall, bringing reality crashing back. "Wild theories will not find my sister. We have these items. The key, the message... We are certain she hid the message. Can none of you... can nobody..."

The woman was losing it and for good reason. Danica could hardly blame her, though relying on this crowd to help her with anything earned some mild criticism. Tori's select group of pseudo-detectives would hardly be helpful moving a couch.

Tori clicked her remote control. In response, Huelo hustled into the hall a moment later, carrying sheets of paper under his massive arm.

"The updated schedule," said Tori. "We will enter the music room next, followed by a search of the garage..."

The idea of searching the car circled around Danica's head, along with splitting up. They'd never find Sofi moving at this slow speed. Going around room by room in a group meant that everyone moved at the same pace. And seeing the garage in print — along with hearing the unhelpful grumbles of the other investigators — solidified her new plan: break away from the group and sneak into the garage.

To pull it off, she'd need a distraction. Even while shuffling through a room full of instruments, she was sure to be missed. She looked at Lorena, who was canoodling with Marty by the stairs. Their heads leaned together as Marty pointed to his phone. Danica crept over to get a peek.

On screen was a video of Lorena, speaking directly to the camera. The background resembled the bookshelf in their bedroom. Marty kept the volume low, but Danica picked up a few words: "great things," "your future" and "look into your mind."

It was a promo. A commercial. They must have shot it during the snack break.

Marty caught Danica watching and whispered, "It's just a temp version. Nothing official yet. What do you think?"

She didn't want to tell him; they didn't have enough time, plus it didn't seem appropriate to scream at them in front of Tori.

Marty didn't wait for an answer anyway. "Have the two of you ever thought about doing a series together?"

First Joy and now Marty. She'd managed not to gag at Joy's proposition of building up her online presence for her non-existent psychic career, but Marty almost got a face full of laughter. And the idea of her and Lorena in a continuous partnership? They'd barely spoken about their *pretend* partnership. The prospect of spending more time — willingly — in the presence of Madame Lorena made Danica's stomach turn.

And yet somehow, Marty made a video series with her and Lorena *not* sound like the stupidest idea ever. He actually meant it. Sincerity and enthusiasm flushed Marty's face and Danica realized he had that winning mix for success in the entertainment business: courage to start projects and naiveté to ignore all the reasons why they should fail.

As Lorena beamed at the prospects of becoming an online sensation ("And you *can* make money doing this?" she asked three times), Danica asked for a moment alone with her. Marty politely pulled himself from Lorena's clutches and joined Tori at the music room door.

Danica leaned over to Lorena. "I need you to cover for me."

"Whatever for?" said the older woman.

She explained her plan: to run to the barn garage, where she presumed Sofi's car was kept, and dig through it ahead of anyone else to get a leg up.

"...Whatever for?" said the older woman again.

Danica didn't expect having to explain the advantages of cheating to someone of Lorena's disposition, so she stuck to her immediate need. "When the group goes to the music room, I'm gonna run for it. Keep up your whole show thing going. Make a big deal about it. All eyes on you, OK? And if anyone asks where I went—"

"You're sick in the toilet!"

"Not my first choice, but OK." She looked toward the living area and the front door. "There's a bathroom over there, so that'll be our cover."

"How long will you be?"

Danica checked her phone's clock. "Give me ten minutes."

"I should say five would be better."

"Seven."

Uncertainty clung to Lorena's eyebrows.

Tori had Huelo open the door and the group began to enter. Lorena put her shoulders back and joined them. Danica watched Lorena's uncertainty waft away as she neared the music room, the stage demanding that her show must go on.

As Lorena disappeared, Danica held back. She let Bobby and the young women, with their pre-investigation re-fills, clamor through. She looked to the front door and started to run.

After two steps, she stopped. Alex was still in the living area, staring at the whiteboard. Staring at the words scrawled upon it: "CAGED" and "CAGE." She looked at Danica with a kind of vulnerability, her face softer than it had been since this party started. Any other time, Danica might have taken this as an opportunity to get a little info out of this enigmatic creature, but not now. Not when she had subterfuge to perform. She checked her clock again.

"How'd you and Marty hook up?" said Alex.

Danica knew what she meant, and what she didn't mean. She *meant* 'How is it that you came to be one of Marty's support inspectors in this strange investigation?' But taken another way — and given the history between Alex and Marty along with the circumstances that possibly connected her to the entire operation — the words 'hook up' came specially loaded. Danica's toes began to sweat.

"He's a client of Madame Lorena's. And I'm her assistant. And he asked us." Nice one, genius. Danica kept her eyes off the door.

"Is that what you do?" said Alex.

"Yup." Danica tried to swing it around. "What about you? I mean, what do you do?"

"Prop maker. Can I ask you something else? What's with your boss? No offense, but she's a train wreck."

"Uh..." A part of Danica had wanted this question to be asked the day before, while another part warred with that first part for fear of having their secrets revealed. "Not sure what you mean?"

"She rolls into every room like it's Broadway or something. She just did it a second ago. The moaning, the deep breaths and the whole thing."

The fury behind Alex's words pulsed, ready to explode.

Ready for that explosion, Danica gave only a non-committal, "Yeah."

"But you don't seem like that," said Alex. "You do your own thing. Your own way at least."

While not technically a question, Danica got the message. Alex was perceptive and Danica's acting wasn't as solid as she may have hoped.

Alex turned back to the whiteboard, still studying the writing. She shook her head. Her hundred-mile gaze put her concentration somewhere else. The same look she had in the game room, staring at that foosball table. Whatever annoyed this woman the most, the information on the whiteboard was tied for second place.

"I don't know if this'll help," said Danica, "but that stuff Joy and Kayleigh have been saying and doing? It's not cool."

"Mmm. You tell them that when you were reading their palms?"

Did this woman have cameras set up around the house? Not that they were doing anything sinister, but Danica had assumed they weren't being spied on. Maybe Alex's dark lipstick gave her stealth powers.

As Danica's inner thirteen-year-old wound up a barrage of cheap insults, she held them back for something more mature.

"We're supposed to be in the music room, but I have to... My stomach...." said Danica. She held her belly and shuffled back toward the bathroom, somehow thankful to Lorena for such an effective ruse.

Alex nodded and shuffled toward the hall, toward the music room. By the time Danica had her hand on the bathroom door, Alex disappeared.

After seeing nobody else for all of three deep breaths, she ran out the front door.

CHAPTER NINETEEN

THE GARAGE.

The building was painted to match the house. At a distance, it would be easy to confuse the two. However, standing at its chipped-wood main door, Danica thought the garage was on the edge of collapse. Upon opening the door, she became certain of it.

After a short (and hopefully unnoticeable) creak, she opened the door, slid inside and pulled the door shut again.

She immediately regretted this decision. The rustic exterior should have been a warning sign that the inside was both poorly lit and creepy. Years earlier, when actual farmers or horse owners had used the building as designed, perhaps they had filled it up with useful, life-affirming tools and supplies. Modern, horse-free life required none of these things, leaving an enormous void to house an unsettling eeriness.

Danica's thumb flipped her phone's screen active. Its faint light found three large, car-shaped somethings under gray parachutes. Under the first two were older-model cars with a little rust here and there. The third was a white BMW with the vanity plate 'SOFITRY.' She recognized it from "Sofi Tries to Parallel Park."

She reset the front of the parachute and slid to the driver's side door. Danica ducked under the chute to the door handle. It opened and she dipped inside, latching the door behind her. She even locked it out of habit. The dome light faded out, so she tripped it back on, casting a beam over Sofi's last known location.

Separate waves of panic rolled through Danica's body. Could Lorena warn her if anyone noticed her absence, or came outside? What was Danica even looking for anyway? How much time had passed, since talking to Alex took at least a minute?

Focusing on her most immediate circumstances, she accepted being a beggar and not a chooser; she would look for anything she could find that might be useful or clue-like.

The keys were still in the ignition. A bag of fast food garbage was tucked under the passenger side's foot area. The rest of the car looked like it had been used primarily as a snacking area, with crumbs, loose fries and empty bags of chips sharing the space.

Finding nothing of particular interest from the front seat, she climbed over the arm rest and into the back, bumping into a water bottle in the beverage holder. She found more of the same kind of clutter; from the rear seats, she noticed a couple pens stuffed between the cushions. Danica pulled one free and — noticing another chewed cap — wiped the cooties off her fingers.

Her bravery allowed her hand to reach under the seat, unearthing a treasure trove of trash. Lollipop sticks, gum wrappers, old pop corn — all the greatest hits of drive-time snacking. Digging under the driver's seat, her wrist cut against something firmer than any mere wrapper. Not part of the seat, not a wire or any cushion material. She pushed at it, forcing a separation at her fingers.

Paper.

Danica felt around the edges, then pulled out another Mead notebook. This one had a black cover. She had just opened it when —

Noises. Outside. Footsteps clumping on the porch. Maybe they weren't coming to the garage. Had she been followed? But where else would someone be walking? She turned off the dome light.

The steps got louder. Then stopped. The person walking had made it off the porch.

Danica opened the passenger door and, after a brief fight with the parachute, extricated herself from the car, immediately regretting her decision. At least in the BMW, she wasn't exposed in the wide open.

On the other side of the thin barn walls, shoes shuffled against the concrete and pebbles. Then a murmuring voice. A man's? A woman's?

Her heartbeat doing double time, Danica quickly assessed the space and chose to duck back under the BMW, her back sliding against the dirty concrete. Compounded panic continued her sliding, as she assumed anyone coming to the garage would be likely after the BMW. She jabbed her body out from beneath the BMW and under the middle car. She clasped her hand over her mouth, wrestling back her breath.

The short creak from the garage door silenced her even more, as the heavy footsteps clomped inside.

The voices returned. Whispers maybe, and close by. They were almost whispers to themselves.

Beneath the middle car, Danica could only see dark shadows against darker floor.

Cloth moved, but not above her. A door opened, but not

the car she'd picked as a shelter. Still, the whispers. Stifled breaths fought for air.

Another creak. The car — probably the shocks. Someone was in the BMW.

Then they closed the door, clomped away and creaked the front door again.

Danica counted heartbeats. Listened for the whispers.

After six heartbeats and no more voices, she heard the footsteps on the porch again. She pushed herself free from under the middle car. She told herself not to rush out of the garage, to check before exiting, in case whoever had come in was still out there.

She checked and saw only an empty porch. There was no one in sight. She counted another half a heartbeat, the sprinted across the yard.

Once again, nobody greeted her, stopped her, or called her out for snooping. A burlap sack didn't drop over her head, she was not clubbed, tased or otherwise acknowledged in a hostile manner for her intrusion. The only thing that greeted her was sunlight.

Danica made it to the front door while avoiding the clompy porch steps. The instant she reached the knob was when she realized she still had the notebook in her right hand and the chewed-up pen in the other. She tucked the pen in her jeans pocket and the notebook in her back waistband, under her shirt.

CHAPTER TWENTY

The Music Room.

Her phone showed eleven minutes had ticked away. She shuffled her feet down the hall, hoping the music room would be easy to find. When it was, she slid up to the doorway, trying her best to strike a pose like she had always been there, observing clues from afar, as if such a thing was possible. This, to her, meant lifting one hand against the door frame and squinting around. It made sense in the moment.

Not quite as sprawling as the living area, the music room still managed to impress in its scope. They were behind the kitchen, but by the looks of its expanse, the room reached deeper into the mountainside. Its floor recessed as well, with three steps around the edges, like a mini amphitheater.

Guitars lined one wall, hanging above a pristine-looking electric drum kit. An antique pump organ rested quietly next to shelves of CD's and vinyl.

The tranquility of the music room was cut by the rummaging about of every other person who hadn't just run from the garage. They were peering into, under and behind every musical item. The CD's were getting a once-over from Joy and Kayleigh, who looked with curiosity and judgment. James rested his coffee on top of a speaker cabinet, the price of which Danica could only imagine. An actual investigation had been occurring and Danica had missed it.

It also appeared everyone in the house was accounted for; even Tori had taken her position of watcher near the pump organ. Whoever had come to the garage had returned ahead of her.

"Feeling better," said Lorena, making a big deal out of things just to show she wasn't out of practice.

"Um, a little. Thanks." Danica rubbed her stomach and joined her phony master, trying not to look at Marty. She didn't need his sincere sympathies right now.

Lorena ran her fingers around the cymbals as Danica said, "Find anything?"

"Very little. Nothing quite as thrilling as the preceding rooms." She lowered her voice. "No luck yourself, I assume?"

Danica scowled. Why would Lorena assume she'd failed? Because she hadn't come in with a parade of marching bands and circus animals to announce her success *like some people?*

"Later," she said. She wouldn't let her get the better of her, baiting her into blowing her score for cheap gloats; she'd save that for after dismissal, thank you.

Tori announced they had one minute left. Danica slid her fingers along the snare drums, acting as cool as someone sweating from running inside after almost being discovered sneaking around could act. At dismissal, Tori addressed them all with distinct frustration.

"I feel we need another break. This is very disappointing that you cannot find anything worthwhile." She kicked the bottom of the organ. She gave the final bell from the hallway, disappearing in a huff.

Danica let herself exit behind Joy and Kayleigh and after telling Lorena she had to go back to the bathroom, ran there to examine her findings in peace and quiet.

The pages were filled with writing. Scribbles, really, accented with doodles, drawings and any other kind of free-associative work someone might throw at a page. She flipped around, finding notes with little direction to them:

"Tired. Gotta find way to nap on set. Won't let me. Still.

"ST: bathroom attendant [star star star]. Tricky. Would have to find place with lots of space. Place in WeHo? Might be closed down. Good? They didn't have an attendant, but lots of room. Good parking.

"Cherry tomatoes, basil, noodles — penne?, feta cheese...."

It went on, page after page.

Pride rose inside Danica. It might take a while to sort out, but the notebook held potential, offering real insights into Sofi's secret side. She imagined cutting out pages, discovering patterns within patterns, deciphering just where more clues had been hidden.

She flushed the toilet for appearances, washed her hands for sanitization, then returned the notebook carefully to its place against her back. Danica opened the door in time to catch Joy staring her way, arms folded, with a smirk on her face. Did she know? Had she snuck out, too, and caught her?

Before Danica could think any more about what that meant, Tori breezed by with purpose. The woman paused for the briefest of moments.

"We will investigate the car now."

Danica nodded, totally fine with this set of plans, adding a nod for emphasis.

The group gathered on the lawn, with the main gate behind them. Danica joined them, each step filling her with more and more confidence. Getting ahead of the game was a bad-ass move she hadn't known she could do. And jumping the line for her own selfish purposes? Never. She felt like a cat-burglar, or a Fortune 500 CEO.

Against her better angels, she searched for Lorena to rub it in. To show that her plan had worked, that they'd found an artifact that could contain— *did*, did contain — a multitude of personal information about the missing girl. A clue the rest of the crew of greedy non-detectives would have missed and now *definitely* would.

Though someone might have had a chance. Danica's heart had just stopped pounding, allowing her to think a little clearer and remember the person who came in to the garage. She'd been so concerned about almost getting caught that she had not considered why that person had come in at all.

"Did anyone else leave the music room?" she asked Lorena.

She knew the answer before it came. "I did not notice. I was too busy...."

Danica let her prattle on. Of course she hadn't noticed. Lorena wouldn't notice if a semi-truck humped her leg. She made a quick count of the group, noting everyone was accounted for.

Everyone except Huelo. He was at the garage, swinging the big doors open. A couple moments later, he drove out the white BMW and parked it a few feet from the group. With its parachute removed, it appeared cared for despite the dirt around the rims.

"This the car from 'Parallel Parking?'" said Bobby. He knelt at the front, inspecting the plates for God knew what.

He'd said this to Marty, who responded, "I think so."

"It is." Bobby spoke immediately after Marty finished his

three-word response. "Before your time. Well before." The mix of Bobby's speedy retort, lack of eye-contact and measured superiority was missed by no one.

Tori stepped up to the car first and said, "Please be careful. This is my sister's car and she prizes it. But it was the vehicle she drove to the desert."

The group engaged in a polite attack of the car, opening all doors and the trunk. Joy and Kayleigh gasped at the water bottle.

"Her favorite," one of them said.

"Iknowright," said the other.

"How'd you get it here?" said James.

Marty answered. "She had it towed. Wanted to preserve it as best we could, you know?"

Danica leaned over the trunk area, but had to admit to herself how disinterested she had become. This must be how cheaters felt. Their challenge after securing victory was in presenting as if they still had struggles ahead of them. As she leaned into the nearly empty trunk, she scrunched her eyebrows, careful not to drop the prize pressed against her back.

Who could've come in the garage? Huelo seemed to have keys to everything, but he appeared physically incapable of sneaking anywhere. If Bobby or James had snuck away, then James would have (or should have) told Danica about it. And when Danica arrived to the music room, Joy and Kayleigh were ankle deep into their CD dive.

Marty had been occupied with Lorena and Danica had seen Alex off.

Lorena joined Danica at the trunk. "Looks empty. Did you want to—"

"Here!" said Bobby. He was on his knees, leaning in the backseat. He struggled a bit more and with a final defiant tug, pulled his hand back. It held *another* black Mead notebook.

Everyone's eyes looked at the trophy in his hands. Danica was glad for it; they'd miss her jaw hitting the ground.

She closed her mouth and thought, 'So what? Good. Another notebook. More information means more insight, but we'll have both of them — a complete picture.'

Marty looked over Bobby's shoulder. They stared at the pages.

'Great,' thought Danica again. 'They look shocked by what they've found. That's fine. It's a lot of work ahead of us. It won't be easy, but that's what it takes sometimes.'

Lorena had moved behind the gawking crew. Danica considered warning everyone to hold onto their wallets, but she didn't. She watched the older woman's face transform from opportunity-seeking curiosity into utter horror.

"Please," said Tori. She held out her hand. Danica jogged over to the group just in time to see the notebook close.

Tori opened it and her expression mirrored Lorena's. The blood vanished from her cheeks and her lips trembled. Was Sofi's handwriting really that awful?

"This... uh...," said Tori. Danica had yet to see this woman at a loss for words, much less a loss of composure. Her eyes darted across every page she flipped, unable to look away. She ceased flipping and stared for a lifetime at one page.

Tori adjusted her orange jacket and nodded to Bobby, keeping her eyes on the notebook. "First of all, thank you. For finding this. We have, I feel, a major clue."

'*Two* major clues,' Danica patted herself on the back.

"This notebook clearly belonged to my sister. And...."

She broke off. Her lips danced like they had words, but nothing arrived. She handed the notebook to Marty, whose eyes became saucers.

"Do we have a projector?" he said. "Something that... so we can show everyone... everybody will... they should...."

"Yes, inside," said Tori.

Marty searched for something steady and his eyes found Danica. Their weight landed heavy on her. He turned the notebook out for everyone to see.

The writing was large and jagged. Blue ink filled the page, but the passage at the top warranted the most attention:

"SOMEONE IS FOLLOWING ME."

Danica caught only a glance of the subsequent paragraph, dense as it was, but the words 'unsafe' and 'scared' leapt off the page. The style of the handwriting reminded her of the other book, only with more passion behind every stroke. Largely written in cursive, many words were accented with random capitalization. Many others were underlined. And all of them appeared much more dramatic, sensational and important than the collection of half-thoughts and recipes currently slapped against Danica's waist.

Lorena nudged Danica in the back. "Show them," she said.

"I don't think—"

"We are falling behind." Before Danica could mount a protest, Lorena reached beneath Danica's shirt and pulled the notebook free. She then rushed back to the car. With all eyes on the new, dramatic notebook, she ducked into the trunk without much fanfare.

"We found something, too," she said at last. "It's another notebook."

"Lorena, this might not be a good idea—"

"Really? Where?" said Marty.

Lorena held the notebook high in the air, but looked for Danica to answer the questions.

"The... the car." Danica wasn't fully lying.

Madame Lorena presented her treasure to Tori with a slight bow. "Perhaps this will offer further illumination."

Tori looked as confused as everyone else. She glanced at a

few pages. "This is... interesting as well." The words came out wobbly. She must have seen one of the several grocery lists.

Lorena must have missed the signals and pressed on. "I feel this book combines with the other in perfect harmony."

"The corner!" said Joy. "Look."

Suffice it to say, Joy had not been excited about anything remotely close to the notebook Danica had found. She was pointing at the other one — the dramatic one. The one that held the fearful scrawling of a terrorized young woman. Specifically she pointed to the corner of the front page where Tori had stopped flipping.

"Yes," said Tori, almost attempting a smile. She cast aside the notebook Danica had found, shoving it at Huelo with all the importance of an airline magazine. Then all eyes watched her as she concentrated on the other book.

While the front page remained completely blank, the bottom-right corner was missing, ripped free, leaving a jagged edge.

Tori reached into her pocket and retrieved the scrap of paper from the foosball egg. Unfurled, 'CAGED CAGE' fit right into the corner spot.

A perfect puzzle piece.

Nobody spoke. Danica assumed nobody wanted to. Joy and Kayleigh looked around for someone to say anything.

At last, Tori did. "We should go inside. There is lunch."

CHAPTER TWENTY-ONE

"Look, no offense, but that's pretty damn racist."

A long table had been set up in the living area, near the back by the kitchen. Lunch was composed of pita wraps circling a green dip. Individual bags of chips lined themselves next to key lime pies and yogurt parfaits. The desserts, too, had been made into individual portions, with the key lime pie crust burned in such a way as to make it look like a full-sized pie shrunk down by sci-fi magic.

The only thing that could possibly stop people from eating such a delicious-looking spread was the conversation near the couch between Kayleigh and Alex. Though Danica had missed the introductory statement, the players and scenario appeared plain as day: two white women arguing about whether something one of them had said was or was not racist.

Easy stuff.

Danica tried to ignore the almost-certain flare up by fixating on her own insecurities. How had she missed that other notebook? Did it really come down to a 50-50 shot where she had just found one and Bobby found the other? On the long walk back to the house, she'd tried to avoid Marty, for fear of disappointing him even more, only to end up next to Lorena again.

To her surprise, the older woman seemed stunned silent — she only had one dessert in front of her and it was barely touched.

"So... quite a find," said Lorena.

Danica nodded. "I didn't say we should tell people about it."

"I thought you said it was good."

"I thought it *was* good."

Lorena held a glob of yogurt on a spoon, suspended in thought. "So you found *that* book, but not... not the other one?"

Danica nodded again.

"It was useless."

"You don't know that," said Danica. "It might have insights into... Sofi's... life or something."

Lorena leaned back in her seat. Her eyes shot across the room to hit anything else.

Danica worried if other people had heard. So what if they had? What, were they going to be jealous that they hadn't found a notebook full of Sofi's shallowest thoughts? Was anyone else clamoring to read the not-so-detailed details of Sofi's trip to the LA Zoo (spoiler alert: the koalas were sleeping)? Not one bit.

Marty appeared from the kitchen with a fresh drink, then headed for the food. Danica's disappointment in herself wouldn't let her look at him. She was supposed to be the one with experience. She was supposed to be the one finding things nobody else could find. God, how had she missed that notebook? How had she guessed so wrong?

"They just want identification," said Kayleigh, still arguing. "It's the president. It's a big deal."

"That's not why they're asking at all, genius." Alex dropped her fork to rid her hands of a possible weapon.

"It is! You have to be, like, a citizen of the country to be president. It's in the Constitution and stuff."

Alex snorted her laugh snort. She glanced at Danica, almost like she wanted back up.

Kayleigh brought her bare leg up and leaned it on the coffee table. "I'm not racist."

"I didn't say you were. I said the idea that you said was racist."

"But I'm not."

"I hear you."

"I voted for him."

"Congrats, you're a total Freedom Rider."

"...A what?"

Another snorted laugh. Part of Alex seemed to enjoy tormenting Kayleigh, who was growing beyond flummoxed. The girl threw up her hands and opened her mouth to spit more ignorance. Ignorance which was delayed for all of two seconds.

"All I'm saying is, like, I get what you're saying, but... like...."

"'Like, like, like, like.' You're a walking Facebook button."

"It's just," said Kayleigh, avoiding repeating that word again, "we don't know for sure about him."

"Did you know for sure about Bush?"

"I didn't vote for that guy."

"What about McCain? Did you ask for his birth certificate?"

Kayleigh flummoxed again. She turned toward Joy, the only Black person in the room. The only non-White person.

Danica sensed the house go dead, like they'd been in a space capsule with a sudden air leak. It was a wordless moment speaking volumes. Kayleigh looked at Joy for validation — some "Not a Racist" certification.

Notably, Joy didn't appear the least bit surprised. How could she be? She took a bite of key lime pie and said nothing. Every now and then she looked up at Danica and cast that same smirky grin.

Kayleigh ignored being ignored. "I'm sorry. I'll drop it. I totally get it, let's just drop it." She threw back the clear liquor in her cup and went to get another. Totally dropping the subject, as evidenced by the tension in her shoulders.

With perfect timing, Lorena nudged her way next to Danica again. "That other notebook has mention of many terrifying things."

"I saw some of them." She let her eyes go to Marty, trying to think of an apology. Bobby had joined him at the food area, discussing something she couldn't quite hear.

"I did not get to see the whole of your notebook, but it appeared much more tranquil. Less... useful in the present moment."

"I get it, Lorena. Fine. I'll put it back if you want."

"I don't mean any disrespect."

"Whew."

"I get the distinct feeling that our partnership is nearing a termination point."

This stopped Danica mid-bite. She'd been feeling this for a while, but she wasn't about to tell Lorena that. That old crack pot didn't get to end this — that was *Danica's* job! If anyone was going to enjoy the moment of storming away, too upset to continue this charade any longer, it was her, not Lorena.

Tori entered and sat at the table, her mind elsewhere. She still carried the book Bobby had found, flipping through pages at random. She would look at some, then close it and have a drink to build her stamina, then open a new page only to repeat the whole process.

"If that's how you feel," said Danica.

Lorena picked up her plate and moved without explanation. There was none to make. She instead slid down the table and invited herself into the seat next to Tori. The psychic reached for Tori's hands and Tori reciprocated.

"I didn't make it a race thing, you know," said Kayleigh, back at the couch.

Alex responded with a torrential civics lesson, drowning out the conversation at the end of the table. Danica could only watch as Lorena and Tori inspected the notebook, marveling at all there was to marvel at.

She turned to face Joy and her knife-sharp focus staring back. Amidst the noise clutter, Danica leaned across the table to her. "Is there something you need?"

"Nope," said Joy, giggling a little to herself. "Nothing that *I* need, that's for sure."

"Well, I'm kinda picking up on some hostility radiating from your way. If you wanna tell me something—"

"You wanna do this here and whatnot?" said Joy. "Let me say: you don't."

At this, Joy got up from the table, heading for the whiteboard area. Danica followed her, worried she might have to block a punch.

When she reached the board, Joy turned around. She held her phone like a police badge.

Danica glanced at the screen and recognized the same Blogspot basic Arial font, same muted aqua color scheme.

ForWhatItsWorth's blog had struck again.

"I don't know... what that... is."

"You've been busy." Accusation clung tight to Joy's voice. "Your email address helped a bit. I know you didn't write this stuff, but were you going to tell Tori you are a private eye?"

"I'm not. Not really. It was just one case."

"You have a 'relationship' with the police," Joy read from the screen. "What kind of 'relationship' are we talking about here?"

"It says 'complicated,' doesn't it?"

"Pfft."

"It's fine, Joy. Really. I don't do that any more. And so what if I did?"

"So what?"

As Joy finished her question, it sat without answer. And in that halted moment, Danica realized the truth: yeah, *so what?* So what if she had worked on a case prior to this one? So what if she had solved it while almost getting killed? She had still solved it. And survived. She still did what everyone thought she couldn't have done. That work — and it was work — had been enough to not only get her involved with the present crazy predicament, but it had inspired some rando to write about her.

It was nothing to hide and nothing to be ashamed of.

And Joy was jealous.

"There's not really anything to say, Joy," she said. "You can read it all right there. And if you're worried about Tori finding out, I'll tell her myself. Right now."

She turned and stormed back to the table, letting Joy stew. So what if she had a past and a possible relationship with a cop and could actually bring some helpful insights into this case. This missing person's case. This strange case everyone insisted on calling a *'missing person's case.'*

The words hung on her tongue, held back by teeth as she reached Tori. She had to tell her everything.

The only thing that could stop her confession was what she glanced from over Tori's shoulder, in the notebook.

It was terrible. The heavy hand Sofi had used filled every page with jagged lettering expounding on her deep fears. In what little she could see, she saw words like "HELP," "GOTTA HIDE," "GET OUT." A shape like a god's eye with strict corners punctuated the bottom of most pages.

Tori flipped the page and horror paused her again.

"HE SENT SOMETHING.

"HE CALLED IT A GIFT.

"LOCK IT AWAY

"MY NECK.

"GASPER WANTS TO TRAP ME.

"HE WANTS TO TAKE ME."

Danica tried sinking through the floor. A mixture of different shames came to her: shame for not finding this juicy clue herself, for not being able to look past her own failures and concentrate on what was actually important. Shame for not being capable of collaborating.

And the shame for her arrogance about her choices, and her position in the house. She had experience — more than Lorena at least. She should have been leading the investigation. A woman's life was at stake after all. Why would Danica let it slide into the hands of amateurs?

Other conversations at the table had gotten louder, all around the this or that's of accusations. Even in Joy's silence, her accusatory look screamed across the room. She would expose Danica's secret, try to position it as a hinderance.

Unless Danica did it first.

"Tori?" she said. The woman turned to face her. The light behind her shadowed her face, yet tears still shimmered. "I have to tell you: I have experience with this sort of thing."

"Um..." said Lorena.

Danica ignored her. "I've solved a murder. I did it last

year, last fall. And, I mean... I think I've got a knack for this kind of thing. Recognizing when stuff is just, sorta, off but connected to something else? And this whole notebook thing, plus that video? This name, Gasper. And the hidden messages and the key? It all seems...."

She rummaged through her vocabulary for a descriptive phrase better than 'weird' but came up empty. 'Weird' didn't feel like enough to cover it, but it was one-hundred percent accurate.

"I know you don't wanna say it, but I gotta say... I keep thinking that... with everything we've found... This situation... the reality of this situation is...."

Tori stared into her eyes and her expression transformed into a kind of serenity, as if a magician's curtain had lifted away to reveal the trick, explaining all things.

"Miss Luman, do you think this a kidnapping?" she said at last.

Relief washed over Danica. That idea had been dancing around the entire case since the beginning, had seemed so obvious that it almost hurt to consider. She had questioned herself for even imagining it, chalking it up to her burgeoning penchants for heroism and dramatics.

But now, it was out there. Someone had said it — the most important person in the house no less. It could be dealt with. They could now look at the facts, as puzzling as they were, with new eyes and face what needed facing.

"Yes. I think so."

The room had gone quiet, continuing Danica's streak of poor timing. Everyone had heard them and all eating and chatting had ceased. Tori turned away from her, back to the notebook, closed it and put her head on her hands.

Then Marty punched Bobby.

CHAPTER TWENTY-TWO

The Living Area, Near the Treats.

It happened in a flash. Marty's hand went right into Bobby's eye. Bobby fell onto the food table, pulling desserts with him to the floor. Marty jumped on him and delivered a barrage as the rest of the house slowly processed what in the hell was happening.

He'd gotten in five good shots before Joy of all people threw her tiny 112-pounds-soaking-wet frame at the fray. She wrapped herself around Marty's right arm. This slowed him down all of two seconds, but enough for Bobby to mount some kind of defense.

Marty knocked Joy off of him and she slid on the polished floor.

Danica shoved chairs and people aside. Compulsion took over; compulsion to save Marty from his own temper. She would be no use in physically removing him unless she utilized her not-quite-high-school-level understanding of physics to its maximum potential.

In essence, if she ran at Marty really fast, her force would generate enough power to move his mass. Or something.

She put her head down and drove her shoulder into Marty's side. A full-on, open-field tackle.

They hit the door to the kitchen. She wrapped one arm around his neck and shoved the other against his punching arm.

"He tried to kill me!" Bobby yelled. "You all saw him. He's a psycho!"

"I'd be doing everyone a favor!" Marty's punching arm flailed again and delivered its blow to Danica's back. She groaned but held tight.

Marty swung again, rolled onto his knees like he could stand. Danica's strength was no match for his, but she could at least make his attempted rampage more difficult by playing the part of human backpack. Dodging another swing from Marty's free arm, she grabbed his head and then grabbed his hair.

Sofi. Standing on a hotel balcony, filming herself with a small camera. Then waving to people below. She smiled at them, then at him.

The scene changed to the lobby. Sofi was mobbed, signing autographs. Sofi pulled the pen cap off with her mouth and signed for a young girl who screamed her head off.

Sofi giggled, then disappeared as Danica released her grip. She fell against the table leg, giving her back another bruise. Through the stars in her eyes she managed to see Bobby crawl to his feet and hustle toward the main exit.

Alex held her hair in her fingers. "What... what the crap was that?"

Lorena's face was ashen, dancing from Marty to Danica and back again.

Marty remained on the floor. Tori had kneeled on his

shoulder, a professional-looking disarm. When Marty wedged his arm free, Tori caught it at the wrist, pinching hard.

"Turn the assailant over," said James Van Owen, quickly recovering from Cop Mode with, "I think I've seen something like that done before. Somewhere. I think."

"Find Huelo," said Tori. James made himself useful for once and jogged away.

For too long, nobody said anything, all the while wanting to say everything. Joy and Kayleigh held each other, unable to look away from the rage monster on the floor. Alex's hair pulling continued unabated. Even Lorena was at a complete loss for words.

If they'd seen half of what Danica had seen, they might have exploded. The new vision of Sofi, happily interacting with her fans, tumbled around with the frightened, wandering, voice-disappearing-and-talking-about-cages version she'd seen just a couple days ago. The handwriting on the book — the scary diary — matched the first vision, but not the second.

People were complicated. They could be happy or sad, or happy *and* sad. A person was not one thing all the time, unless they had become a literal brand. Sofi might have been slipping away before someone took her.

She remembered: Tori had said the word, 'kidnapping.' She'd accepted the possibility.

Danica's eyes went to Tori's. They were waiting for her. Behind the hurt and anger, Tori's face fractured. Her lip trembled, wanting to tell Danica something, but knowing she couldn't say it around anyone else.

Together, they recalled the conversation they'd just had a moment ago. What she'd just said to only her and Lorena and to nobody else. What she meant:

Tori didn't trust the others.

She suspected them. She wanted them here so they could be found out.

Huelo came sprinting in, keys smacking his massive leg. He wrapped his fingers around Marty's shoulder and kneaded it like Grandma's dinner rolls, pulling him to his feet.

Tori stood as well and straightened out her orange jacket. She spoke with calm menace. "I will not have this behavior here. Activities are postponed until further notice. Everyone go to your rooms, please."

She gave another tiny look to Danica, but Danica understood completely. She had work to do.

The kidnapper was in the house and Danica had to figure out who he was.

Or she was

Or they were.

She backed up, back to the table to gather her things.

The other notebook — the lame one of doodles, half-baked ideas and never tried recipes — had disappeared.

CHAPTER TWENTY-THREE

UPSTAIRS.

Joy and Kayleigh protested the loudest. Charged up with post-adolescent rebellion, they resented being sent to their room and let Tori understand this completely. As Danica ascended the steps, she lost track of everyone else, but there was no losing Joy and Kayleigh.

With the argument soundtrack behind and beneath her, Danica paced the upstairs hall. James and Bobby's door hung open, but she avoided it. The stolen pen in her pocket reminded her that she needed to find some accompanying paper — something to keep these thoughts from slipping out of her brain.

Her head already hurt. She'd only had the initial sip of alcohol on the first night; not nearly enough for a late-presenting hangover. Perhaps Marty had thrown her into the floor harder than she knew.

Crap, Marty. Her endorsement for being in the house at

all — her sponsor — had just attacked someone for no good reason. Someone had to know why.

Why was he envisioning Sofi during the fight? Why didn't anyone do anything to stop it? Why would someone take the lame notebook — the one of little to no substance? Why did the name Gasper seem so familiar?

The blog. That fan page she'd read — the one talking about the "real" Sofi with its clear and disgusting fan entitlement. That had come from someone named Gasper, hadn't it? Without any way to capitalize on that information, how would it help?

It all ate at Danica as she made her third lap around the hall. The variety of vague half ideas dusted before she could solidify anything into a cohesive thought. Somewhere beneath her, a one-sided,-two-voiced argument had devolved into a tantrum. As she stood near the guest bathroom, Danica could still hear Kayleigh's full attack.

Opportunity smiled, or rather continued to scream indignant tirades downstairs. Without those two to hog it, their odd treasure of a bathroom was open for snooping.

Etiquette made her lightly knock before entering. With no answer, she knocked again as she opened the door.

She found a standard bathroom, possibly the most basic part of the entire Starr residence. The ceiling hovered low and the fan failed to turn on when she flipped the switch.

Danica closed the door behind her and locked it (again, etiquette), then gave the room a proper staring at. The toilet and vanity appeared to be a rudimentary Home Depot special, picked off the shelf and plopped into place. The tiling was multi-colored and looked mostly cared for. A rug in the middle held very little resemblance to the over-used and under-cleaned variety currently holding space in Danica's home apartment.

As she studied the room's underwhelming qualities, she

considered the distinct possibility that some people actually did have more fun than she did, and that they were capable of enjoying the differences a bathroom to themselves had to offer. It made her a little sick and she sat on the edge of the tub. Took a breath to calm herself. She'd been in a fight, sort of. Come close to violence. Her wrist ached. She took another breath and stared at the tub.

Three dark lines ran near the drain. Scuffs, like from a shoe. Danica slid the curtain to the wall and rubbed some of the scuff away with her thumb. She turned the cold faucet to let some water wash it away.

No water came.

She turned the other knob. Same result. She examined the drain and felt its dryness. This shower had not been used for years. Maybe never.

Danica stepped back a bit and absorbed. Joy or Kayleigh could have stepped into the tub to give one or the other space, but that didn't suit their style.

The knobs wobbled like they might snap off. She tried them both at the same time.

The cold knob became solid and clicked, at which time the wall opened. A door emerged, one to a small dark pathway, just large enough for a skinny woman to slip through. Three feet beyond that wall was daylight.

Danica gaped around the rest of the room and confirmed her reality by catching her reflection in the mirror. It was real and she was really there. She sucked in her stomach, squeezed through the opening and within two steps walked onto a balcony overlooking the forest.

She looked behind her again, at the door, like it had anything to say for itself. If the balcony had been attached to any of their guest rooms, it would have made sense. Even if it had been attached to a bathroom with a window, she could have seen that happening. However, the idea of a secret hole-in-the-shower balcony defied reason. Her image of Warren Beatty became clearer (the Warren Buffett image as well). Above the balcony was a small awning, with a thin steel line running from it down into the dark trees below. Like a grounding wire.

As if invited to surprise her even further, Danica's phone exploded with text message alerts. She quickly silenced the thing, then remembered that it hadn't made a peep since entering the proclaimed dead zone of a house. The vibrating plastic in her hand tickled her palm.

"It's a hotspot," she said to the trees. This was how Joy and Kayleigh looked her up, how they had managed to survive these terrible hours with poor cell service, and why they had been sneaking into the bathroom at every opportunity.

Her first text was from Gabby, but she ignored it for the one below it. From Freddie.

"Your roommate called me but didn't give details. Do I need details?"

She could sense the concern. Not condescending, but genuine apprehensive thoughts about her wellbeing. Despite Freddie's sincerity, Danica decided to leave it for the moment with Gabby's text. No reason to worry a completely platonic friend with her troubles. Not yet.

She checked her saved pages and found the Kutman blog, then held her phone closer to the satellite magic above to bless her with signal.

Thy Holy Signal's will be done, hallowed be Its name, Danica's search drew results! The page opened on the sparse site she recognized, with its dark green background and terrible, tiny font.

Danica checked that the page had loaded fully. It took ten scrolls before she finally came to its finish. Then she climbed back through the door and replaced the shower wall into its normal position. She checked her phone again; the blog's text remained, but her phone carried no signal.

A quick check in the hall to hear any voices. They had stopped. Joy and Kayleigh would likely be coming to draw from the signal well soon. Danica washed her hands to sell the act and returned to the hallway, spring thoroughly returned to her step.

As she walked, she read:

Sofia Stornelli may have created her YouTube account near the turn of the century, but "Sofi Starr" made her first true appearance in 2005. Other blogs and boards get it wrong, only focusing on the "official" videos. Those things fall in line with her curated persona of a fun-loving girl. Those writers and "fans" are willing to swallow anything put out by the Sofi Starr brand, incapable or unwilling to discern the product from the real Sofi.

The first of these products came in 2008 from a video titled "The Court Room." It's a low-budget comedy skit where Sofi plays all parts in a crazy trial. Clearly shot in the living room of her Van Nuys apartment, Sofi jumps into each role with both feet, layering herself with copious costumes. Sofi the Lawyer wears a mustache and suspenders while Sofi the Judge bangs a gavel on an entertainment center. It's got a wildness and a kind of joy, like early Peter Sellers.

But it's not her. Not really.

A few more of these skits have appeared in recent months and while her fans support Sofi's stretches into the fanciful and her attempts at new avenues, it's difficult to relate this performance from the woman we've all come to know. It all comes off as desperate. Certainly, internet-based comedy comes as a mixture of amateurism and hard work (it is not subtle), but it does not suit OGS.

There are many fingers to point with and I have to

agree most should aim at her team up with PowerWorks. They're a conglomeration of like-minded content producers, striving to cross market its products (ie stars) to produce viral videos (ie get more clicks and more money) to make even more products and push them to produce even more videos. The cameos and crossovers started right away, with comedian KaseyY appearing as side characters in Sofi's skits and even a few of her "Tries" videos. KaseyY does nothing but ham it up, with all the soul of a wet sandwich.

And yet, here we are, years later and all the surprise cameos have not stopped. They must be working for someone. Some bean counter money man who doesn't even watch these videos, has no respect for the arts or the artists and tries to push as many commercials in front of the camera as he can.

PowerWorks is happy, of course. They dominate the front page of YouTube, using all their paid-off money to do it. They even got in early with Facebook and have recently been talking to major phone companies about developing content exclusively for phones.

And in the opinion of us true fans, it's all artificial and disposable. They're trying to rip Sofi's heart out and mass market it, forcing her away from her true work — the reality videos and the "Tries" series — while shoving those stupid skits in front of our eyeballs. The artificiality stands out so bad it hurts. When you try to make things look authentic, we only end up seeing the strings.

There's still hope though, and it lies in Sofi herself. Somehow, her spirit has persevered. Somehow, her spark still shines. She continues to release new videos — TRUE videos of her true self — despite all opposition. PowerWorks and YouTube are trying to bury the true Sofi by forcibly "printing the legend."

We are here for her. For Sofia. We will do whatever it takes to save her.

It ended with a place to add your name to the list of supporters. It was a petition.

Danica checked the date: December 11, 2008. The user's avatar was of an old Lincoln Log cabin package. Next to it was the name GKutman.

Context changed things. As she re-read the blog, what had previously been mildly creepy now carried sinister subtext. The ownership of Sofi as something this person could posses and keep, the undercurrents of resentment at change, the mild sexism around gazing at and cyber stalking a woman. Danica had missed it before, or seen it and permitted it to blend in with all the other misogyny around her, but she couldn't miss it now.

"You get a signal up here?" It was James. He stood in his doorway, leaning. He slurped his apple sauce in the cup like a thick broth.

"Just looking at something."

James' casual façade dropped when he motioned for her to enter his room. Despite thinking better of it, Danica accepted the invitation and was immediately struck with an overwhelming scent of Axe Body Spray.

"Real quick," he said. "Alex used to work as a prop maker."

It took Danica far too long to catch up, so James jumped in again.

"Our deal? Trading what we find out. I found this out. She's in the business, like Sofi and Tori and all of them."

"I actually know this already."

"Well did you know she made magic props?" James remained impressed with himself. "Like for magicians and live shows and stuff."

"So... she made Sofi disappear?"

"No," said James, his crest discreetly fallen. It rose again with his next though. "But that's how they met. Her and Marty. She made some custom jobs for folks and they were on the same shoot."

Danica shifted her hips. She wanted to be nice and nod along, but it was difficult to take James seriously in any setting, let alone his double-bachelor room. As she scanned the room, she asked, "What makes this information valuable?"

"Hey, I'm trying here. It seems like something's there. Marty was dating someone else before Sofi and before Alex. Don't know anything about that person. When he met Alex on a shoot, he dumped her. Then he met Sofi, dumped Alex, and here we are. Got anything for me?"

"Are you interviewing people or..."

She stopped as her eyes pinpointed into the contents of his luggage. Amidst the jeans and socks, a dark cardboard corner stuck out.

The notebook. The lame one, the one Danica had found. There it was — hidden among travel clothes.

Danica pushed the socks aside and pulled the book out. "How'd you get this?"

James stammered. It was one of his super powers.

"This is the one I found. Someone stole it from downstairs during the fight."

"I didn't... That wasn't..."

"This is your room, right?"

"Well... yeah." James' face sagged into a sad potato.

She tucked the notebook under her arm. "Real good at sharing stuff, man."

"It's useless anyway, right?"

"That totally justifies stealing it." She didn't wait for another of his lame excuses. Danica stepped out of the room, pulling the door shut as hard as she could.

The rush of emotions mixed with the flood of questions. Her hand instinctively opened the notebook to search for a clean page. She'd felt so untethered without being able to jot some of her thoughts down. The pen flew into her hand, but she stopped for two reasons:

First, it seemed like a violation to write in someone else's notebook, even if the topic of one's writing focused on locating the missing owner.

And second, something created a lump inside the notebook. It had never been in the best shape, but this lump felt more solid than from mere paper creases.

She folded back the back pages and found a cheap-looking silver pendant and chain, taped in two places to the back cardboard flap.

Danica pulled it free for an examination. Inside was a picture of Sofi, smiling, as in a screen grab from one of her videos. The picture oozed with creepy familiarity. A cursive inscription on the back said "The Stuff," adding to her ever-growing sense of perplexity.

James St. Sticky Fingers must have pinched this thing from a bedroom drawer and not known what to do with it. Not that Danica had any ideas either. She flipped through the notebook again, looking for other lost treasures, finding none.

As she reached her room and opened the door, the unmistakable sound of Huelo climbing the steps rang out. She stuffed the pendant in the middle of the notebook, promising to return it to its owner eventually, and shoved them both under her pillow.

The security guard knocked on her door frame.

"Just you in here?" Danica nodded and Huelo continued. "There's matters that need discussing, concerning your relationship with Mr. Dole. Tori needs to talk to both of you."

"I don't know where Lorena is."

"Find her, please."

"Are we getting sent away?"

"Find her, please," Huelo said again. "Come to Tori's room in ten minutes." Then he left.

In that brief moment of solitude, Danica sensed the resignation waft over her. It was finished. All the sneaking and lying and snooping and, sure, the do-gooding had finally come to an end. They were going to get kicked out.

CHAPTER TWENTY-FOUR

Once Danica had eliminated Lorena's chief hiding place (the kitchen and snack areas), she swiftly excused herself outside, to the general expanse of the grounds.

Two figures stood at the far gate. Since the wind was whipping one of the figures' scarves like a flag on a clipper ship, Danica obliged to head in that direction.

She didn't want to find Lorena. She didn't want to get kicked out. In the search for a positive spin, all she could land on was, 'At least I don't have much to pack.' Her *Dookie* shirt itched.

Through the oak leaves, she saw the sky above the city, a layer of green smog cradling nothing. The trees lining the barrier created a cool blanket around the house, dipping down to the closed front gate.

Lorena and the other person stood in the tree's shadow by that gate. She couldn't hear them, but they were definitely conversing.

And smoking.

It was Lorena and Bobby Utz. Together.

Smoking.

Danica stopped walking, then tried to resume her pace in as casual a manner as she could, as if she hadn't just seen Marty attack the man ahead of her; as if they weren't being called inside for disciplinary reasons. No, she just happened to be strolling by when — oh! — there they were.

The couple at the fence stopped talking to nod at Danica. She tried not to watch at the cigarette smoke rollicking above them, or at Bobby at all, or at the house where Marty was currently detained. She considered covering her eyes with her hood.

"Hello there, my dear," said Lorena. "You found us at last."

The filtered cig was clenched between her lips. The woman spoke with kindness; either their relationship had not reached a termination point, or its termination had stalled to allow Lorena access to greater opportunities. Danica rolled with it.

"Huelo and Tori have to talk to us."

"Concerning the altercation, no doubt." Lorena turned to Bobby. "She tackled Marty, you know? Ran across the room and threw herself into his ample frame."

Bobby nodded. "Thought so. Guess I owe you some gratitude."

He reached into a side pocket of his cargo pants and withdrew the pack. He offered one to Danica.

"Oh, no, I don't... not anymore... don't smoke," said Danica. "How's your face? And everything else?"

"Probably be alright," said Bobby, putting the pack back in his pocket.

"We were just talking," said Lorena, "about everything Mr. Utz has seen."

"It's not much—"

"Come now. It's plenty. He's very motivated to solve the case."

"I know you wanna get Sofi back as much as I do. I mean, you're fans."

At a few Hollywood parties she'd attended, Danica had encountered this kind of assumptive talk. Especially at release parties. There, partygoers gathered to experience someone's masterpiece — a movie or album or magazine article — with the presenters' general consensus being that the attendees felt just as excited about the piece as those who made it. Which they did not. In Danica's opinion, the attendant crowds consisted of people who prized drinking free wine above any artistic endeavor on display. The circumstances fell in their favor where friends of theirs offered access to said free wine. They cheerfully accepted the invitations and made appearances. She also suspected that, deep down, the creators of these masterpieces knew this truth as well. And yet everyone moved along, pretending. All part of the hype system.

The thing Danica came to learn from those parties was that even though most attendees were free-wine-enjoying-non-fans, the few who were fans were *super* fans. Those people didn't just get into the parties for snacks, drinks and chit-chat; they went out of their way to be there for the artist. They found ways into those parties to experience that particular artist's vision, picking the fruit from as close to the vine as possible. They built days and even weeks around these events, dropping everything to attend and they assumed everyone else at the party felt the exact same way. They'd tell others as much. And a few times, years earlier, Danica had been part of those conversations.

There, standing by the fence, with the smell of cigarette smoke in her nose, listening to Bobby talk through a fat lip,

Danica got the distinct sensation that he might be one of those Super Fans. His bold and brash assumption of their mutual fanship, the passion in Bobby's voice when he spoke about Sofi's work, referencing the use of the car in past videos, or the talk of Sofi herself... it all tracked with fanaticism.

And in her experience, when confronted with a Super Fan in one of these assumptive moments, the best response — the only response — was the one that Danica said next:

"Totally."

Bobby gave a solemn nod. He bought it. Danica got her ticket for tackling Marty, but she got her street cred from Bobby for being a fan. She decided to use it.

"So... what did happen? Why'd you guys fight?" said Danica.

"Not a fight. He just attacked me."

"Why?"

"I don't know!" Bobby waved his arms, reaching for anything stable. "We were just getting food and chit-chatting, then he jumps me outta nowhere. Been riding my hide the whole time we've been here. I've known the guy before and we've never been what you might call close, but this whole trip? On my behind."

"Mr. Utz and I were just discussing it before you arrived," said Lorena. "We have decided he is... what was the word, Mr. Utz?"

"A tool box. Look, no offense to you guys. I know he's your friend and all...."

"He only invited us into the house, my dear. He is but a client, little else."

"I kinda figured that, too. He only ever wants the money. It's why he's with Sofi in the first place."

Lorena shrugged. "Don't you? I mean, won't you take the money yourself if you find the girl?"

"I volunteered. When I heard Sofi'd disappeared, I volunteered to help. Only found out about the money after the fact."

The smoke trickled from Lorena's hand and mingled with the cloud above Bobby's shoulders. "You may be the only one here for truly noble reasons."

"Not you?" said Bobby.

"Perish the thought," said Lorena. She laughed, inviting Bobby into the joke. Danica chimed in for a while before Lorena started coughing. "I am half kidding of course. We were commissioned, so we would take our cut. But only if we earned it."

"I get it," said Bobby. "Appreciate the honesty. More than we've seen from this crew. Even James. He just wants to get paid, but I ask you: did he jump in to save me when Prince Perfecto attacked me? Nope. Just stood there. Some stuff you gotta do 'cause it's right. And if you're not in it for the right reasons, it shows. Boy, it shows."

Danica ignored the nicotine temptation and wondered if Bobby knew about James stealing the lame notebook. Instead, she bounced back to another thought. "I'm sorry. You said you volunteered?"

"Mm-hmm."

"To who? I mean, did you know when Sofi disappeared?"

"Welp, Tori canceled a shoot couple days back. And Tori never cancels shoots. I pressed her on it. I could tell something just wasn't right. Anyone could tell, that is, if they actually cared about people."

He took another drag. His tone and willingness to talk was telling either of Lorena's skills at customer manipulation or a deep loneliness.

He pointed his cigarette at Lorena. "Be real with me: you guys trust Marty?"

"I did," said Lorena. "Until all that ugliness."

"I'm gonna say something nobody wants to have said, but I'll say it anyway 'cause it feels like the truth." He leaned in. "I think Sofi was kidnapped."

There it was again! That word. Danica hadn't made it up, Tori wasn't paranoid, it was getting around for a reason.

She reset her deadpan expression and tried not to high five anybody. "So if it is a kidnapping, is Marty your main suspect then?"

"Honestly, no. Between you, me and the fencepost, I was leaning more towards Joy."

"Joy?"

"Why not?

Danica could not tell him why not, but tried anyway. "She's... a friend of hers. I know she's been around Sofi for only a couple months, but that's not enough to build any grudges or anything."

"It's not long enough to build a relationship either. Only seven weeks by my count. I remember distinctly when those two showed up. You ever hear about that purge of the Power-Works crew a couple months back? I was the only survivor of that. Next time I show up, I saw all new faces, including those two useless ones. So, yeah, she hasn't known Sofi long enough to be angry with her, but she also has nothing person- ally at stake to stop her from betraying her either."

Bobby's powers of persuasion and paranoia perplexed.

He continued, "Plus her mom's a big tech guru."

"Joy's mom?"

"No, the other one. White one. Kayleigh? Her mom's super-duper connected in the business. And Joy's been chat- ting up some up-and-coming social platform where it inter- faces with Facebook or something or other. That's why Joy's friends with Kayleigh to start with. Kayleigh's the money, Joy's the brains. Joy knows her stuff, man. It's how she reached Sofi. Through some big tech shin-dig. Heck, Joy probably traced Sofi around to 'accidentally' bump into her. Meet cute and all that."

The memory returned of Joy asking for Danica's email address. The energy behind capturing it so quickly — plus Kayleigh's encouragement — gave her a retroactive start.

Bobby continued his musing. "They got their fingers in something big. Maybe it's gone beyond their reach, I don't know. But that Joy girl? She's a shark."

"She is tenacious," said Lorena, adding, "and whatnot."

Bobby laughed while Danica waved away another exhaled cloud. "Sorry. But how's being a shark make Joy a suspect in a kidnapping?"

He leaned closer. "She wants Sofi to push her product onto her viewers. To influence them."

The idea rattled against the logical side of Danica's brain. "That sounds like a reason to keep Sofi safe."

"Yeah, but you're thinking like a human, not a tech head. To tech heads, people aren't people. They're just products or numbers or content. When Sofi's disappearance becomes news and spreads, it's gonna be big news. And if you had a platform where you shared news, that means clicks. And if you were close with the celebrity who disappeared, then it would mean even more clicks. It would make *you* the influencer."

Danica ruminated on this. She didn't see the explanation as air-tight, but that likely had more to do with the fact that she didn't know any of it prior to thirty seconds earlier. Ambition could cloud anyone's judgment, or focus it in disturbing directions. And Joy didn't seem like the warmest individual, judging by the ways her concern focused more on available wifi than on the wellbeing of her supposed friend.

"But now this," said Bobby waving toward the house. "I'm back to thinking Marty had something to do with it."

"Since just now?"

"I've known him for a while. He's the most contemptible man God ever made, when he wants to be."

Bobby's eyes danced, waiting for a reaction to his sentence. Danica had none, but she saw Lorena's face light up.

"What is that from? *The Thin Man?*"

"*Maltese Falcon.* Still Hammett though, so partial credit."

The two of them shared a giggle over old media, the kind Danica remembered trying (and failing) to have with her stepfather. He'd show her old movies, keeping one eye on the screen and the other toward Danica, as if expecting applause.

Bobby went on. "Marty, he ain't right. Did either of you see any more of that notebook? The diary one?"

"Only a little," said Lorena before Danica could speak. "I saw some scary bits, but only in pieces."

Danica circled back to her immediate circumstance. "If you think Marty's dirty, do you think he's the stalker people have talked about?"

"Sofi's stalker?"

"Yeah. I've heard chatter about a stalker. Plus I found this blog."

"What blog?"

"If I could get online, I'd show you. But something about it reminds me of what Sofi's been writing about."

Bobby looked toward the smog over the city. "Well... I kinda doubt Marty's inclined that way. To writing, I mean."

"But if he's in on it..."

Behind them, the front door of the house opened. Huelo stepped outside with Marty at his side. The two of them walked to Marty's car. They said something before Marty got in. He started it up, pulled out of his spot and rolled down the driveway. The gate opened and Marty drove away.

"Shoulda' got arrested," said Bobby.

A loud crackle broke the air and Tori's voice came from

some unseen speaker: "Attention everyone. Please return to the house and remain indoors until further notice."

Bobby stumped out his cigarette with his toe. "Look, I know Marty's your guy. I just think you should be careful. You know, if he's around again."

He moved to leave, but Danica stopped him. She thought back to that vision of Sofi signing autographs. A happy time, not a rage-filled punch-fest. "Wait. Marty hired us and all, but if you know he's dangerous...."

"I didn't say all that."

"Sofi's his mealticket. Why would he want to do that?"

"I don't know."

"Then why are you accusing him of kidnapping her?"

Bobby shrugged. "Why not?"

"'Why not?' Why would the kidnapper hire people to solve the kidnapping?"

"I dunno," said Bobby. "Creeps do all kinds of weird stuff."

The tension jackhammered into Danica's shoulders. She tried rolling her head a bit, but it did nothing for her. It also didn't help that Huelo was walking straight for them.

"I think I need to get some ice for my head," said Bobby. He hobbled toward the house.

Danica almost reached out for Lorena's hand as they awaited their execution. Out of the corner of her eye, she saw Lorena stub out the cigarette with her toe.

"That was more than ten minutes," said Huelo, reaching the fence area.

"Sorry," said Danica.

"Ms. Tori would like you to return to the house now."

Lorena and Danica gave a small nod and followed the giant man back to the house. As she reached the door, she allowed herself one final moment of waiting for Lorena.

The woman unclenched her jaw long enough to spit on the rocks and curse the taste of nicotine.

CHAPTER TWENTY-FIVE

AFTERNOON. THE LIVING AREA AGAIN.

Huelo's gargantuan hand pressed against the middle of the door, slamming it shut. What little existed of Danica's hair blew back in the breeze. Huelo locked the door, then stared toward the living area, telegraphing their path.

The mess of the food area had been partially cleaned, with only the two empty tables remaining. Alex and Bobby sat at the bar while Tori stood. There was no sign of Joy or Kayleigh, or James Van Owen.

Danica apologized for being late, but Tori shook it off.

"I have already informed the others that Marty has been excused from the house."

"We saw this," said Lorena.

"I cannot tolerate such behavior in my home. Certainly not now. However, despite his exclusion, your services are still welcome here."

"I... don't know what to say," said Danica, and she truly did not. She wanted to leave, but had no amount of appropriate words to express this desire. As she looked around the room at the others, sussing them up, she wondered how much Tori suspected them. Or Marty. She must have trusted him to let him leave. Instead, she looked back at the door, at Huelo and his keys.

"Are you locking us in?"

Huelo said nothing as he delivered the keys to Tori.

"I have decided," said the host, "that we cannot waste any more time. I am speeding up the timeline. Instead of two days left, you have until tomorrow morning. Then I feel I must contact the police."

"But the door..."

"For everyone's safety and in the interest of fair play, I have locked the door. You have come so far, I do not want someone to miss out on such an opportunity. Some people have found this to be disagreeable."

The smirk on Alex's face as she sipped her drink told Danica that by 'some people,' this meant Joy and Kayleigh. The premise of the game — the controlled investigation game — had empowered Tori to keep all her players in line, but some of them were not pleased with the new boundaries. Somewhere upstairs, a fit was being had.

"The interior rooms have been unlocked and you have free rein to search as you like. Please hurry." At this, Tori turned and left, disappearing down the ground-floor hallway, as if there was nothing more to explain.

Lorena clapped her hands together. "Well, shall we?"

Danica yanked her voice down to a whisper. "This is jacked up. We have to call the cops."

"And lose the money?"

"As opposed to our lives?" The group at the bar shuffled away, but Danica kept her voice low. "Even Tori believes one of these people is connected with the kidnappers. We could be in real danger."

"We have come so far already while staying on Tori's good side. Now with Marty's... situation, my inside scoop for a web-based business is in jeopardy. My additional windfall opportunity may have dried up. This is our only chance so, no, we shall not be calling the police."

Danica looked out the window, at the cars, ready to floor it down the mountain, any way she could find. She quickly remembered she hadn't driven herself so she checked her phone. Still no service, no way to contact Gabby.

Not in this room anyway.

"Joy and Kayleigh are upstairs," said Lorena, eyeing the steps ahead. "I am going to see what I can pry out of them, if anything."

"Just because Bobby said so?"

"And because it seems like a good step. I'm sorry I didn't acquire this info using your sources."

Danica felt the edge to her words. "What does that mean?"

"You and that other man, James Van Buren or something. You've been sharing secrets. Were you waiting until a better opportunity to tell me what you've learned?"

"James didn't have much—"

"But it was something. And you kept it from me. For yourself. I got information from Bobby and let you share."

"After I found you!"

"But I kept it up! I even smoked that awful cigarette to keep him chatting. He gave us a lead and now you don't want to use it. I'm going to talk to them and see if I can get more out of them than you did from your previous encounter."

"Hey. I... I learned stuff. That they'd only been friends with Sofi for a little while." And that Kayleigh's dog had died, but Danica didn't add that part.

"Ah, yes, that valuable nugget of information. I'd almost

forgotten, what with the excitement around the notebook of doodles."

"You dragged us into the deep end here, Lorena. This was just supposed to be about finding a missing person, not a *kidnapped* person. Now there are fights and our sponsor is a possible suspect? This is too much."

"For you, perhaps. But I for one am not going to squander the opportunity we've been given." With that, she hiked up her silks and hoofed it to the stairs. At the top, Lorena turned back. "Are you coming?"

With folded arms, Danica relayed a silent response to this invitation with a sulk. It was the move she'd made as a kid and to make her mom's blood boil. It provided the desired effect as the staircase showcase whirled away to leave her alone at last.

Danica took three steps toward the hallway before noticing that the bar was, for the first time in what felt like the entire visit, empty. She'd been silently judging everyone's alcohol consumption; with the end of her stay so near, she decided to get her own money's worth. Leaning against the side, Danica helped herself to the most expensive looking bottle she could reach. A silver thing with slick brown liquid. Just what she needed.

'Locked in the house,' she told her glass. The liquid fought its way down her throat and she pretended it felt good.

The general hum of the house had settled around her. Somewhere, feet clomped around in one or more of the rooms they'd investigated. The ones she'd wanted to go back to, now available to her, and she didn't want to anymore. Screw them.

Somewhere above her, voices chattered and even giggled. Lorena had made a connection with Joy and Kayleigh, making wonderful headway with her new targets. Good. Screw them, too.

She threw down another sip and tried not to throw it back up. Something had to drown all this out, along with the thoughts.

Thoughts of Joy's rising internet empire and Marty's anger management skills rested in Danica's brain as she stared at the glass. Kayleigh's money. Joy's ambition. Alex and Bobby's distaste for the young women. Tori's desperate control. She wanted to write it all down. She wanted to forget it.

Her glass stared back at her. She spun it in her fingers, coaxing the liquid as close to the rim as possible without spilling, like she'd seen gangsters do in movies. Maybe all those times, those characters were also trying to suppress their own annoying tendencies to seek out answers when nobody had asked.

Danica poured out the rest of her liquid courage and jogged to the downstairs hallway, ready to bravely quit.

The lights in the hallway were on, but the dark walls absorbed their output. She walked carefully, passing the game room and music room, confirming both to be wide open and inviting. That pump organ hulked in the center, little curlicues lining its legs. She left it. Someone was moving around the game room. Good for them. Let them search for answers when there weren't any. Let them nose around in things they should have left to experts.

To the left of the master bedroom another door sat slightly ajar. She found a room similar to hers and Lorena's upstairs, only with even less window light. And with the door open, the sounds from the hallway and upstairs and in her own mind dipped out, replaced by a new sound.

One of crying.

Alex sat on the foot of the bed, but the tears were not coming from her.

They were coming from Tori.

For a moment, Danica stared at the unbelievable sight. Tori had been a glacier, a kind of emotionless organization machine. Seeing a glacier cry would stop anybody in their tracks.

Even Alex appeared softened; she didn't throw anything at Danica, too occupied rubbing Tori's shoulders.

"Is there anything I can do?" said Danica, unsure of what that could possibly be.

Tori shook her head and let Alex continue to rub her back. "It's all messed up. Everything is messed up."

A notebook rested open in Tori's lap. The scary one. The torn-corner page stared at her, begging for answers nobody had.

Finally, Alex sent a scolding look. "I got this. She wants to be alone."

"It's OK," said Tori.

Danica sat next to her and Tori laid her hand on hers, as though she had something important to tell her between the tears.

"We'll find her," said Danica, surprised at her inclusion of herself in that equation.

"I'm glad you're staying. I trust you."

A mixture of relief and reluctance came over Danica. On one hand, she enjoyed being included in things, even ones marked with danger. On the other hand, she was on her way to quit already and Marty's eviction had provided a nice excuse to get out of this place. To ditch Lorena, call the police and get some actual problem-solving processes going here.

Tori choked back a sob, then literally choked. It brought Alex to her feet.

"I need something to drink," said Tori. "I haven't had my vitamins either and you know where..."

"Alright." Alex looked at Danica when she said, "But I'll be right back," then the goth girl jogged out of the room in pale bare feet.

Alone at last with the host, Danica gagged on all the questions she wanted to pose. As more tears arrived, Tori looked up from her hands and into Danica's eyes. She had her sister's eyes. Maybe it was the low lights, but she resembled her lost sister more and more. Seeing the video of Sofi in distress gave Danica a glimpse to how the Stornelli family handled stress; they cried. If the burden of the last several days hadn't slouched Tori's shoulders, she would have resembled her sister even more.

Danica processed all this while staring back at Tori's eyes. She had only met this woman, but she was still a woman in need of help. Thus it was Danica's duty to help her face the truth.

The notebook slid off Tori's lap and onto the floor. It opened to a page of scrawled vitriol. Danica glanced at it for a moment before reaching out to Tori's shoulder.

"You need to allow for a bigger investigation, Tori."

"She is all I have." Tori clenched her fist, clinking the gold bracelet against her jacket button. "I'm all she has. Her image, we have fine tuned it. If this were to get out—"

"Not to be, you know, flippant here, but people — celebrities — get taken. Sometimes, right? Wouldn't her fans, like, be on her side?"

"You don't understand fans. Internet fans especially. They want the same thing, all the time, every time. Until they don't. Then they turn. Sofi is an internet celebrity. She's not seen as a person to them. First will come the jokes, then they will dig. And dig and dig."

Danica heard the words, but couldn't grab the meaning. Letting the possible reactions of anonymous fans drive decisions around a kidnapping investigation struck her as an ineffective strategy.

"I'm not trying to pry, but are you, like, afraid of bringing in the police because they might find something else? About her? Or you?"

Another set Stornelli family tears emerged.

"Our father," she said. "He is deceased, but he was not a nice person. We traveled much of our childhood for his work."

Danica paused and pressed. "Was that work, um, nasty work?"

Tori nodded. "You are a good detective. The man was an entrepreneur."

"Okay."

"Have you ever heard of the security firm named Blackwater?"

Danica had. Carla complained about them often, referencing some newspaper article she'd dug up online. It had been a kind of pet project: Carla would read aloud the latest scandals surrounding the mercenaries for hire purchased by the US government to "clean up" places like Iraq and Afghanistan and Danica pretended to understand. Her big takeaway from those one-sided conversations was that Blackwater types were, scientifically speaking, bad dudes.

If her father's legacy with them was enough to scare a hardened businesswoman like Tori, he must have been a real peach.

"We all have secrets," said Tori. "But my family?"

The tears returned, crumbling the woman deeper into the carpet.

"You want to quit, don't you?" Her words came flat. "Everyone wants to quit and leave me here. Alone, without my sister."

Danica paused again to recognize her own impulses. The

reason she hadn't just shouted 'I quit' and left this woman to her weeping. She couldn't leave.

She was a do-gooder. She had to accept it. She had to help.

"You know who I am? I mean, for real?"

Tori nodded. "I looked you up."

"Before this all started?"

Again, Tori nodded.

"And everyone here, everyone you invited? You suspected they are somehow involved with Sofi's disappearance?"

It came slower, but Tori nodded once more.

"Okay then. We don't have to go wide with everything yet. But we gotta go another way with this investigation."

"We have. I've loosened up." On Danica's look, she added. "I have! A little. I had a plan. It's not like the kidnappers wrote it all out and…"

Tori heard her words and stopped. She stared at Danica, then to the notebook on the carpet.

Danica grabbed it and flipped the pages, looking for the section they'd stared at before Marty punched Bobby. She found the passage with "…CALLED IT A GIFT" scratched onto it.

"This gift could have come from the stalker, from the kidnapper, right? Do you have any idea what this gift she's talking about might be?"

"We get so many things. I don't even know how they reach us."

"All the more reason to look. If someone went to the trouble to find your address, then they might go to the trouble to do other stuff, too."

"It'd probably be something small," said Tori. "It cannot be too big, or Sofi could not have hidden it."

Her face transformed to a far away look. Tori pushed away from the bed and ran to the closet. It was smaller than her sister's, but held the similar set of order. Tori shoved aside a few jackets and rummaged on the floor.

Danica leaned over to see. The floor of the closet was covered with cardboard boxes. Little ones in big ones, piled on top of various sizes.

"We were keeping these for a shoot. A stunt maybe, or one where Sofi would build a coffee shop with boxes or something. Here it is!"

She emerged with a box and the widest smile Danica had seen her give. The box was slightly smaller than a shoebox, with only the sending address on top.

"This came few weeks back. At least a month, I think. But I remembered it for this." She pointed at the address, at the name: Ms. Sofia Stornelli.

"Sofi's real name," said Danica. "Not her stage name."

Tori nodded. "We get mail to 'Stornelli' all the time, of course, but more like advertisements and credit card bills, those kinds of thing. Not full packages. Not from fans."

"OK. So someone knew her real name and her real address."

Danica took the box from Tori and opened it. Inside was a mess of newspaper confetti with a blue jewelry box resting in the center. She wiggled at the blue box and it barely moved. Removing some paper revealed a wooden stake glued to the bottom of the cardboard.

"They centered it."

"I think to keep the jewelry from jostling around," said Tori. "I left it for Sofi to open — it had her name on it after all. But when I came home, Sofi was scared. Upset. Talked about firing the whole crew. Wanted to quit making videos. I asked her why and she wouldn't tell me. Later I found the box in the recycling."

Danica opened the jewelry box, finding it bereft of

jewelry, with two small holes near the top back and an indented circle looping around the fuzzy floor.

"It's for a necklace."

Danica studied the box, in hopes that she could spontaneously develop a special fingerprint-seeing skill along with access to the FBI database. While she waited for that to manifest, she looked back into Tori's bedroom.

"Just a sec," she said. She ran back for the scary diary and brought it to the closet, reading it carefully She read aloud: "'LOCK IT AWAY.' No subject."

Tori's mood of abject realism and impatience returned for a moment. "Are you diagraming the sentence? Like from junior high English class?"

"Grammar school, actually. All these other sentences start with 'He' except for this one. Who is she talking to?"

"Herself, I assumed."

Danica continued her staring contest with the page, neither blinking for a good long while. It wasn't past tense, like Sofi *had* locked it away. The writing did appear to be talking to the reader...

"Locket."

"Sorry?" said Tori.

The words reached into Danica's memory, taking her upstairs, to her bed, to the contents under her pillow.

"I found a locket. Silver, on a long chain."

The color left Tori's cheeks. "Where?"

Something held her back from throwing James completely under the bus, so she said, "While I was investigating. It's upstairs. And this?" She tapped the page. "I think she meant 'Locket.' It's the only sentence without 'He' at the top, so we can assume the subject is the reader. And if Sofi's so into codes and puzzles and all that, maybe it's a word play. Reading it aloud it sounds like 'Locket.'"

"But 'Locket Away?' How does that work?"

"'Away from my neck.' There's no period either. Like it's all one sentence. I think she got a locket from this person. But… if the thing I found wasn't hidden, are we supposed to be looking for another one?"

Tori mulled, for a good minute. "Alex is coming. We should—"

"Keep this a secret." That's what Danica assumed she was about to say as Alex returned, holding a glass of water and some pills. Tori sniffled and grinned at her, but did not share the information she and Danica had just discovered.

"The bathroom's tapped for aspirin, so I had to dig into my own stash."

Tori thanked Alex. "Would you mind if I have some privacy? Ms. Luman was just leaving and I would like to lie down."

Alex almost looked insulted, but she acquiesced and pulled back to the door with Danica. As they entered the hallway, Tori called for Danica one last time, then handed her the empty box. With a bit of a stare, she said, "Would you mind taking that away?"

Danica, in fact, did not mind. She accepted the empty jewelry box and avoided Alex's admonishment, hustling back into the hallway. She waited all of five steps before turning into a full sprint, up the stairs.

CHAPTER TWENTY-SIX

5:01PM. LORENA AND DANICA'S BEDROOM.

Danica entered without knocking, not that it mattered. It was supposed to be her room, too. Besides, Lorena was somehow mercifully missing.

She stabbed her hand under her pillow, retrieving the lame notebook.

The pendant was still inside.

She opened the locket again, hoping someone had slipped an answer key inside. Finding none, she slid the chain around the circle of the box, with the pendant resting in the lower indentation.

While possessing no skills or experience in the world of fine jewelry, sizing up the thing did not take much of either. It wasn't a right fit. The pendant was far too small — a dime size object in the space for a silver dollar — and the chain strung around loose where it should have been snug. She stared at it, trying to force it to fit, force it to make sense, but failed.

The locket couldn't be *nothing*. It had Sofi's picture in it after all, yet Danica had to admit to herself that the "Stuff" pendant had likely not arrived in this box.

Her proximity to so many possible solutions had once again given her a rush with none of the nutrients. This didn't connect to the stalker, to the blog, to the person leaving comments. She'd been so certain a moment ago, only to now feel as steady as a deer on an icy lake.

The adrenaline exited her body as she flopped onto the bed. What would she tell Tori? That she'd disappointed her *again?* She had been so certain of having something, so focused that she hadn't closed the door behind her. Joy and Kayleigh's voices grew louder, but Danica didn't care if anyone saw her or her lame findings. They'd discovered the key to nowhere. An ornate key that resembled a go-nowhere key hole on a foosball table's belly. They'd had just as much success with the weird codes and hidden 'CAGED' messages. All they'd found was Danica's online presence. Apparently they could find out about anyone, except for Sofi Starr. Or Sofia Stornelli.

Ms. Sofia Stornelli.

"Hey, Joy!"

Calling for Joy surprised everyone, including the caller herself. The younger women stopped at the top of the stairway, eyebrows cocked and loaded, ready to cut down whatever Danica had to say.

Danica greeted them with an open hand and held out her own phone.

"Huge favor: I need you to find someone." When they looked confused, Danica added, "Online."

More confusion ensued, or at least the performance of confusion. Joy scoffed and Kayleigh gave a small chortle as though she'd heard the funniest, shortest thing.

Danica pushed past it. "There's a video. One of Sofi's. It's called 'Sofi the Judge.' And there's a comment in there that calls her 'Ms. Stornelli.' It says something like, 'NOT OUR SOFI' for a title. I wanna know who wrote it."

Joy's scoff continued. "Why do you think I can—"

"Because you did it to me. You did it in that wifi hotspot down there." She tipped her head down the hall, toward the guest bathroom.

Instead of scoffing again, Joy switched to a tongue cluck. "I can't just get the name of the dude if YouTube doesn't have it available and whatnot. I'm not all *CSI* and stuff."

"But you can get *something*, right?"

"Well... yeah."

"Great. I'll take something. I have to talk to Alex, but I wanna know if that commenter is related to this blog." Danica held out her phone, displaying the Kutman page.

"Please," she said. "It's to find Sofi. For real."

Joy scowled, scrunched her lip, but then shrugged. She looked at Danica's phone, at the open website and the challenge presented. "You shouldn't just hand your open phone to people like that? They can steal your data and whatnot."

"I'm trusting you."

Whatever schemes may have been cooking in Joy's brain diluted in a blink. She took the phone, then headed toward the guest bathroom.

Kayleigh started to follow as always, but Danica held her back.

"You play music, right?"

Alex leaned outside of Tori's bedroom, a guard dog in bare feet and black pleather. As Danica and Kayleigh rushed toward the sullen woman, their momentum disarmed any swear words Alex might have flung their way.

"Why were you so interested in the foosball table?" said Danica.

She raised a dark eyebrow. "Are you deranged?"

"Yesterday, when we got the message out of the foosball table. You were just staring at the thing. Why?"

Alex stammered.

"Did you make it?"

Alex's alabaster cheeks went Pepto color. "N... no."

"Pfft. Lie." Kayleigh was an affective hype man.

"I'm not. It was just... it was weird. I did make a table, once. And it kinda looked like that one, but that wasn't it."

Danica nodded. "But you *did* make one. Once."

"Yeah."

She led the group to the music room door and pointed to the pump organ. "The table you did make — was it like that?"

Alex frowned. "I never made an organ."

"No, I didn't say you did. But did you make anything *like* that? Look: you and Marty met 'cause you made props, right?"

"Yeah?"

"And you made special props. With compartments and stuff."

"...Yeah."

"So this table you made. Did it have compartments? Like for a magic show?"

Shock raced across Alex's face. "Yeah. It was for a show. Some outdoor 'Phantom of the Opera' theater-in-the-park failure."

"Oh, I love 'Phantom,'" said Kayleigh.

"Was the table about that size?" said Danica, pointing at the pump organ.

Alex's memory strained as Danica invited herself into the music room. They circled the pump organ, sliding fingers around the curly decorations painted around the edges.

"Yeah," said Alex. "About this size, maybe. But — and I

keep saying this like you're going to get less dumb and understand — I didn't make an organ."

Danica stopped near the back and motioned for Alex and Kayleigh to join her and see what she'd found.

A key-shaped hole, near the center bottom of the rear panel.

A new level of paleness hit Alex's complexion

"You recognized that wall plate thing, didn't you?" said Danica. "From under the foosball table. It was like an antique and didn't fit in. But it would fit here, right?"

"I... I don't understand. I didn't make this thing."

"But you made something *similar?* I'm not asking if it was this exactly, but was it close? Close is gonna count for something."

After a torturous breath, Alex at last said, "Yes. I think so. It was an antique desk. About a year ago, maybe less."

Danica felt around the corners of the bottom, beneath the key hole. She pulled at the panelling. It came off as loose as a present wrapped by an eight-year-old. Beneath the ornate panelling was a plain dark brown wood, a color which drew a gasp from Alex.

"What the hell? Why is... what the hell?"

"I think your prop was repurposed. Like they took the idea from the thing you originally built, but then remade it here."

"But why?"

Danica stood, hands on hips, then looked at Kayleigh. "You still have that key?"

She said she did, then pulled it from her tiny, mildly-scratched purse. While Alex's mouth made fish noises, Kayleigh asked, "Why?"

"It's how you turn it on," said Danica. She looked at Alex. "Right? When you saw that key hole without a hole, you made the connection. You recognized something in it, but couldn't quite explain it. Your work turned on with a key. Your work looked similar to the foosball table, but wasn't the foosball table."

Danica took the key and returned to the back area. She inserted the key and turned it. The organ fired up as it had been waiting for an excuse, sending its excess electricity shivering through the rest of the room.

After a quick glance for any surprises, Danica hopped to the side to face the keys. "What's it supposed to do?"

"How should I...." Alex pulled more hair. "I mean, my design had a door open where you typed in a code. But this thing? Who knows what they did to this thing."

Danica stared at the instrument, focusing on the keys. The whites had yellowed with age, while the black ones shimmered even with the low ceiling lights. She pulled down a page of sheet music and retrieved her pen. As she wrote, she said, "Kayleigh, which one is 'C?'"

Kayleigh pointed at a whitish key near the center. "Why?"

Danica held up her writing: C-A-G-E-D-C-A-G-E

"The message from the foosball table," she said. "It's notes."

"Let me do it," said Kayleigh. The pseudo surfer positioned herself before the keys, flicking her wrist into a pianist's claw, the thumb resting near the center white key. She played the nine notes in quick sequence, blurting out a low hum from the instrument. Once she finished, the three women stepped back to wait.

When nothing happened and they finished saying so, Danica looked from the instrument back to Alex, who was as confused as anyone.

"Do-over," said Kayleigh. She tried in the same middle position, then with higher notes. Then again with lower notes. All performances yielded no results.

Alex demanded a closer scrutiny of the paper and Danica

handed it over in a stupor. Had Lorena been right? Had she been getting too cocky, too up her own butt about being right that Danica could have missed something?

"They weren't in blue ink before," said Alex.

Kayleigh laughed. "There's no such thing as blue notes, stupid. It doesn't matter what ink they're in."

"But the original note? Most were in black ink..."

"And one was blue," said Danica."

"The second 'A.'"

Kayleigh followed the exchange as her mind drifted somewhere else. She repositioned her hands in front of the middle keys and set her fingers to work. Kayleigh started the same tune, but when she got to the seventh note — the "blue A" — her long finger reached up to the black key. At this note, the tune fell apart, drawing out a depressing howl from the brown box.

At the final notes, Kayleigh held it for a beat of emphasis, then let the organ go dead quiet again. The life which had been coursing through the antique instrument suddenly vacated. For two excruciating seconds, it sat as if refusing to awaken.

At two-point-one seconds, the organ's lower casing released a low rumble, similar to a jawbreaker rolling down a dispenser's chute. Everyone's eyes followed the sound to the floor, near the pedals.

Right on cue, a panel above the right pedal flapped open and there, on the floor, appeared an off-white ball.

"Is that," said Alex, "the lost foosball?"

Danica picked it up, instantly hearing the rattle from inside. It was more spherical than the egg found in the game room, but this ball was just as hollow. A light squeeze cracked it open.

A silver chain spilled out and onto the floor, drawing with it a heavy pendant. It slapped Danica's toe.

Kayleigh snatched it but shared a look with the others. The pendant was another locket. To Danica's memory, its shape seemed more appropriate for the empty box from Tori's closet. Kayleigh wiggled the lid.

"Empty. And the piece of crap won't close."

Danica scanned the object. It was similar to the pendant in her pocket — similar in its unremarkable design. Its shoddy design had allowed a larger-than-needed hole below the clasp. Like the other, it too had an inscription within its lid.

"'The Dreams,'" Alex read aloud. "That supposed to mean something?"

Danica dug into her pocket, extracting the smaller locket. She placed it in the shell of the larger one — the Dreams — and positioned it so the chain would run out the hole. Then she pulled the larger one's lid down.

It latched, holding the smaller inside.

"It holds it," said Kayleigh.

Danica re-opened the larger Dreams locket, then opened the smaller Stuff locket, showing Alex and Kayleigh the picture of Sofi inside.

"No. It traps it." She gripped the locket tight. "I found this smaller locket upstairs. It was in a notebook of Sofi's — the one I found. Someone stole it, but I found it in someone's luggage. And when I took the notebook back, I must have pulled the locket out with it."

The wheels inside Alex's brain began to roll. "Whose room?"

"James and Bobby's."

"So the locket was in those morons' stuff. They must have had it before stealing the notebook. Whose bag was it?"

"I thought it was..." The image of the suitcase upstairs flashed before her, of James' confusion around her accusation of his thievery.

Joy broke up the moment by bursting through the door, looking both triumphant and put out. She handed Danica her phone and said, "Found it. Name is 'Gasper Kutman.' And before you ask, no, that's not a real name and whatnot. It's another dead end. I checked. Got one of those 'Did you mean' things from Google."

"Like what?"

"I think it was 'Casper Gutman.' Some old dude from some old movie."

Danica nodded at her. "Was the movie *The Maltese Falcon?*"

Joy paused, at last reading the room around her. "How'd you know that?"

Ignoring the question, Danica looked back at the locket set. The Stuff in the Dream. When combined, they approximated into a version of 'the stuff that dreams were made of.'

"It was Bobby's luggage," she said. "He stole the notebook. He had the locket."

Kayleigh's wheels spun slower than others. "Why would someone steal a stupid notebook though?"

Alex and Danica shared a wide-eye, no-blinking glance.

Danica spoke first. "To collect stuff. Like a fan. A super fan."

Tears welled in Alex's eyes. "Let's find Tori."

CHAPTER TWENTY-SEVEN

5:22PM.

The four women galloped through the hallway, with Alex pointing the way to Tori's bedroom. Just as Joy and Kayleigh got off an all-too-loud befuddled exchange ("Who's Bobby again?" "Duh, that guy with James?" "His name is Bobby Withjames?"), Danica made a demand for quiet.

"We cannot let him know we're onto him."

Alex stepped into the bedroom and returned just as quickly. "Not there."

After a deep breath, Danica headed toward the living area, with the others close behind. Every corner felt larger than before. Darker and more capable of hiding anything. The shadows swarmed around them, joining forces with the corners to conceal deeper things. She became aware of the house's quiet, too.

Danica cleared the kitchen door without drama and moved on toward the general living area.

Bobby sat in the sunken couch. The white board had been

moved to that side of the room. He stared at the notes written there, transfixed.

Joy gasped and Danica spun back in time to see James Van Owen emerge from behind the refrigerator, a La Croix in his hand.

"Whoa, easy. Calm down, ladies." Never a helpful turn of phrase, but Danica let it go.

She whispered, "That wasn't your luggage upstairs, was it? The one where I found the notebook."

"No?"

"So it was Bobby's?"

"Yeah?" James spoke at full volume, inviting a slew of shushes from the group before him. After finally catching on, he whispered, "What's up?"

The four women ceased breathing as they watched the hallway ahead of them.

"He's in there," said Danica. "The living, big-giant room place. Stay with him. Keep him in there and don't let him get away."

James' eyes looked to Danica's hand, to the locket. "What's that—"

"Just keep Bobby in the front room and keep him calm while we find Tori. And for once please be cool?"

James nodded. He turned back to the living area, jammed one hand into the pocket of his pressed jeans and sipped his fizzy water. He almost looked believable.

"Now what?" said Kayleigh.

"Tori must be upstairs somewhere. We find her and get word to the police."

Alex led the way to the stairs, button-hooking at the edge to allow as little of herself to be seen from the living room. The rest followed her on their tip toes.

They fanned out to quickly survey the guest rooms. They just as quickly found no Tori.

Alex tapped her bare toe into the carpet, thinking while looking around. She checked the room next to the guest bathroom again. Danica snuck in with her to a small office with barely enough supplies for an intern.

Lorena emerged from her room. Whatever powers of deduction she possessed kicked in as she surmised the grim excitement of the group before her.

When the older woman inquired about their business, Danica allowed the others to hash out the details. She didn't feel like talking to Lorena. The woman had already distracted her enough. Once the fortune teller received the full rundown, she glanced over the railing and into the front room area. Doubtless, the jealousy raging within her compelled her to check Danica's work.

"We have that James Whatshisface keeping Bobby Whoever in there now."

"But there is no one down there," said Lorena.

Danica rushed to the banister. Thanks to the aggressively open floor plan, she saw the sunken couch area. A few steps downward and she viewed the back wall. And a few more steps down to the ground level, she confirmed that James and Bobby had vacated the front room.

The others fell in behind her.

"Where'd they go? They were just, like, so here." Kayleigh grabbed the railing.

Grim theories floated around to explain their disappearance. But one came to Danica's mind as she turned from the empty living space toward Lorena.

"He knows," she said.

No one disagreed. They flooded into the living area, spreading like billiard balls as if to find someone playing hide and seek behind the sparse interior decoration.

"Let me get this straight," said Joy. "Y'all think Bobby What's-His-Name is dangerous and a kidnapper stalker guy?

And that he's, like, on the loose and we're trapped in here and whatnot?"

"I don't know about 'trapped,'" said Alex.

Joy, in an instance of practical argumentation, walked to the front door and wiggled the handle. "Locked. Trapped."

Snotty tone aside, Joy's summation had still done its job, the subtext drawing from the river of bafflement raging the collection by the door. What had happened to Bobby? What had happened to *James*? Was he attacked, drugged, wooed away with a shiny toy? If he had been attacked, was he dragged away? Where had Huelo gone? The guy who had been watchdogging everyone for two days chose *now* to vanish? Danica looked around more to stumble upon what to do next, her focus so erratic she could not settle on one course of action.

Her mind snapped into complete focus when the lights suddenly turned off.

Kayleigh screamed. Joy did, too, but it was muffled slightly by her friend's shirt, their embrace a result of terrified self-preservation. The entire group gravitated toward the front door, some of them trying the doorknob again to see if Joy had been pretending. She had not.

Danica's left hand was seized by Kayleigh. Her free hand groped against the wall until it tripped on the floor lamp. Useless as a light source, Danica pulled it free from the wall and held it before her, the closest thing to a weapon she could imagine the room providing.

"Whaddowedo, whaddowedo, whaddowedowhaddowe- do..." Joy's muffled voice ran on and on as the afternoon light deserted the house.

"Stay together," said Lorena. Her parental tone reminded Danica of Carla.

A strange cool air shivered through the gloom. Danica stared at the hallway and stairway ahead, ready for anything to emerge, hoping to see Huelo, hoping against seeing anyone else.

"Alex," she whispered. "Is there another way out of here?"

"How... How would I..."

Danica spat a look her way, as if begging Alex to keep up the pretense that she *didn't* know her way around the place, and that she *didn't* have a friendly relationship with Tori."

Alex got the message. "It's on a locking system. Same as this."

"Keys then? Somewhere else?"

"Why would she know that?" said Joy, more to Kayleigh, though neither she nor anyone else answered.

Alex said, "Tori's room. Bedside table."

Danica's sigh set the mood for her next question. "Back down the hall again, right? Can you do that with me?"

A tremble invaded Alex's voice. "But she'll be back soon. She has to—"

"*We* have to get them," said Danica. "Us. Understand?"

Alex gave a final shadowy nod.

Danica turned toward Lorena. "All of us."

She received another nod, accompanied by the jingle of cheap earrings.

CHAPTER TWENTY-EIGHT

6:14PM.

The last drips of outdoor light flickered through the kitchen door as women shuffled by. It left them in a step or two deeper into the hallway. Danica's phone pointed screen-side out provided little substantive help.

No sound came ahead.

As they made it to the hallway proper, Danica wondered if they should have pulled together more weapons — *any* weapons. A couple more lamps maybe. Or a chair. They would be passing the music room soon and some of those things had looked heavy. Like any of it would do much good against a highly-motivated man set on not being caught.

Her right hand felt the wall, tripping on one door frame, then another. Her breath bounced off the walls. Just as her hand felt another door frame, Alex moved ahead of her.

"Here," said Alex. A door creaked open and she stepped inside. Danica looked back at Lorena.

"We'll stay here."

She remembered the bedroom from moments ago, but it might as well have become a black hole. A light switch made a noise, but the darkness remained. Danica assumed the biggest dark spot in the middle of the room belonged to the bed, but her memory couldn't account for the others.

Danica offered her phone's dim light to Alex, but she either didn't see it or didn't need it. Despite the darkness, Alex moved with confidence through the room, past the bed and toward the wall. Her silhouette danced against the curtained window. She bent down a bit.

Wood slid against wood. Danica heard the familiar jingle of clutter shuffling around. The noise echoed through the room and out the hall, announcing their location for anyone to discover.

"Should be here," said Alex. She continued her rummaging.

Then she screamed. Twice.

Danica ran to the dark bedside. Her phone's light pointed at the floor near the window. Even with the low light, the orange vinyl jacket could not be mistaken. So it was with the person in the jacket as well, lying motionless and face down.

The light found a sparkle on the carpet. Dark brown and growing from underneath the short bleach-blond hair to mat into the thin shag.

As the Earth ceased its rotation, the others joined them. Joy joined her phone's light to Danica's. She screamed, then caught herself when Lorena put her hand over her mouth.

"How... How..." was all Kayleigh could say. She stumbled back and hit the dresser.

Lorena shushed them. "Listen... Someone is coming."

Dense footsteps headed their way. Danica's chest tightened as her eyes strained at the door, waiting for something terrible to emerge.

The footsteps ran to the bedroom door and Huelo entered. "Everyone alright?"

He charged inside, carrying a large flashlight in his hand. Whatever natural sense he had for distress pointed him to Kayleigh and her emerging panic attack. It wasn't until she pointed at the floor that he noticed Tori.

"We found her like this," said Danica.

Huelo's shadowy form kicked into full soldier mode. After a moment's study of his employer's body, his knees bent and placed him into true action position, ready to strike in any direction. He flashed his light on the drawer. "Anybody find the master keys?"

"Don't you have them?"

"Tori's instructions. Only one set. Don't worry. We're gonna get you all outta here. Everyone, with me, in the hall. Let's move careful now."

Joy and Kayleigh required no further invitation, scooting into a huddle and moving out of the bedroom. Lorena joined as Huelo continued his instructions.

Alex, however, did not leave. She knelt in the evening light, staring at the absence. Danica put her hand on her, feeling a tremble at the touch.

"We're gonna take it slow," said Huelo. "I want everyone to—"

Two gunshots interrupted him.

In one motion, Huelo shoved Joy and Kayleigh across the hall, into the adjacent bathroom, then grabbed Lorena and ducked in the bathroom as well. Danica stumbled back from the doorway, but could still see Huelo in the open bathroom door. His flashlight's spill showed a silver pistol in his hand.

Another shot rang out, then another. The noise pierced her ears, yet it sounded closer than before. In the hallway.

Danica covered her ears. They screeched to the back of her skull even when the shooting paused. Joy and Kayleigh might as well have been screaming at the top of their lungs or made a vow of silence — Danica's ears were trained only to hear gunshots.

A few more shots came, followed by the briefest pause. In that pause, Huelo made his move. He spun into the hallway, fired three times, then turned back.

Even in the dark and across the hall, Danica saw Lorena's eyes staring into hers. The older woman's face stiffened with full concentration. Danica returned the look, memorizing the last face she might ever see.

She counted breaths. Only after reaching twelve did she realize all shooting had ceased.

"Hold tight." Huelo held his his weapon out as he walked toward the main living area.

Danica blinked and broke her gaze with Lorena, then stood. She snuck another glance back at her lifeless host laying behind the bed, then peeked into the hallway.

Huelo's flashlight swiped around the stairs, toward the sprawling front room. It stopped near the end, illuminating a spot near the steps. A pair of work boots stuck out of the side, toes pointing up.

"We're good," he said.

Cries floated up from behind Danica, from Alex, still near the bed. She knelt at Tori's side, pulling at her own black hair, trying to make the world disappear.

Lorena leaned into the hallway, the fear on her face needing no flashlight.

"Did he get him?" said Joy.

"Who?" said Lorena.

"Bobby. Duh."

"Yes, I believe he did." Lorena sighed and slumped to the floor, her courage calling a full retreat. She let out a labored breath before re-locking eyes with Danica.

"I hate to mention it..." said Lorena, then nodded toward

the bedroom.

Danica raised a hand. She returned to the bedside, to the whimpering woman behind it.

"Alex?" Her voice reminded her of her mom, only less convincing.

The vamp turned to face her, finding the phone's light. Mascara had raccooned her eyes and cheeks.

"I'm so sorry but... the keys? You think they might be, um, in her pocket?"

Alex sniffed. Her mouth trembled out something like, "Maybe."

"Do you want me to get them?"

A grunt was the answer.

"Madame Lorena, could you help in here for a second?"

Lorena sped across the room with as little flourish as possible. She reached out to Alex to help her stand. "It will be more comfortable in the kitchen, my dear. More windows and light and all that."

Alex moved at zombie speed, entranced. Shocked.

Danica had been around dead bodies before, a fact she reminded herself with a deep inhale. A portion of her brain made note to stop making such interactions a habit, but she shoved that jerk to the side. Save it for therapy; excuses and shoulda's were no help now.

The brutality before her gave her pause. The fresh openness of the head wound represented new territory for Danica.

After a couple self-motivating shakes of her arms to make sure they still worked, she knelt where Alex had been and checked the back pockets of Tori's pants, hoping keys were there. Hoping for a miracle.

No such miracle occurred. To check the front pockets, she'd have to turn Tori over.

'Just like CPR class,' Danica told herself. 'Turn it over, on the back. No big deal.' She pictured all the times she'd taking

CPR training — all two times. Position the arm. Bend the knees at a right angle. Pull the bent knee to roll the victim over. Easy. Just like class.

Easy.

Simple.

E.Z.

Danica positioned the limbs and pulled. The body wheezed when it lifted from the floor, letting loose an empty groan when it landed on its back. The face area hung slack in all the wrong ways. Even in the dark, Danica could tell bad things had happened.

Focused on her mission, she ceased her breathing while reaching inside the orange jacket pocket. Her left hand steadied on the floor.

Her right hand found something metal inside the jacket while the tip of her left thumb stretched out and nudged something hairy.

Visions didn't come from the dead. In Danica's (admittedly limited) experience, it seemed that once life left the body, it took whatever the hell kind of super magic juju psychic connection with it. She had tried it before and received only black nothingness.

However there, on the bedroom floor by the window, digging through jacket pockets of her mortally-wounded host, Danica received considerably more than nothingness.

She received darkness, with a pinhole of light. The sound of a heaving breath, restrained. Then extreme light.

Danica pulled her hand back and felt Tori's chest. It gave the slightest motion.

"Hey! Someone! She's still alive!"

But not for long. Someone in the real world beyond the bedroom said something, promised something else, but Danica ignored it. How much time would they have — did Tori have? She put her hand fully on the dying woman's head.

"Tell me," she said.

Back to the darkness and the pinhole light. The color of the darkness changed to a deep grey wall right next to her face. A bare leg — *her* bare leg. Then more darkness — not the darkness of "no psychic signal received." This was in-vision, from-memory dark. Something covered her eyes, or had fallen over her head. But something else moved.

She was struggling, her arms held.

The mask moved. She wiggled some more and the mask came free.

A bedroom. This one.

The room blinked away and she was suddenly back on the mountain, the same one where she had talked to Marty. Walking.

Then screaming.

Then blackness one last time. At last, true nothingness. No signal received.

Danica opened her eyes, readjusted her grip and closed them again, but saw nothing more. Tori's chest sat stone still under the vinyl. She had finally fully died.

The lights turned on around them, sending with it a strange mix of elation and despair. Huelo ran in and pushed Danica aside. She fell into a sitting position, leaning against the wall beneath the window.

"She's gone," she said.

Huelo ignored her. He picked up his employer and carried Tori out of the room, promising help.

Danica rubbed her eyes. When she opened them, she saw Lorena's hand offering to help her up.

Instead, Danica gave her Tori's key chain. She forgot she'd found it.

CHAPTER TWENTY-NINE

9:?? - 11:??PM.

Once the electricity came back online, Kayleigh went through the house and turned on every light she could find. She even managed to re-plug in Danica's weapon light. The resulting illumination was both comforting and oppressive.

The two younger women were having an informal therapy session in another room, to work out all they had just experienced and how they just couldn't handle it, but they just did, and they just couldn't believe they even had to, but they just really did do it, and that they'd *never* come this far west of the 405 again, and how they just needed to find some cool people to hang with and on and on. Their voices soundtracked the entire house, verbal white noise nobody could escape.

From the floor, Danica leaned against the fire pit, holding a cup of water she didn't drink. Lorena marched around the room, matching Danica's silence, unwilling or unable to offer any kind of comfort.

Someone knocked on the wall by the stairs. James Van

Owen waved as he approached, holding a bag of ice to the back of his head.

"Land line's back up. I called my commanding officer, so we'll have somebody here soon. How are you two doing?"

Danica's mouth opened from social obligation to offer an instinctive "fine," but the weight of the situation reached her jaw muscles in time to prevent it. Instead she said, "What happened to you?"

"Hit from behind. I had just seen you guys off, went to find Bobby when he jumped me. Must've been listening at the doorway or something. Next thing I know, I'm in a dark room, claustrophobic and hot and my hands are tied. Turns out I'm in that closet by the door right over there."

Danica didn't have the heart to make fun of this.

"Kayleigh and Joy filled me in on what I missed."

Lorena cleared her throat. "Where did they move the, um... did they keep her... did...."

"Taken care of," said James. "I blocked off a couple rooms at the end for the authorities, but outside of those, everyone's got space to move freely."

"Then I'm going outside," said Lorena. She opened the door, filling the room instantly with night air. Joy and Kayleigh came hustling from the kitchen, kicking off their shoes to give their toes some late-night grass time. Danica watched the older woman pace on the porch, still concentrating, still processing. Poor thing must've been so in shock from seeing a dead body that she forgot to ask about how they'd get paid.

James bent down to sit on the edge of the fire pit, moving like it cost him years. He nudged Danica with his knee. "Thanks for the help. Again. I'd tell you not to make this a habit, but you're getting a little too good at it to stop. Pretty soon you'll get one of those doors with your name on it like in the movies."

Danica recognized his words as playful. She wanted to josh around with him and make light of everything. Instead she could only watch Lorena walk around the porch and think about Tori's dying dreams of bound arms and darkness.

"We still have to find Sofi."

"Oh, I'm such a turd. HQ already sent people to Bobby's place. I thought word had already gotten to you—"

"Where?"

"L.A."

"But *where*?"

He fumbled with his ice bag, weighing the options of sharing sensitive information with a woman so clearly on his side. "Lake Balboa. Some apartment building on Sherman."

Danica ran a map in her mind, calculating drive times. James' face held a different kind of scrutiny. "You thinking about why he did it?"

"He was a nut bag."

"A nut bag who *hired* you."

James looked like his head needed more ice. "Yeah, but he even did that in a nut bag way. He sent a letter. I'll never forget — it said, 'Requesting your services.' Who sends letters anyway? Paid in cash before we even met."

"When?"

"Months ago. It was for another thing that went nowhere. Security stuff around Sofi. Guy was paranoid. I was supposed to tail someone. After it dried up, he still paid."

Cops really did have the best scruples.

James kept going. "Must've kept me at the top of his list, 'cause a few months later, when this came up, I was in line. Got me by text this time. Must've upgraded or something."

"So," said Danica, turning to face him square, "you think Bobby hired you to help find a person that he himself kidnapped just 'cause 'he's a nut bag?'"

"Hey, that's not my theory. It's yours, remember? The stuff

about the locket and the stealing notebooks, the stalkery blog and all that? You're the one who made the connections. I feel dumb enough getting suckered like I did, so don't pin it all on me."

Through the window, the tops of Joy and Kayleigh's heads bounced up and down like kids skipping home from school. All the while, Lorena continued her contemplation laps.

"By the way: *was* a nut bag," said James.

"Huh?"

"'Was.' Bobby *was* a nut bag. Past tense. Guy's dead now."

Was.

James left her to get more ice for his head and she went back to watching Lorena.

God would forgive her if she had a cigarette. Under the circumstances, all things considered, when it was all said and done, a backslide would be totally understandable. But digging through Bobby's things seemed tacky.

Her fuzzy hair felt like it had grown an inch since last morning, bending in odd, chunky directions against the wall. Even now, it grew between her fingers. She wanted long hair so she could pull on it.

Without a cigarette or long hair, her thoughts returned.

When would the cops actually find Sofi? What if she wasn't at Bobby's place? What if she was hurt, or starved? What if the place had booby traps? What if Bobby had a partner who worked with some strange network of creeps, abducting celebrities to inflict whatever kind of power trip they desired onto them?

What if she was dead. What if Sofi *was*, the same as Bobby *was?*

Her fingernails scratched down her scalp and dug into her ears.

She had to get out of this house.

She had to stay.

She had to see if Sofi was OK.

'Don't overthink,' she told herself. 'Cops can do their jobs. Occasionally. Don't think out the map, about how they could make it to Lake Balboa in only a few minutes, or how that might not even lead to Sofi, or how she might have been moved to some yet-to-be-known location by some yet-to-be-discovered accomplice. Or how — if they *did* find her in Bobby's place — the cops would want to question her, get her medically examined, take all the other steps of a thorough going-over before even thinking about sending word of her status to the house, let alone before actually releasing her.'

Some relaxing inner voice.

She checked her phone. How long had it been since Huelo shot Bobby in the hallway? An hour? Three weeks? Time slipped and slid. The sides of her eyes ached.

But when she closed them, all she could see was Tori, dying in her hands. Danica hadn't moved to help her; she had just sat there, sucking up the woman's last moments like some kind of memory vampire. All for herself.

Those last moments replayed, as did those last images. The not-total-nothingness dark, the light, the pinhole, the outdoors. Should she tell Sofi this when she saw her.

If she saw...

Danica shuddered and stood. Her energy returned. James had the phones hooked up, but the mission was not complete. Nothing felt settled. They had to find the missing woman.

Pushing herself to her feet, Danica moved to the bath-room near the front entrance. She left the lights off and the door open, focusing what little brain power she still had on getting to the sink. She ran water over her face. Even in the dark, the mirror did her reflection no favors. She washed again.

Outdoor lights brightened the bathroom, but only for a

flash. Danica turned off the water and listened. A loud door shut — not the front door, but another one, from deeper in the house.

Danica opened the bathroom just in time to catch Lorena's eye.

"She's here," said the older woman.

CHAPTER THIRTY

Giggles exploded, echoing off the high living room ceiling.

Danica's face dripped onto her shirt. The *Dookie* shirt had seen better days — inside out or right-side out — and was certainly not in any state to meet a celebrity. She considered running upstairs to grab her slightly-less-used pajama top.

Lorena had her back to her, moving as if entranced, toward the kitchen doorway. The palm reader paused near the steps, her long skirt drooping onto the first step.

Light from those enormous windows poured across the floor, brighter than they'd been in days. A small group of people huddled around the sunken couch.

Among the group were two uniformed police officers talking with James. They stood on the floor, above the sunken couch. Marty crouched near the center, his good looks still very much intact. Though his smile held weariness, it brightened when he noticed Danica.

James lunged to the side, demonstrating how he had been

attacked from behind. His move revealed Kayleigh and Joy sitting in the deeper seats. They were hugging someone in a patented sorority sister maneuver: the choke-hold hug. Their arms covered their hug victim, whose longish blonde hair dripped onto Joy's shoulders.

Marty gently intervened. "Don't overwhelm her, OK, guys? She's been through a lot."

The woman faced away from Danica and the stairs. Joy and Kayleigh managed to extract themselves from the hug, revealing a puffy white vest under all that hair.

James looked up from his reenactment and focused on this woman, disbelief oozing from his open mouth. He spoke to the cops, but his gaze remained on her.

Marty leaned over, whispering something through the blonde hair. Then he motioned to Danica and Lorena. Danica's instincts turned her head around the room, in search of support. All she found was Alex, leaning by the front door with more shock on her face than her dark lipstick could mask.

Danica's hand had a mind of its own. It grabbed Lorena's. She had never been the hand-holding type, yet there she was, holding the hell out of this one — *Lorena's* hand! The psychic's wrist went tight and two of her bracelets slid down her wrist, smacking Danica's fingernails. She only held tighter.

"These are the two who helped find you," said Marty. "I knew they could do it. I just knew it. This is Madame Lorena and Danica Luman."

The pair moved as if drawn by a super-powered magnet. Danica's mind fired off paranoid theories as her pent up adrenaline released its last gasps. All those clues and patterns and puzzles, begging to be solved. That energy searched for a way out, manifesting in Danica suddenly shivering on the left side of her body.

They stopped walking a few feet shy of the woman as she turned to face them. Her lower lip was swollen. She had two black eyes, a fact her make-up only highlighted. Her smile strained.

With Marty and Kayleigh keeping her steady, she stood and stepped onto the sunken couch seat, ascending to floor level. She seemed to be the same height as her sister was.

Was.

"Hi," she said. "I'm Sofi."

Her voice was a husky whisper, reminding Danica of the confessional videos.

She extended her hand to shake, limping as she walked. Her sweatpants had "LAPD" printed down the side and her sockless ankles had scratches just above the tops of custom Nikes.

"Easy, Sof," said Marty.

Sofi connected with Lorena first, somehow finding her lighting from the recessed lamps above. Despite this professional star move, she still looked like a special kind of exhausted. 'All cried out,' Danica's mom used to call it; past the point of feeling everything, but not numb to the hurt.

Lorena ended the handshake, offering a respectful (if a little curt) smile.

When Sofi turned to Danica, the star would not allow for another quick exchange. When their hands connected, she pulled her in for a hug.

Marty smiled, at the hug and at everyone else. The grip on Danica's shoulders got tight.

Sofi said a low, tearful "Thank you" into her ear.

After a few awkward moments, Marty said, "The medics want her to rest, so...."

Sofi pulled herself away from Danica and reached back. He took her hand and escorted her down the hall toward the master bedroom. They scuttled away, with Sofi under Marty's arm, her head resting near his armpit.

Danica sensed her gaping mouth. The only thing that closed it was the sight of seeing Lorena climbing the stairs, off to pack her things and move on with everything.

An hour later, Gabby came to get Danica, fortunately bringing a spare shirt. They left without saying goodbye.

CHAPTER THIRTY-ONE

Thursday, January 22, 2009. 10:40AM. Earl's World of Curls.

"Where do you think Marty went after he got kicked out?"

For someone who didn't care about Danica's detective work, Carla had developed an impressive habit of diving into the details. She interrupted Danica's opening-time drawer count to continue a conversation they'd begun before Mrs. Simmons had arrived for her touch-ups. Now, with Mrs. Simmons barely out the door, Carla picked it right up again.

Gene, the other co-worker who claimed to have no interest in Danica's crime-solving, chimed in. "Old boy was probably hanging around down the hill all dang day. One time, Samosa got kicked out of a birthday party for hogging the wine. We sent his ass packing. Well, he left, but didn't go home. He just drove down the block and parked at the Arby's, thinking he could come back after a while. Your thing might've done the same."

"Marty is not her *thing*," said Carla.

Gene scoffed. "Either way, old boy missed his girl. He was concerned."

"You call fighting a guy 'concerned?'"

"If the guy was a stalker? Hells yeah I do."

"I'm just saying Marty came back real quick for a banished dude."

"But that makes sense. He wanted to be close to the action."

They carried on this way, discussing the last couple days of Danica's life like fans of "Lost" debating island theories.

Gene finally looked Danica in the face. "Exactly why are you here? I mean, aren't you rolling in it now."

"Leave her alone, Gene." Carla spoke to the wall.

"If I got a fat check, no offense, I'd be outta here so fast, even my shadow would miss me."

"They haven't sent anything yet," said Danica. She assumed as much for Madame Lorena, seeing as how the mystic hadn't been bothering Carla. Ostensibly, Danica's plan — such as it was — had worked.

Gene tossed his things into his kaboodle. "I got another coming soon, right?"

Danica scanned the schedule. "In about twenty."

"Is it Georgette?"

"Georgette."

"Then I'm stepping out. She's always late." As Gene sauntered by the reception area, it might have been the perfect moment for him to lean close to Danica and, just under his breath, utter something like, 'Good to have you back' or 'thanks for helping the place out by putting your life on the line.' Instead, he pulled his charger from the outlet and left with less than a blink.

It didn't matter; whatever risks she'd undertaken, she certainly didn't do it for Gene. It had been two days since rescuing Sofi Starr, two days of processing and attempting to bask in the victory. She'd been hugged to the point of chest compression by her friends. Even her step-dad called:

"You all right?"

"Fine. Now."

"Mmm... that was some trouble, huh?"

"Yeah."

"...Yeah."

It lasted almost seven minutes, a record for their phone calls. Yet even with all this attention and the displays of concern, Danica moved in a daze. She'd gotten up at a reasonable hour, showered, dressed, arrived at work. Her movements qualified as productive without registering much impact. Her mind remained fully elsewhere. During her ample free time, she checked her phone for the news. Each check yielded a scold from Carla. "Torturing yourself" was what she called it, but Danica had to know.

A few stories popped up concerning the events at the Starr Residence, but if Danica hadn't searched them out, she might have missed them entirely. Of these, two major stories found bits of traction. *The Times* reported that a funeral would take place, noting it would be "small, with only a handful of friends and family." More detail came from the *Daily News,* which listed out some of Viktoria "Tori" Stornelli's accomplishments with a dash more fanfare than the average obituary, but not much more. It also dedicated some ink to the events of the house, stating, "...though her life had been cut down by the person responsible for her sister's kidnapping, the star was found safe."

Danica searched again, searched yesterday's paper and news, hoping that somewhere in the wall-to-wall inauguration coverage there was more to be found. She wanted the cold face of newsprint to push away the dream-like state of her memories, the images of that body lying on the carpet. The empty resolution of finding one Starr while losing another.

The news only made things stranger and no such respite emerged.

She switched to YouTube, to Sofi's page. After a few seconds of random "Sofi Tries…" misadventure, Danica searched for that old Tori short. The woman's last strange mark on the world where she zip-lined into a pool. It had been removed.

Carla said something about a customer, Danica made an 'uh-huh' sound, then put her phone down. Frustrated, she grabbed it again, as though answers lay within if only she stared at it long enough. No, not answers. Merely more questions. Enticing queries hooking deep within her psyche. Something was missing. She felt incomplete, along with a deep need to fill some kind of hole.

Customers arrived, paid, left, all leaving that hole unfilled.

CHAPTER THIRTY-TWO

Friday, January 23, 2009. 10:32AM. Island Estates Apartments, Van Nuys, CA.

Her reward check arrived at her apartment via FedEx, along with a letter.

Dear Ms. Luman,

I cannot fully express my emotions or gratitude at this time. I'm sure you understand. Marty has not stopped talking about how helpful you and Lorena were. To honor my sister's wishes, I've sent you the full reward that was promised.

I hope you can do something nice with it.

You are my hero.

It was signed: *Sofi*

Danica slid the check out, like unsheathing a samurai sword.

"I've never seen this much money in one place, in any

form, in my whole damn life." Gabby reached out her hand, magnetized toward the check. "It even smells wealthy."

Danica stared at the letter; stared through it. This should have been it: the completion of her mission and the reward — literally! — for all her work. Holding the prize in her hand should have arrested her attention while wiping away all other distractions and focusing her mind to a single, clarity-inducing point.

It was only paper and ink and it meant little else.

Gabby noticed her distress, first offering jokes and then another of those hugs everyone seemed to think she'd been asking for.

A lump grew in Danica's throat. She gave it air.

"Why can't I stop?" she said. Gabby inquired further and Danica continued. "We solved it. Bobby did it. We stopped him, we got rewarded. This is what I was trying to do. It's over."

"It is. And you were right!"

That didn't help. "But it doesn't *feel* over. I've been, I guess, antsy. Ever since coming home, since you picked me up. It was the same when I got there, to the Starr house. I just can't stop." She shook her head. "I can't stop thinking of her body."

"That's natural. It's traumatic and scary and all that."

"Yeah, but I can't stop thinking about *why* it happened. And how it happened."

Gabby opened her mouth, almost smiling before catching herself.

Danica spoke for her. "Yes, it's the Solving-Stuff Buzz."

"Oh, baby, I'm so sorry. I'm not making fun of you."

"I know. Nothing feels whole. Even though it is! I can't stop... why can't I stop?"

"You can. You just gotta stop seeing what's wrong with *everything*, Dani."

"I don't think I do that."

"What about that woman in Arizona? The one you 'helped' with her car? She didn't ask for it, but there you were, nosing in. And you're back now and, I mean, you're wearing the same clothes, right?"

Danica looked down at her shirt, which stared back with a blank blue color — no *Dookie* to be seen.

"Those pants are pretty ragged at least," said Gabby, tugging on the knee.

"I've worn other pants."

"But you haven't washed these."

"It's expensive!"

"Alls I'm saying is you gotta learn to accept things as they are and move on. You don't have to constantly challenge and change everything."

She shook her head again. "I know. But I can't. I'm tired but can't sleep. All I wanna do is stare at this thing and search for answers."

"That's phone addiction. I read about it."

"It's not. Not exactly. I will not let this case go — I'm even calling it a case! I just keep digging, even when there's nothing more to find." She buried her head into her arms and tucked her legs up. "I wanna see Bobby's apartment."

"You can't do that."

"Why not?"

"You don't even know where it is."

"It's in... Lake Balboa."

"That's not very specific."

"But... I have to know."

"Hey, I get it. I know you. You look out for me and your friends. But there's nobody to save at the moment. Tori died and you gotta accept it and move on." Gabby rubbed her roommate's back, going full mother mode. "Did you talk to Lorena? Is she feeling this way, too?"

"Nope."

"Haven't talked or she isn't feeling this way?"

"Haven't talked."

"Maybe that would help."

"I don't know. Talking to Lorena has *never* helped."

"What about someone else?"

She looked up from her self-made shell. "Is this why private-eyes drink?"

"Probably," said Gabby. "Do you want me to get you someone?"

Danica nodded and Gabby flew into action. She grabbed her address book and made a quick search, promising the therapist was recommended by her parents and of the highest reputation.

The check and the letter had fallen to the floor. A personal check, with 'One-Hundred Fifty Thousand and 00/100' written carefully in capital letters. The signature matched the letter, but with a business touch of including her last name.

"Actually," said Danica, "I was thinking of talking to someone else."

CHAPTER THIRTY-THREE

Friday, January 23, 2009. 1:40PM. Van Nuys Streets.

"AT. THE. NEXT. STREET. TURN. RIGHT." Gabby grumbled at the navigation machine as she made the turn.

"I cannot believe I let you talk me into this," she said.

The route to the shoot resembled the one they'd taken the prior week, only with more sunlight. Danica concentrated on keeping her cool, trying not to jabber, not to look excited or worried or anything. Poker face.

"What's Freddie think of all this?" said Gabby.

"Haven't talked to him about it."

"Hmph. I bet I know why. I can imagine it perfectly. Let's just say it would not be encouraging."

Danica didn't want to agree with her driver, but she did. Freddie would have ranted at her, listing off a scolding litany of reasons why dropping in on a PowerWorks shoot was a terrible idea. The list would have likely included:

- she was not invited
- she was not hired
- she might not have the right location
- the people she wanted to see were probably not there, and even if they were...
- she should not bother them.

"What if they're not there?" Gabby pulled into the storage area, while apparently reading Danica's thoughts. After a couple turns around the lot, Danica became inclined to agree with her roommate, and her mood dropped through the bottom of the car. This desperate lunge for closure via gatecrashing would not qualify as a strategy for success, if it qualified as a strategy at all. It would garner lower marks if Sofi's crew wasn't even there.

However, the third turn revealed a U-Haul truck surrounded by college-aged adults milling about, at which time Danica's heart jumped. Three young-looking men in cargo shorts handled items in the truck's back. One of them carried a large pipe-like object.

Gabby parked almost ten doors down. "Don't gloat."

"You wanna get closer?"

"I mean... I *could*, but I... what if they see me and...."

"I can go by myself. It's fine." Danica unbuckled her seatbelt.

"No, no. I'll come."

Danica didn't recognize anyone in the milling crew. As expected, a whole new group of bad beards and baseball caps hustled about, speaking that set-based language she did not understand.

A tall man walked out of the open garage and Danica stopped, as did Gabby. It was Marty, stretching his arms and soaking up some sun. His own luminary qualities shot warmth across the lot and into Danica's face. Next to him was a woman with blonde hair, sipping a fashionable drink.

Sofi. In the flesh and in her element. Even from a distance, Danica could see the make-up applied to her face and legs to cover the bruises. She wore a trademark vest and held a pen which she pointed at Marty, then back into the garage.

A well of tears came to Danica's eyes. She wiped one eye but gave up on the other. The sight of Sofi Starr back at work, alive and healthy... Danica had been thinking about it for so long, but to actually *see it* became too much. She cursed her stupid brain for wanting more trouble, for actively seeking it out, for not letting good enough *be* good enough, for her strange wanna-be-a-hero streak. She had accomplished something nobody else could have done; who was she to ask for more?

"It's... her," said Gabby, a little overcome, too.

"I know."

"So... Do you want to see her or talk to her or...?"

"I'm not exactly sure," said Danica.

"Is this always how you operate?"

"I'm not exactly sure," she said again. She hadn't planned much of anything for the last couple days, mostly because her headspace had not been equipped to do so. Sofi and her sister had been all she could think about; just their mere existences, not how to see her or engage with her. Seeing her again was nearly enough.

They watched as Sofi re-entered the garage, unencumbered and completely at home.

Alone, Marty turned and squinted their way. His million-dollar smile appeared, switched on as if by a light switch.

Danica took Gabby's hand and whispered. "Follow me, OK?" She did not wait for Gabby to respond.

"So great seeing you," said Marty. His arms were wide as

he made it across the span of the parking lot. "I didn't know we got you back on the roster."

"I'm not," said Danica, accepting the hug. He smelled wonderful. "I actually, um... this is so lame, but my check got damaged."

Gabby remained notably quiet as they watched Marty go from happy beaming to sad beaming. "Aw, man, really?"

"Yeah. Like I said, so stupid, but is there a way I could get it replaced?"

His smile's sparkled dipped a fraction before he refreshed it. "I'll see what we can do...." He looked back to the garage.

"That'd be awesome. I know it's super awkward. I could come back later?"

"No, no," he said, then looked back to the garage. "I think... let me check. Gimme a sec, OK?"

He smiled again — that perfect switch — and jogged into the garage. He could turn on that smile so quickly and decisively....

Gabby gave him four seconds before she said, "Your check got messed up?"

"Not exactly." Danica reached inside her jeans pocket and extracted the folded check. Gabby gasped a little at the sight of it.

She gasped a little more when Danica ripped it in half.

Gabby choked and sputtered, trying to talk through her thoughts. "I... you... that..."

Danica stuffed the two halves back in her pocket. "Just stay with me." She led Gabby into the garage.

Near the back, Marty's head bobbed above the wave of grips and best boys. A fresh-faced make-up person studied her phone in the same corner where Danica had worked that earlier shoot.

A large brown man with short black hair stepped up from the food area and flexed. It wasn't Huelo, but it could've been his protege, studying at the University of Giant Muscles and Gruff Facial Expressions. As he approached, Danica moved faster. Not a sprint, to avoid warranting security's interception; she merely kept her eyes forward, focused on the green wall area ahead of her.

At the green wall stood Marty and Sofi, in an intense conversation. Sofi jabbed her hand at Marty's chest. He may have had a foot of height on her, but the guy grew smaller and smaller the more she spoke. He kept putting his hands up, motioning to himself and then to some far off thing, all while Sofi's face grew more taut. As she spoke, a muscle in her perfect cheek danced.

The security officer reached their side and said, "Help you?" just as Danica said, "Sofi?"

Her blonde hair whipped at the sound of her name. Sofi's stare landed perfectly onto Danica's face. A kind of terror sat on Sofi's face, most likely from hearing her name spoken by a voice she did not recognize; it dissipated once she registered Danica's haircut and smile.

"Hello!" she said. "Come here! I'm so glad you dropped by."

Danica's gambit weighed as heavy pieces in her pocket. There had to be easier ways to talk with a celebrity. At least less financially risky ways. Yet something about Sofi's smile — like Marty's switch-on-demand — gave Danica a tinge of confidence.

"Do you have the pieces?" said Marty. "I mean, not that we don't trust you."

"No, I get it. They're here." Scraps were produced. "I could have taped it, but I think banks are, you know, careful about what they accept. Especially when it's this much."

Marty thanked her and handed the pieces to Sofi. She reached into a large purse to grab a thin brown check book.

She tried writing, then scribbled the pen against the

ledger. "It's out of ink." Sofi tossed the pen on the table. Gabby showed ninja-like speed and caught the pen as it skittered off the table while Sofi returned to her purse for another search.

Without thinking, Danica reached into her pocket and drew another pen. She must have done it too fast, too vigorously, because when it emerged, a clear wave of fright ran across Sofi's face.

"Dani, the girl's been through a tough experience," said Gabby. "She doesn't need your sword-looking pens."

"Sorry," said Danica, hiding the chewed pen cap.

Sofi blinked and said it was fine, then accepted the working pen. She spread the scraps of the check onto the table and began writing a new one.

"Sorry about all this, seriously," said Danica.

"Don't worry about it at all," Sofi said, head down. "Least I could do. I owe you."

"And I'm sorry about Viktoria."

Sofi's pen stroke froze on the date line. It couldn't have lasted more than a half of a second, but to Danica, time ceased, all sound dipped out, nothing breathed and nothing moved.

A moment later, everything resumed to normal. Sofi finished writing the date, then tore the check free and handed it and the pen back with a smile.

Danica tried to smile, too. Her cheeks burned, but not from embarrassment. "Thanks."

"I'm so glad you came," said Sofi, smiling again. "I'm sorry things are so busy, otherwise —"

"No, no, we should get out of your hair." The words slid out of Danica, barely in her control. She stared at Sofi, who stared right back. Gabby said something, they all waved and promised to stay in touch. Then they left.

"There you go," said Gabby as she buckled her seatbelt. "I

didn't think that would go nearly that well, but I was wrong. She seems fine. You were right, this idea was good, so let's go get Fatburger." Gabby realized she was still carrying the dead pen and dropped it into the cup holder.

Danica nabbed it. "Actually, could you take me to work?"

CHAPTER THIRTY-FOUR

She asked to get dropped off on the corner, making an excuse like she was doing her a favor by not having her turn left. Danica promised to call Gabby if she needed a ride home, then hustled away. She pretended to check her phone as Gabby's Prius drove away, then pretended to walk to Earl's. Once traffic swallowed the Prius, Gabby did what she hadn't been able to do since getting back from the Starr Residence: she walked to Madame Lorena's place. She stayed tight to the wall once she saw Carla's car in the lot, but she made it to the door without attracting attention.

The door was unlocked and the beaded curtain parted without tangling. Lorena sat in her parlor and appeared unsurprised to have a sudden guest. She blinked when she recognized Danica, but offered no protest.

Danica sat on the same farting vinyl seat as she had the first time she'd been there and for a moment all the two women did was sit and breath the incense hanging on the air.

"Haven't seen you for a while," said Danica.

"Likewise." Madame Lorena hesitated, twiddling her fingers.

"Were you this uncomfortable back at the Starr house?"

Lorena said nothing — no words, though she did tilt her head as though jogging a memory.

"When Sofi came back. Actually, before that. Before we'd fought, you seemed... uncomfortable."

"I'm not certain I would use that word, but if that is what you saw..."

Danica held up her hands. "Sorry. Let me start over. I think I owe you an apology."

Lorena stayed silent, her eyes open and expectant.

"You were doing your best to search the house and find Sofi, and I bit your head off for it just because it wasn't the same method as mine."

"I didn't find her though," said Lorena.

"But you found something."

Lorena shrugged. "Useless distractions, as you said."

"I did say that, but I don't think that was right either." Danica regrouped. "I went to see her today."

"Sofi Starr?"

"She was filming something and I... I had to. I haven't been able to stop thinking about everything, especially that last night, over and over again. It's been driving me up the wall. I thought if I could see Sofi just being herself and living, that I might be able to move on."

"How was she?"

"She was fine."

"So it worked for you?"

"No! That's the thing and that's why I asked about you. Like I said, I couldn't stop replaying the last night in my head. At first it was all about Sofi, but then it became about you. You and your discomfort. You couldn't hold still."

"Well, it is not every night that I experience gunfire and a dead body. Two dead bodies, in fact."

"You were like that earlier though. When you saw me running around solving clues and stuff, you were either somewhere else, or you were distracted."

"Do not rub it in."

"I'm not. I promise. I just want to know why you felt that way."

Lorena rubbed her fingers together, working up her courage. "I did not agree with your line of investigation."

"I get it," said Danica. "Even when it was working."

"Yes. It was curious. I saw you and those girls running around, figuring out this and that, finding clues to puzzles, but something about it did not feel... it felt..."

"Off."

"Precisely."

"I was on the other side of it," said Danica. "Running around, I mean. When I was in the thick of it, everything was clicking into place. Everything had an answer, no matter how strange the clue or the question. We were told Sofi liked puzzles and we— I just bought it."

"That came from her own sister."

Danica nodded. She tapped her teeth for a moment, loosening the words. "Thinking about it now — and like I said, I've been thinking about it all a lot — things might have been too easy."

"*Too* easy? I never pegged you for a braggart."

"I'm not. Think about the clues the group found. That old key was in a vest in the closet — a bright, shiny vest with a spotlight on it. Joy and Kayleigh found it simply by having functional eyeballs. It was set up to be found.

"Then you found the note in the foosball table. How hard did you look?"

"I... well...."

"I'm guessing not very hard. You heard the thing rattling when you nudged it. Again: you found it because you were there. Then there's the notebook."

"Which one? The scary one or the lame one?"

Danica swallowed her pride and continued. "Right, *that* one is part of this whole thing. The scary notebook was found by Bobby just by looking in the car. Again: he had eyes and saw it. So how did I miss it and end up with the lame notebook?"

"I wondered that myself, dear."

"When I was in that car, I turned it upside down searching around. The stuff I found was wedged in the cracks of the seat. Then someone came into the garage and got in the car. I never saw who, but they must have planted the scary notebook in the backseat *after* I had been in the car."

"Why?"

Danica paused, weighing her options for a moment. To stop here meant keeping her money and moving on. It also meant the likelihood of more sleepless nights and nagging brain chatter.

"Tori said that nearly everyone she brought to the house was a suspect, right? Why would anyone do that?"

"To catch them," said Lorena.

"Yes, but why would the suspects ever accept the invitation in the first place?"

Though she tried to find one, Lorena had no response,

"I think this is what tripped you up, Lorena. You've been reading people for a long time, reading situations and all that. You could smell it. No matter how badly you wanted the money, you could tell something was up. It was all a set-up to point at one person."

"Mr. Utz?"

Danica beamed. Lorena must have been thinking it, too, for nearly as long as she had been.

"I'm still unclear," said the mystic, "about how the 'lame' notebook you found fits in. If everything was so easy and targeting Mr. Utz as the suspect, then why plant something so obtuse?"

"They didn't. Don't you see: the scary notebook was the one that mentioned a stalker and Sofi being scared and all that stuff. It was also put in front of our eyes to make sure we all found it so we could see it. But the lame notebook? That one nobody but Sofi really knew about. It was a legit find."

"But it had no clues."

"Exactly," said Danica. "If we were dealing with a set-up, then the clues without clues are more truthful than the clues *with* clues. Because those were just planted there. Planted to be discovered by the group."

Lorena did not kick Danica out of the building, but she did crook her eyebrow. "I'm sorry, dear, but I'm afraid I do not understand what you want from me. We've gotten our rewards. Surely, you received your check, right? That's all I signed up for. We have the money and we can sort out our issues with the building, so I am not certain what these theatrics mean. For us, for Sofi, for anyone, frankly."

Danica dug into her pocket and pulled out the new, folded check, fresh from the shoot.

Madame Lorena's grey eyes stared at the check, transfixed. However, Danica did not see dollar signs or money bags dancing in her eyes as she had earlier, like when they'd agreed to take the assignment, or when Marty offered to help her become a YouTube sensation. Instead, Lorena's eyes held the kind of focus that came with soul searching and decision making.

"Have you cashed yours yet?" said Danica.

After a few more moments of searching and making, the older woman leaned behind her and pulled clunky purse from the shelf. She unzipped a side pocket and her hand emerged with a check of her own, with a matching dollar amount.

Danica beamed. "I knew it! It doesn't feel right, right?"

"So," said Lorena, that indecipherable accent popping up. "Let's just *entertain the notion* that I am agreeing with you. That I *might* agree with your *theory* that this is all 'too easy,' as you say. So what?"

"It means we agree, that's so what. We agree because we are thinking the same thing. We have two of us — two experts, first-hand witnesses — who feel something weird is going on. And because we're both thinking it, it could be true."

"But how can you be so certain?"

"'Cause today I went to see Sofi. Saw her and Marty. They smiled perfectly — too perfect. Too easy. They handed over the money, too, and did that too easily. Easy because it's what they wanted to do. What they'd planned on doing. They paid us off."

"But... and I am not disagreeing with you, mind, I simply must inquire... *why?*"

Danica opened her retrieved the pens from her pocket.

"You've been collecting?"

"I stole a couple here and there. From the Starr House." She started with the blue one. "I found this pen in Sofi's car. Same place I found the lame notebook — the *true* notebook of the true Sofia Stornelli. The cap is all chewed up, right?"

Lorena nodded.

Danica switched to the black-ink pen. "I got this other pen from meeting them just today. Look at the cap."

The low light and increasing haze made for a lousy criminal science lab, but Danica worked with it. She set the pens in the center of the table.

"They're both chewed up," said Lorena.

"But not the same, right? This one —" she pointed to the

blue one from Sofi's car "—is mangled, like a wolf got at it. But this other one —" she traded for the black one from the shoot "—is barely touched and only at the very end."

"Molars versus incisors." Lorena scrutinized the two pens, then looked back at Danica, waiting for more.

"Bobby was set up for the kidnapping and we were brought there to help pin it on him. He was kept around the PowerWorks sets because he was a target; perfectly uncool and easy to suspect. It was all run like a show. A fake." She tapped Lorena's check. "That's why we didn't cash these. That's why we were so uncomfortable the last night at the Starr house. We didn't buy the show."

Lorena stared back at her. Danica didn't know whether she would attack her, hug her or throw up. The older woman's lips trembled; at first, Danica thought they were about to let out a sob, but then she saw them shift gears and become barriers. Lorena's lips wanted to speak, but they also wanted to hold back what she was about to say.

"It's OK," said Danica. "I just threw a lot at you, but I think we're thinking the same thing here. The clues, the puzzles, the two notebooks the body, the complex set-up, being hired and paid off, the managing of the 'show'... and the different bite marks on these pens... You're thinking what I'm thinking, right?"

Speaking her thoughts aloud, sharing them with someone who went through the same challenges at the Starr Residence, the clouds in Danica's imagination began to dissipate. An idea, one whose seeds had been planted the night Tori died, broke ground and began to sprout. Ever since Danica looked into that bleeding woman's mind and saw her last fitful fever dreams, the idea had been grasping for air, praying for nutrition. It had spread, this idea, grabbing more control over Danica's entire being. The idea was the reason why she'd returned to the PowerWorks shoot, why she'd ripped the check, and why she'd gone straight to Lorena afterwords.

It was, by all accounts, a stupid idea; one barely clinging to logic or sense. Spending so much time thinking about it embarrassed Danica. She took a cue from her partner and did some deep breaths. The parlor air had become thicker and she coughed; Danica told herself it was because of the incense and not because of nerves.

As her eyes anchored to Lorena's, Danica self-doubt mounted a counter attack against the idea reaching her mouth. Butterflies twittered in her stomach and her breath grew shorter. She had manifested this idea for days, but there, in the hazy parlor, could not speak it.

Fortunately, as Lorena's eyes released tears, the old mystic spoke the thought for both of them: "I don't think the real Sofi came back."

Every emotion rushed through Danica's body — relief, elation, concern, confusion, mild hunger. Most of all: recognition. That nagging bastard of a half-formed thought that Danica had been wrestling with, unable to name or speak? Lorena had it, too.

Danica wanted the older woman on her feet so they could share in a rare hug.

More tears rushed for Lorena's cheeks. After forcing a few sharp inhales, the mystic said, "We'll need to prove it. All of it. And the heat will come down upon us with a furious tumult. They will come after us. If they could do such manipulation, then their malice has no limit."

"I have a friend we can contact. I trust him and he believes me with these kinds of things." Usually, Danica said to herself.

"Call him," said Lorena. She stood slowly, with an ache. Then she sat back down, holding the side of her head. "Head rush."

Though she'd made the offer, Danica had not put any real thought into her first call with Freddie in months. How could she possibly start that wouldn't immediately bring a scolding through the other end? "What do you think I can say to him?"

The older woman wasn't looking at her, just at the floor. She blinked, then smelled the air again, this time in short bloodhound bursts. She stood again, still sniffing. After two steps toward the beaded curtain, Lorena stumbled against her table, falling into one of her shaded lamps. Her hand reached for the table top, finding only the fringed table cloth. It followed her onto the floor.

Danica moved to catch her, but her legs disagreed. Her eyes drooped. The haziness of the room seemed excessive, even for a palm reader's place. The trail from the incense darkened as it rose, collecting at the vents. Not leaving, but collecting. Building. The intensity of the smell burned her nose.

Lorena had shifted from kneeling next to the table to moving on all fours. Crawling and coughing.

Even in a fuzzy condition, Danica's brain processed an important data point:

The room was filling with gas.

She tried walking, but her legs were still iffy on the subject. Danica joined Lorena on the floor. The air at carpet level was less thick, but by the thinnest margin.

"Gas leak?" said Lorena, coughing as punctuation.

Danica scurried through the beaded curtain to the front door.

Locked. Or blocked. Smoke gathered on the glass, clouding the sunlight outside. Beyond the door, a car engine rumbled away.

She looked above and saw another ceiling vent with a dark cloud around it making no attempt to push through.

Not a gas leak. As she crawled back to into the parlor, she found one of the pens that Lorena had thrown to the floor.

They must have followed her.

Lorena was in the same spot, on her elbows, head down. She looked at Danica with bloodshot eyes.

Danica groped in the haze at the table. Her phone had been there before Lorena wiped it out. It had to be nearby. Her hands found the vinyl booth and dug around in the cracks. Only thing she found was the other pen.

Lorena's seat yielded a few soft things (likely scarves), but no phone.

"Land line?"

Lorena shook her head and coughed in response, doubling over again.

Danica grabbed the spilled table cloth and pulled it to her own mouth, then brought the other end to Lorena's. Their coughing slowed, but barely.

"Back... door..." said Lorena through the cloth. Her voice had a serious wheeze.

Christ. Her asthma.

Danica's head swam. Her directional sense sagged along with her eyesight. She headed for what she thought was the rear of the building, her fingernails digging into the thin carpet in the center of the room. She traced her way beyond the table, chair and rug again, to the linoleum flooring and finally found a wall. From her knees she groped for a doorknob.

Behind her, Lorena's coughs became steady and endless.

Danica's hands circled over the wall, knocking into whatever hung there. At last they slapped something metal and round. She turned the knob.

It moved, but nothing opened. Something on the other side had seen to that, from the alley. Danica pressed her ear to the door and heard a low, mechanical growl. The coughing behind her grew louder.

She wiped her eyes with her sleeve, a strategy that didn't help much. All she saw was swirls of gray from floor to ceiling. Her nostrils smoldered. Her mouth opened to compensate, but did so too quickly, punishing her lungs with another coughing fit.

Staying calm was no longer an option. She screamed to Lorena, with full panic in her voice, as she crawled back to the table.

Lorena lay on her back. The coughs and heaving chest were the only positive signs of life.

Danica felt around Lorena's sides. The fleeting hope of finding Lorena's inhaler — that it might somehow save her — died when Danica found no pockets in her dress.

She took Lorena's hand and scanned the room again. For anything.

The opening. The trap door crawl space thing Lorena had used to sneak to and from Earl's. It had to be somewhere nearby. The useless vent above them was way too small to fit a person, but Lorena's secret might be somewhere in the smoke.

"The vent, Lorena. You climbed through it from Earl's. Is it here? Where is it?"

Lorena's hands trembled and her mouth opened, but only gasps and chokes emerged.

Danica moved her fingers to Lorena's neck and cradled her head. She closed her eyes.

"The vent. Think of the vent, please. Think of where it is."

Once, years earlier, Danica cut the hair of a full-on hippie who must have either been on something strong, been mentally ill, or both. These hypotheses were the only ways she could justify the swarm of colors and swirly weirdness she'd witnessed while linking to his mind. She thought she'd seen herself at one point and wondered if she had experienced the telepathic version of a mystical psychedelic journey.

Back on Lorena's parlor floor, holding the old woman's head and drowning in smoke, Danica experienced much the same as she did from that hippie cut. She saw Earl's with the walls dripping into lakes around the floor. The scissors and razors vibrated like players on an electric football set. Everything drifted, expanded and bubbled with no discernible pattern. Danica — or whatever she'd become in this branch of reality — elevated up and into the ceiling. She passed through it like the liquid metal T-1000, squirting back together again inside a bright silver shaft. Hundreds of teeth lined the tunnel ahead of her.

Was this death? Was this her soul failing to find Heaven and settling for something worse? She'd always settled, never valuing herself. Was this to be her punishment? It didn't feel like Hell. It only felt like a nightmare.

She drifted forward as a hum grew around her. Then a drumming. Then a rhythmic bang. Still she drifted, until reaching the other end of the tunnel where the drumming had transformed into a banging cacophony.

Looking down she saw herself and Lorena on the floor. Surrounded by smoke and praying for their lives. The angle was high, over her right shoulder.

On the floor and in true reality, Danica opened her eyes. Death and Hell disappeared and reality slammed back inside her. Her head throbbed as she released Lorena's scalp. The air had grown thick and smothering as a wet beach towel.

"Lorena. Get up."

Lorena did not. She only coughed, a fractured beat which matched the rhythm of the banging during Danica's trip.

Danica strained her eyes, up and to the right. Over a shelf

in the ceiling's flimsy panels. Through the smoke, she could just make out a discoloration on the wall. Dirty, like skid marks from a tire.

She ripped the table cloth in half, lay one part over Lorena's mouth and stuffed the other into her own. She bit down, freeing her hands from her makeshift mask. Danica drug the table to the shelf wall and righted it. A pedestal table with one big center leg. Wobbly.

No choice.

Her fingers pushed against the table top, keeping it steady. She lifted her right leg onto what felt like the table's center. Her thigh ached and made her promise that if she survived she'd stretch or do yoga or something.

She coughed and the inside of her skull stung. She would have to frog it up, onto the center of the table and hopefully maintain balance. She coughed again, as though her lungs had their doubts.

Lorena. On the floor, still coughing, but slowing down. No time left.

Danica's left leg tightened, then pushed her up. Her right leg pulled at the center of the table, keeping her momentum going. When her left foot reached the table top, her hands stabilized her. She'd made it to the top of the table.

That was the easy part.

Her wrist made a sharp pain, reminding her of past mistaken attempts at heroism. She transferred her hands to the wall as she rose. The world turned musty, yet she could hear air coming through the ceiling. From the passage, up and to the right. She reached her hand into the darkness and found the ceiling.

But no door. No vent, no hinge, no trip switch. Nothing.

Where was it? Lorena's vision had come from this area. It also had teeth inside a metal tube; the vision could be wrong. But she'd seen it here. Hadn't she?

She could've been wrong, too.

Danica closed her eyes. They weren't doing her any good anyway. Her hand moved, frantic, feeling only styrofoam and ceiling tiles. Nothing that would hold a person.

She took a breath to calm herself. Mistake. The fumes and smoke filled her lungs and she gagged. She had to be close. It had to have come from this direction...

Another frantic hand sweep met pain. Something had cut her finger. Something metal.

If Lorena had made this trip a habit, then there had to be a latch or some manner of accessibility. Something.

After another swipe, Danica found it. Tripped it. Something hard whacked the side of her face. The door had dropped. She added its sting to her throbbing headache, spasming thighs, mistreated wrist and burning lungs to a list of ignored ailments. She released her grip on the wall and put both hands into the hole above her. Warm steel met her fingertips. A hot breeze flooded in, with no vent to slow it down.

The bend of her fingers barely reached the seal. She'd have to jump — blind — then catch the sides to pull herself up.

Danica ran her fingers around the edge one last time to get an idea of the target. Then her fingers let go and bent her knees.

No coughing came from the floor.

No time for debate.

Danica jumped and splayed her arms. Her palms smacked solid metal. She quickly wiggled to the corner, forcing her forearms into position, holding her in an awkward iron cross. She tucked her knees up and into the hole. Her left arm went numb. She cut her ankle on the metal edge. And the table cloth mask was lost to gravity.

But she made it inside the ceiling passageway. Specifically into an air vent with silver walls and a rattling echo.

The tunnel before her presented two directions. Her dizziness wasn't helping to place her location, or the proximity of Earl's or anything. She saw no guarantee that the tunnel went straight to anyplace better than a dead end. The left direction held darkness with some smoke while the right had more smoke, becoming a full-on billow. It also had more breeze, which carried an unnatural smell. A familiar odor.

She chose the direction to the right.

Sliding on her knees, she pulled herself along by pressing her palms against the walls. She paused a moment to pull her shirt collar to her teeth, trying to eke out some semblance of protection from the smoke. Soon after, her collar fell free and she ignored it. Or tried to between gags.

The tunnel banged a steady rhythm as she crept along. Was that really happening, or was she remembering what she'd heard from the vision? Either way, it gave out after a few more feet and she was left with a deathly silence.

Her progress slowed. She couldn't feel her toes, nor her legs. Her fingers weren't doing great either, truth be told. As she pulled and slogged, Danica thought of her mom. She thought of the teeth she'd seen around the vision vent and wondered when they would bite. To take her legs or take her completely. At least she would feel no bite; she couldn't feel anything.

The tunnel became darker as she slid deeper into the smoke. Ahead of her appeared a wall. A dead end. Or maybe more smoke. She felt so tired. Sleepy, really.

One last push and it would be over. She had tried. They couldn't say she hadn't tried.

Her arms latched on the walls and then she fell. The crash roused her while the stinging in her back assured her that she was not in the afterlife. Her toes tingled above her, and her knee pressed against her face. Yet the darkness remained. A kind of total darkness, not the smokey cloud in Lorena's place or the tunnel.

She felt dirt. And metal. Cans maybe. Fat ones, like for paint.

And the familiar smell returned, stronger. And wetter.

Cleaning supplies.

Shampoo.

Danica pushed against the pile of whatever she'd landed on, putting her faith in a wall presenting itself. It did, as did a doorknob. And unlike prior knobs, this one worked uninhibited.

Light swept into her eyes as the door flopped open and knocked over the supply product shelf. Someone screamed — a woman, she thought. And a different woman — Carla, she hoped — swore a blue streak as Danica fell into a pile of fine Happy Spatty products on her way to the cold floor of Earl's.

After a single breath of clean air, she said, "Smoke. At Lorena's. Call someone."

CHAPTER THIRTY-FIVE

7:30PM. 405 SOUTH. LORENA'S KIA.

Weekday afternoon traffic proved unforgiving. Lorena's car shook as if it, too, had been trapped in a room filled with carbon monoxide.

Unlike her prior rides, Danica kept a close eye on the cars behind her this time. For a few blocks, she thought she saw a small pickup truck keeping pace with them for no good reason, but it pulled off when they got on the highway.

"And you know this person?" said Lorena.

"I do."

"Even though you've never been here before and you stole the address."

Danica hadn't *stolen* the address; she'd *borrowed* it from the Earl's customer database. Carla maintained mailing records for when she got around to mailing coupons. Danica's password hadn't lapsed, so she snuck online during all the commotion with firemen and ambulances and when Gene gave her a moment to herself. Carla hadn't seen her do it; she didn't think she'd seen her. She was preoccupied with the old car in the alley and how its exhaust system had been linked to the vents.

"Exit's coming up," said Danica.

She'd promised herself she would talk to him. And technically, the initiating phone call handled that part. She'd promised Lorena in her parlor to call her friend and she had. But these were all lies she told herself. She needed to make amends. Ignoring someone for months — someone who may have at one time loved her and God knows how she felt about him — only to pop up out of nowhere asking favors... she had a road ahead of her.

Lorena swerved onto the exit ramp. "And then?"

"And then almost there."

A few blocks from the highway stood a submarine-gray apartment building. Three or four floors, none remarkable. If they hadn't been looking for the place, they would have driven right by.

Lorena targeted a spot near the front gate.

"Not in front," said Danica, checking for another tail.

For once on the drive, Lorena gave little argument. Hiding from murderers merited side-street parking at a minimum. After only a few minutes they found a spot that did not insist on a permit.

They exited the car with the kind of casual air one might see from victims of electroshock therapy. Lorena put on sunglasses and spun her head around with every step. Danica was not much better, pulling her hood up and walk-sprinted to the apartment entrance.

She made it to the callbox, pressed the A-Z button and scanned for the name. Lorena caught up, still shaded, still scanning.

"This person, your friend who lives here... he's just going to let us in?"

"He said he would."

"Because he is, what? A do-good person?"

Danica found the name and pressed the button. "I think so."

"A do-gooder who is not your boyfriend?"

"I told you he's not." The callbox purred.

"Is he your ex?"

"No."

"Because if he is your ex, that might make matters considerably more—"

"He's a friend, Lorena. That's all."

"I only mention it because of something Carla said—"

Freakin' of course she did. "Just a friend, OK?"

After two more purrs, a low voice spoke through the call box. "DL?"

"Yep."

"Third floor."

A loud buzzer sounded and Danica yanked open the door. Lorena swept inside and Danica followed. They took a forty-seven-second long elevator ride in the absence of conversation and Danica was grateful for it.

When the doors slid open on the third floor hallway, they were greeted by a smiling Freddie Ford. "There you are."

Danica waved. She should have immediately responded, then felt bad for not immediately responding. It could have been something simple like, 'Thanks for letting me and my sort-of-partner escape from danger' or even 'You look great in T-shirts.' Words often vacated her mind when Danica looked at Freddie Ford.

"You must be Miss Baronette," he said.

"Madame Lorena." She held out a hand as if protocol dictated a kiss of her rings. Freddie shook it and ushered them into his open apartment door.

Lorena nudged Danica in the side. It was ignored.

Any notions Danica might have held about Freddie living with a significant other were immediately dismissed upon entry to his apartment. He either lived alone, or his roommate insisted they decorate in a stereotypical bachelor style. She stepped over a small mountain of remotes to move into the living room. The hand-me-down couch faced a TV the size of a small continent, with several gaming systems plugged into it. These lined the floor; no room (or need) for a table.

"Spare bedroom's at the end of the hall," he said.

On Freddie's direction, Danica found the small bedroom. Inside was a dresser and a mattress resting on the carpet, already made up with pillows and sheets.

Freddie leaned into the doorway. "When you called... well, it's the best I could do on short notice."

"It's great. Of you. It's all great." Dammit, Danica. She kept her eyes on the carpet and away from his own. And away from his dark arms. And the bed.

"Our deepest apologies for the imposition," said Lorena.

"Forget it. Make yourselves at home. You need anything right now? A drink? I got water? Sprite?"

"Wine, if you have it." Lorena took the invitation to make herself at home to heart. She made her way back to the living room.

Freddie made quick work in the kitchen, returning with three glasses and heavy pours. Lorena leaned back on the couch and Danica joined her. Freddie took a gentlemanly squat on the floor. He looked up at Danica, sending everything away when he spoke.

"I'm glad you're safe."

"Thank you again. We were... we just had to get out of there."

"There was danger," said Lorena.

"She told me. But the police and fire department came —"

Danica held up her hand. "Not them. Until this all gets settled, her place and mine felt…"

"Exposed?"

Danica smiled, appreciating his acceptance and his locating the right words.

"Not to be a bad host, but you wanna tell me just what is going on?"

Bye-bye acceptance. "I told you. Some of it."

"Some, yeah."

"Did you call it in?"

"I did," said Freddie. "But my superiors and the reports I gotta file, they need more than a wink and a smile. I can't just go on faith that you have a good reason, so, please, gimme a good reason."

"But they're going to get them now, right?"

Freddie sighed. "I contacted some friends in West Valley PD. They're going to the house. Nobody's just gonna get arrested — it doesn't work like that. Not unless we got damn good reasons and rock solid evidence. So…?" He held out his hands, waiting for it.

Danica looked at the walls behind him. A desktop computer monopolized what would have been a dining room table. She felt Freddie's look — that Cop Look even he couldn't help but use. The scolding was coming soon, she could tell.

She said, "We were attacked."

"Right."

"And we know who did it."

"Marty Dole and Sofia Stornelli?"

"Well… sorta."

"Oh, right. She goes by Sofi Starr."

"Well," said Danica, "sorta."

"Let's simplify here, DL: you think at least one of those people attacked you, right?"

Danica nodded.

"Was one of them Sofi?"

Her voice box dammed up the words.

Lorena nudged her glass into her arm. "Tell him about the pen."

Danica took a moment. The ache in her lungs still lingered, but the deep breath helped. "I went to the Power-Works shoot earlier today. I ended up seeing Marty there. And Sofi. Kinda. I think one of them — Marty for sure, Sofi for maybe — followed us back to Lorena's, barricaded the doors and pumped the place full of carbon monoxide."

"Why Marty?"

"Well, it wasn't Sofi."

"Because she was working, or because she's a girl? That's pretty sexist, DL."

"No. Let me back up."

"I wish you would."

"Talk about the pen," said Lorena again. She was little help.

Danica stood up and handed her wine glass to Freddie. "Can I stand? I feel like it'll go better if I can move?"

"Sure."

"And don't... y'know, don't interrupt me, OK? Not that you would, but just... y'know, let me get it all out."

Freddie mimed locking his lips with a key.

She began, "About a week ago, Sofi Starr went missing. Lorena and I were asked to help find her. We were asked by her boyfriend Marty, but the whole thing was organized by her sister Tori. Tori asked a bunch of people to her house to help and offered a reward for finding Sofi. She had a reason for not going to the cops, before you ask. Wanted to protect her sister's image and brand and all that."

Freddie raised his hand and unzipped his lips. "I'm sorry,

but just so I get it: Tori Stornelli is the woman in charge of Sofi Starr's productions, right?"

"Right. Just let me do this thing."

Freddie re-zipped and Danica continued.

"We got to the house and followed Tori's instructions. The money dangled in front of our eyes, we had to listen to her. She organized the entire production — that's what it was: a production. She led us to certain rooms at certain times to find certain things. We collectively found a key, a coded message and a notebook all pointing to one person."

"Bobby Utz."

She nodded. "And it was all a set-up."

"Set-up by Tori."

"Right."

"But she died."

"Just lemme keep going," said Danica. She paced. It felt good to move without her life depending on it for once. "This is gonna sound like it doesn't make any sense, but if you just listen and hear it all, it will, so let me get it all out:

"A couple years ago, both Sofi and Tori tried to start YouTube channels, to make it big in that world. They both made videos trying to see what clicked. It clicked big for Sofi, not for Tori. And she got jealous. Not only of her sister's fame, but of Sofi herself. After all, the 'Sofi Starr' persona was kind of a creation. It was her brand, something they concocted. Tori felt she owned it as much as anyone else. She wanted it for her own. She wanted to replace her sister in the role.

"Tori already controlled the Sofi *brand*. Their company and the operations were all under her thumb. That meant she was in charge of who they hired, which friends hung around and where they filmed. That's how this plan worked.

"Late 2008, Tori booked her sister to do more and more solo

stuff, remote and on location. She had previously been doing mostly staged stuff with crews and sets and all, you know, around other people. But for these remotes, Tori sent Sofi to do it all by herself. At the same time, Tori fired their old crew and hired all new people. So while Sofi was away, Tori used that time to step into the part around this new crew — the new audience. They'd never met Tori or Sofi before, so what did they know? They were brand new to Starr & Starr. Tori would arrive on set dressed as 'Sofi,' acting the part, talking like her, everything. They even filmed a few shorts with the same setups, so everyone's stories lined up. It's like she was a stand-in for her sister's life."

She stopped when she heard Lorena snoring. Her head tipped back and the empty glass resting on her knee.

"Stand-in, like for movie stars?" said Freddie.

"Yeah. All so when she finally *did* replace her sister, nobody who was still around would know any different. Even Sofi's 'friends' were new. Joy and Kayleigh only really knew this new version of Sofi, never Sofia. She did all as backup so that after they killed her, she could slip right in and nobody would see anything different. They'd see her as Sofi and think, 'all good.' The one exception was Bobby Utz.

"Bobby was a hardcore Sofi Starr fan. He was a little off and didn't fit in with the crew. He was even kind of incompetent. Why would Tori keep a guy around — especially after a mass firing — if he sucked at his job?"

Freddie sucked back some wine and shrugged.

"Because he was their fall guy. Tori pegged him early on when she tied him to the Gasper Kutman username and the fan blog. He'd written about Sofi Starr for a while. Tori built that blog into evidence of stalking.

"So they had the schedule, the fall guy, then here comes our part: the corroboration. Lorena and I were found by Marty to be witnesses for a frame up. We were hired to 'Find Sofi,' but really we were there to make Bobby look guilty.

"We went through all the paces — I. I went through the paces. I admit, it was almost fun, putting together this wild puzzle and rushing around with clues falling into place. Until the gunshots.

"Once I played my part and pinned it all on Bobby, he was killed. Then they brought in Sofia — the *real Sofia* — dressed like her sister and killed her, too. Left her on the bedroom floor and we all assumed it was Tori.

"We had all the clues," she said, "but they pointed in the wrong direction."

Freddie raised his hand and she allowed the question.

"I think I'm following you. But I'm still waiting for evidence. Did you, y'know... *see* anything?"

He whispered the last two words, glancing at Lorena to make sure she was asleep. He didn't mean 'see' with her eyes, but with her mind. Danica had hoped so desperately that Freddie had forgotten about that little discovery last year. That he'd moved on from believing her to be psychic. That cold-shouldering him for a few months would have made him reconsider the notion and that they could get back to being regular people who didn't know each other's secrets.

Apparently not. His eyes stared truth into her. He still thought she was psychic just as she still sucked at lying to him about it.

Danica wielded the pens, pointing their caps to his face. "Bite marks. One from very recent, another one from a while ago. They're different, from different Sofis."

She scrunched her face, thinking back to Marty's on-camera struggles. "I think they were both good actors. Marty and Tori. The characters they were playing were for real life audiences."

He examined the pens. "Any idea how they managed all this? I mean, moving things around? Their house is in the sticks, in Tarzana."

Danica nodded. "I think they kept Sofi nearby at all times. Once they kidnapped her I mean. There's a storage locker near where they film, that's one place. Then I'm pretty sure they kept her in the trunk of a car, which they'd move around."

"How about getting Sofi in the house?"

"Back door? Window? It was in Tori's room, which is below a bathroom with a trick wall. I bet that's how they did it. Marty got kicked out halfway through. I think he hung around doing the legwork."

"How'd Tori get out?"

She stopped, stumped. She had hoped her charms and engaging personality would cloud his reason. Once again, Freddie proved too good for that sort of thing.

Then he laughed. "Sorry. It was a zipline."

"Huh?"

"My friends have already been to the house. That extra room you mentioned, the one through the bathroom? It has a little balcony, right? Apparently there's a zipline cord hooked up there."

Danica suddenly remembered the 'Sofi Tries...' video showing Sofi — or someone claiming to be Sofi — doing just that into a pool.

"The thing leads to a road, well, near one. They think the killers had a car waiting and then they just Batmanned their way outta there."

She sat on the floor. "So... you knew?"

"Yeah. Well, not all-the-way. I didn't get as deep into the weeds as you, but like I said, the cops have been to the house. They found some stuff." He looked at the pens again. "We could check dental records."

"You can just do that?"

"If we got a good reason. And your grimy pens might be good enough."

Being believed felt nice, especially when things had so often been unbelievable. Danica sunk her head to the floor.

He pointed the pens at her. "You kinda got yourself into this, you know? I've been telling you to be careful."

"Hey, they found me, not the other way around." She leaned toward him. "Thanks to your blog."

His eyes fluttered. They stayed on hers in such a way as to appear unfazed, yet their focus betrayed his confusion.

Danica sat up. "I put it together thinking about how many people might know or even care about what I've done. The list was pretty small. Gets even smaller when you realize someone like Carla or Andrew aren't exactly computer savvy. But the tone of your writing is what really did it."

"Too mean?"

"No. A little, but more... Protective. You tried to hide it, but you couldn't."

He looked away and smiled, caught.

Danica stared a moment, then she scooted a little closer to him and leaned against the couch. "Am I nosy?"

"Yes." He was kidding, but he took it back when he saw her face sag.

"I mean, do I make trouble? Is there something wrong with me where I put myself into these situations just to... I dunno, just to act like some hero?"

"I wouldn't say that."

"Be honest, Freddie: do you think I'm a good detective?"

"Doesn't seem to matter what I think. You're proving that on your own. Making it a habit."

"I'm not trying to make it a habit."

"You're not trying too hard to break the habit either." He saw how that cut her and added, "Sorry. I just think you're gonna need to be more careful next time."

"I'm not doing any 'next times.'"

"I doubt that very much. You might not have tried to fall

into some crazy scheme with life-swapping sisters and puzzle boxes and all that, but *apparently* those people are out there. And so are you."

"I'm so sorry about ignoring you."

"It's fine," he said.

"And not telling you about any of this earlier. I know I said I'd be careful but—"

"It's fine, DL."

"Really?"

"No." He laughed, but his dark eyes stayed on hers, embedding and inviting. "So? What do you wanna do now?"

Danica weighed his question while answers swarmed her brain. She wanted to stay there. To move in, nest and reside for the foreseeable future. M-80's exploded in her mind, listing all her options. To live with and be with this person, to be his, in every sense. It would be rushed and she didn't care. He had listened and always would. He would protect her, but not box her up. He respected her.

He loved her.

She leaned a little closer, thinking of all this while thinking of only one thing.

His mouth opened.

Then Lorena said, "Call it in, man."

The mystic's hair was a mess. Her face, angry. Her arms, crossed. She scowled at both of them for not thinking of this answer sooner. "Call your cop friends and arrest the bastards."

Danica pulled back as Freddie grinned and grabbed his phone.

CHAPTER THIRTY-SIX

In typical times, the salon enjoyed quiet Monday mornings. Everyone involved from Carla to Gene to the customers often used such days to recover from long weekends. And customers who came in often only required touch-up work.

This Monday, however, was anything but typical. It was practically frantic, but this frenzy had nothing to do with customer hair. Building inspectors tended to bring that kind of tension with them, noting problems beyond the impact of the initial call. Carla had the fire department on the scene the moment she saw Danica fall through the closet, so she knew the can of worms she'd opened. She simply did not enjoy the experience of being summed up.

A white man with a white hardhat, clipboard and no sense of humor stomped around the salon, scanning the ceiling area. Every mark he made on his clipboard sent a cut to Carla's skin.

The television on the wobbly card table played highlights of the new president. Talking heads dissected his every syllable, looking for meaning and substance and mistakes.

The hardhat man walked to the back of the salon toward the office. Carla released a gruff sigh.

"It'll be done soon," said Danica.

"Don't know why he's looking back there. Farthest point from Lorena's. There wasn't any fire here anyways."

The locked front door jiggled behind them. Before Carla had time to turn and politely explain that they were closed, Lorena let herself in. She pocketed the master landlord key and swooped toward them.

"Good day, all," she said. Her presence and perseverance was almost a relief to Danica, seeing her back at Maximum Madame Lorena levels, complete with sparkling rings and a new fringy green wrap.

The hardhat man emerged from the back hallway, still staring at the types of things only he found interesting.

Lorena dropped her performance stature for a moment to ask, "How is it going?"

"Moving pretty fast," said Danica. "We can't tell if that's a good sign or a bad one."

"For me as well. He filled out his clipboard and whisked away with barely a moment's pause. I've consulted the spirits and have been directed to take this as a sign of good fortune."

"If you say so," said Carla, trusting it as far as she could throw it. She shuffled toward her chair and grabbed the broom to spy under the pretense of cleaning something.

Lorena lowered her voice even more to Danica. "May I assume you received the same news as I?"

Danica nodded. "I sent my check back today." Not only did the police work swiftly to locate, question and apprehend Tori and Marty, but they moved with equal speed to inform

Danica that her reward check had been presented under false pretenses and that — with the estate being seized — she would have no choice but to return the funds.

"The frozen accounts of murderers are unlikely to thaw." Maximum Madame Lorena, with bonus fortune cookie vibes.

When Danica received her notice, she immediately thought of how this would crush Lorena. The woman had performed heroically for the last week, helping to do right and discovering the actual criminals. However heroic she had become, giving the check back — willfully handing over money — probably felt like cutting off one of her own hands.

With Lorena actually standing next to her, tension burned in Danica's chest. "Don't foreclose on Carla. Don't raise her rent. Give her a break. It's not her fault. I know we didn't get the money, but you need this place to earn it back. Let her do that. Please?"

Less than a week ago, such a plea might have hit deaf, bejeweled ears. Madame Lorena the Shrewd Business Woman would have turned away with some form of 'business is business' shrug and gotten back to turning the screws on everyone in her way.

Yet standing there after all they'd endured together, Danica saw in this older woman the picture of optimism and heart.

"I wouldn't dream of it, dear."

"I know you needed that money."

Lorena said, in a more-chipper-than-it-needed-to-be voice, "It was not to be."

"Not in the stars, you mean? You really should've predicted it."

Lorena nodded by way of laughing. On the TV, the press conference concluded and the talking heads resumed their jabbering form of work.

"And you?" said Lorena. "I understand you will be helping the financial efforts as well. Moonlighting work and the like."

Danica had made some more in-roads with some of Gabby's actor friends. They were interested in starting up their own online content and decided they needed good hair and make-up to do it. Even better: Gabby suggested that they come to Earl's to do it.

"Helping is, apparently, what I do," said Danica.

"Understandable. I've seen your skills."

"Customers seem to like it."

"Oh, I mean your *other* skills."

Something slid into Lorena's tone. Something sly. It made Danica's eyes squint, trying to find the crack. The older woman's eyes turned to Danica's and locked into place.

She wasn't talking about cutting hair.

Nor about detective work.

She was talking about...

The planet ceased its rotation.

"I don't know what you mean," said Danica, after approximately three hours of staring, convincing no one at all.

"Deny it if you must, but I know what I know," said Lorena.

"But you don't—"

"You spoke with such conviction at the Starr House. 'I am a telepath. I channel people's thoughts from their minds' or what have you. You spoke of your gifts without need for elaboration. It held the ring of truth. Because it was."

As Danica stammered, the flowery tone of Lorena's performer's voice stepped side, making way for the rough-edged trickster.

"I can spot honesty when it happens since I am, as you pointed out, a professional liar. And you, my dear? You had honesty in spades."

Danica wanted to deny everything, but her mouth had taken a break from work at the moment, leaving her defenseless.

Lorena straightened her shoulders and the faux-regal voice returned. "I have been contemplating how you gathered your information in the first place. The information from Marty which you so generously presented to me a week prior. He wouldn't have come out and told you these things. Especially if he had been plotting something nefarious. How else would you have acquired these insights if not through some means of, shall we say, extraction?

"And then you saved my life. Our lives. By asking me to think of the passage in the ceiling."

"I could've guessed that."

"Then why take the time to ask?"

Danica's brain joined her mouth for another work break, leaving her with no helpful excuses. Cornered, she remembered Freddie and how he'd figured it out and she'd pushed him away just for being smart. Finally she said, "I don't like people to know."

Lorena winked. "It's safe with me. One professional to another."

The woman's low voice made everything calmer. Despite all evidence to the contrary, with her secret being known by the person on the top of her personal 'Do Not Share Secrets With This Person' list, things felt like they might work out.

"However," continued Lorena, "as you mentioned earlier, we do find ourselves in a financial crunch. Without our windfall to offer respite, I fear we may need to get a bit creative."

"I know the feeling."

"I thought you might. Which is why I wondered if we might work together again. You and I."

Danica had already been speaking in a low whisper. Upon

hearing Lorena's inquiry, she found an even quieter, sub-dog level of volume. "Like... doing what?"

"Being partners. Rather, associates, if you like."

"But associates of *what*, Lorena?"

The older woman became energized. Her eyes sparkled like they had at the Starr Residence when Marty had pitched the idea of doing a web series. Oh God... that couldn't be her idea. Making YouTube videos? After all this?

Somehow, the idea Lorena articulated seemed even worse: "We would bring in customers. Ones with problems which nobody else can seem to solve. We hook them with our abilities and our razzmatazz, then deliver outcomes better than anyone else possibly could."

"I've never been great at reading fortunes though."

"Not reading fortunes, dear. I'm talking about detective work. Working cases. Solving *clues!*"

Yep. Even worse. "Um... what?"

"A customer would arrive at my business, we would concoct some manner in which you might see what they are thinking, as you do. And — poof! — we solve their case. We have to fix the awning already, so it's a golden opportunity to rebrand a bit." Lorena's voice had grown embarrassingly less quiet.

"Lorena, I don't even know how it works. I just, you know, touch a person's head and sometimes, occasionally, I see what's there. It's a pretty limited skill set."

"As someone who owes her life to that limited skill set, I'd say it's very useful. You did the palm reading with Joy and whatshername. You touched them then."

"Yeah, their hands, not their heads. I didn't get any visions."

"So just say you have to read their scalps, their brains, what have you. That could be a thing. A newly discovered mystical entry point known only by your great great grandmother from the old country. Or something like that. Add to that your experience as a detective —"

"Two cases!"

"In a way, three. This Sofi Starr business should count as a double."

Danica folded her arms. "So you're saying..."

"We would open a psychic detective agency."

Fireworks and dollar bags danced through Lorena's eyes, her smile genuine and intimidating.

Danica could see no good way to start this kind of business. First off, she'd learned her lesson of working with Lorena: avoid it. Second, exposing herself to all kinds of shady business practices, fights, danger and the one-hundred-percent certainty of mockery that would come with that work offered no comfort. And third, all of the above.

Carla returned from her mock cleaning and Danica turned away from her former partner. The older woman had not only figured out her most precious secret, but was already set to exploit it. Her trust in Lorena rose for all of ninety seconds before dropping back into the dirt.

The hardhat inspector emerged from the hallway and handed receipts to Lorena and to Carla, offering little fanfare before exiting for his next assignment. Carla's face framed in every level of stress.

"What are we gonna do?" she said.

They'd need money. Earl's wasn't going to just going to magically manifest enough new customers. Not new haircut customers. The repairs facing the strip mall required serious help. Or *someone's* serious to help. Someone open to strange situations and unique opportunities.

Danica hated herself a little for wanting to run away, but forgave herself right back again for knowing there was no way she ever would.

Danica had a problem. Helping others — doing good — was in her nature. No point in denying it now.

On screen, a replay ran again of the first Black man taking the oath of office.

"Don't worry," said Danica. "Lorena and I might have an idea."

Continue reading for a look at
the <u>first</u> Psychic Barber Mystery...

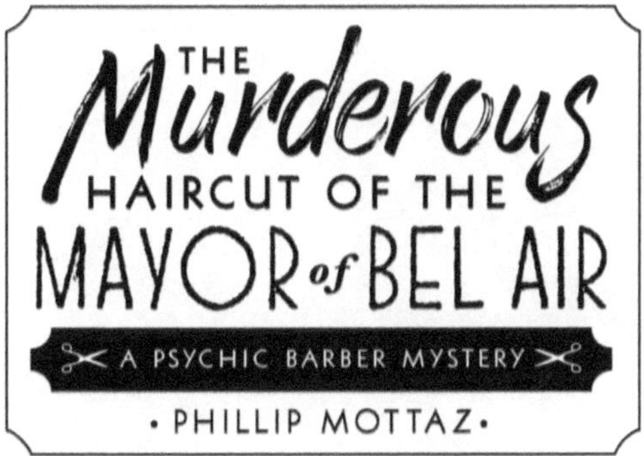

Available everywhere!

PREVIEW — CHAPTER 1

Monday, August 25, 2008. 8:46AM. Van Nuys, California.

The grey walls of the strip mall on Saticoy and Sepulveda seemed even more drab in the rain. Every door had a faded red awning, and they all needed attention, especially the one above Earl's World of Curls. Earl's did just well enough to stay afloat, to fight off selling the business to a corporation, or to hiring awful people. Carla took over the business years ago from someone she would not name, and ran a tight, friendly ship, valuing word of mouth and customer loyalty. Danica was a white girl who could cut Black people's hair, and her sulky realism charmed her way into the position. The fact that she could nail a customer's style through supplemental means helped in her demonstration and she got hired quick.

Danica parked in her spot at the end of the lot, locked her door and jogged past the tax preparer's and the tarot card reader's to the Earl's entrance.

The smell of shampoo and hairspray baked into the linoleum floor welcomed her with a smack in the face. KOST 103.5 FM played low from the one working speaker hanging above the door. Beyond the cash register counter were the two stations against the mirror wall. One station had a customer (an older woman) and Carla Velez stood behind her.

Danica expected a barrage of motherly questions from her manager. "Where've you been?" "How massive was this accident?" "You can't find another route?" "Don't you know I got customers?" Carla cared about her, but she still had a business to run. Add to that the stress of trying to refinance her house, and her mood was wholly understandable.

Yet as Carla's eyes stared over her blue plastic glasses, no such barrage arrived. Instead, a strange smile brightened her face, and her dusty curls might have even had a bounce to them.

"Danica, girl!" she said. "We were just talking about you."

She followed Carla's nudging head and recognized the customer in the chair. Mrs. Roosevelt had been an Earl's regular, and was known in the professional haircutting world as a Handful. She often asked for dye jobs, and usually had big dreams for new styles every time she returned. The desperate smile on Carla's face made more sense.

Danica pulled off her wet sweatshirt to hang it up, apologizing for being late, and Carla shuffled over to her.

"I need you over there." Carla spoke in a hush. "Says she wants something like on '24.'"

"Kiefer Sutherland?"

"Her words," said Carla. She looked lost.

Danica nodded and approached Mrs. Roosevelt. The customer waved from under her smock. "Didn't mean to be disloyal. Just couldn't wait. Big plans."

"Sure thing," said Danica.

Normal social situations prohibited people — however familiar they might be with each other — from walking up to one another and playing with their hair. However, normal social rules did not apply in the shop, and Danica took advantage. She twiddled Mrs. Roosevelt's wispy hair and asked, "What are we doing today?"

Mrs. Roosevelt began a rambling babble of gobbledygook as Danica's finger tips found their place. A sullen young woman appeared in her mind, younger than everyone in Earl's by a decade. She had blonde hair in tight waves against her forehead.

Danica released her grip and said to Mrs. Roosevelt, "You're in good hands," then whispered to Carla, "It's that Eliza Cuthbert actress."

"Elisha Kush-berg."

"I think we're both wrong," said Danica. "Doesn't matter. Just look her up. Tight waves to the forehead, but not bangs. Give as much body as possible."

"You're a lifesaver."

"I owed you."

"Yes, you did. Kush...?"

"Cuthbert."

"What?" said Carla.

"Never mind. All fine. You're welcome," said Danica, and she shooed her boss back to the customer. Only then did she notice the man sitting in the waiting area.

She held up a finger to ask for a minute and hustled to her station. She shared it with Gene, the drama queen who worked nights and told everyone else why they sucked. He and Danica had worked out a system to tell what stuff was whose: Gene kept his things in tidy order, and Danica did not. Despite owning fewer items than anyone on the Earl's staff, her things found a way to be chaotic. Old bottles of shampoo lined the area by her half of the mirror, and her sink held wet towels from the night before. Gene's towels, on the other hand, sat folded in a nice pile on top of his polished tool kit. Danica's tool kit doubled as a rack for dirty aprons.

She flattened an apron against her gray tank top. She hung her last working water bottle on the loop of her cargos and motioned for the customer to join her.

Even after seeing him take only a few steps, it seemed obvious this guy was athletic. Danica's bare arms felt even thinner when she glanced at his poking out of his nerdy polo. His face was new to her, and it held a stiffness in the jaw. He wore jeans that looked like they were ironed, and not in any way remotely cool. The man eased his way into her chair like he had entered an especially hot jacuzzi. Danica took care to spin him slowly toward the mirror for fear he might barf from all the excitement.

Just as she got him facing the mirror, the front door swung open and a tall woman shuffled inside, her impractical vest with the hood down, rain be damned. She held her purse over her hair with one hand, and a coffee in the other.

"Got a sec?" said Gabby. The audition must have been quick.

"Not really," said Danica.

Gabby sidled up to the chair and invaded Mr. Uncomfortable's personal space. "It's important."

Danica looked at Carla. She was talking to Mrs. Roosevelt, but she must have noticed Gabby make herself at home, and couldn't have been thrilled about it.

"I'm busy, Gab," said Danica.

"I got the gig. And I brought you a mocha."

Danica's antennae went up and she looked out the window. Even with the distance and drizzle, she could see Gabby's car. The recent model Prius, a gift from her parents when she moved to LA, parked right in front of the shop doors. The backseat filled with junk. A trash bag pressed against the window, next to a couple of suitcases and various shoes.

Prickles ran up Danica's neck. She looked back to her roommate and wondered if, in fact, she still was.

Gabby bit her lip.

"What the hell, man?" said Danica.

"Customer voice," said Gabby, then immediately regretted it. "The shoot starts tomorrow, so I gotta haul to Moab. Freakin' Utah."

"How long's the shoot?"

"Couple weeks."

"Looks like you packed for months."

"Maybe more than a couple," said Gabby. "But not forever."

"Okay, well, that's great. And they're paying you?"

Gabby nodded.

"Very great."

Gabby stopped nodding, and the prickles ran over Danica's neck again.

"Excuse me a second," she said to Mr. Uncomfortable. He winced a nod and Danica pulled Gabby to the reception area.

"When?"

"When what?" said Gabby.

"When are they paying you?"

"I get paid when the shoot wraps."

"The whole shoot, or just your parts?"

She chewed her lip like bubble gum. "Whole shoot."

"So I'm guessing that's, what, like two months or something?"

"Probably."

"Gab, we need rent for not just this month, but the last one."

"This will pay for that. After the shoot."

"In two months!"

"Yes!" Gabby smiled, but it faded as she looked at Danica. "You're not happy about me making money? We need it for rent."

"Jeez." Danica pictured the pile of red-letter envelopes waiting to attack her mailbox.

"I had to do it. This is the first thing I've got in months."

"And you'll be away." Danica couldn't believe she said it. To be so vulnerable came with weird fear of being fully seen.

"I'll be back."

"Sure," said Danica.

"Y'know, I could probably talk them into hiring an on-set stylist. You could come."

Despite all evidence — high cost of living, dangerous, enormous, full of douche bags — Danica claimed Los Angeles as her own. She won it in the separation from Tommy. He took the music, her favorite plates and the TV, and she took the city. Leaving her adopted home would count as a defeat and there was no way Tommy would win that one. She shook her head.

Gabby handed a wad of cash to Danica, but she pushed it back. "It's OK. You'll need gas."

They hugged. Gabby made a squealing sound, then broke it off and handed over the mocha. It weighed expensive.

With one last pouty face, Gabby stepped outside, back into the rain, and jogged to her car. Danica turned back to her station. She could hear the Prius' familiar hum grow loud, then quieter, then gone.

Numbers swirled in her brain. She had months to plan for and past months to pay for. Even moving to a cheaper place would cost money she didn't have. The numbers gave way to plots and schemes, as though she was the type of person who could invent something to sell that would be not only desirable but on the market by September.

"Everything OK?" said the man in her chair. He'd heard the whole thing.

"Forget it," said Danica.

"Do you need something?"

She didn't need his condescending voice, that's for damn sure. She needed this guy to tip well and get out so someone else could get in and bring twenty friends.

"You're Danica, right?"

She nodded and washed her hands. "Someone recommend me?"

"Someone from work," he said.

"They say good things?"

"Yes. I understand you do," his voice lowered, "dye jobs." He said it like a dirty word.

There went the prospects of a good tip. In her experience, old people and dye jobs were notoriously bad at tipping. Her eyes ran over his tell-tale salt and pepper temples. She should have noticed it earlier.

"What's your name?"

"James."

"Don't worry, James. I happen to do the type of work you're looking for." Before he could ask, she added, "Discreetly."

James' resting glower gave a flicker of what, for him, must have been elation. Danica turned him to face the mirror and started playing with his hair, moving her hand to the "Intake Position."

"What else are we doing today?"

She planted her fingertips under the bump of his skull. He began speaking as she closed her eyes and gave the oncoming images her full attention. If she could nail the look he wanted, perhaps he would buck the low-tipping-dye-job stereotype.

She saw a dark field. Lots of grass, at night. Short hair on the sides, dark brown. A flashlight on the ground. Longer on top, flat. Someone's shoes, walking. The light pointed at the ground. Someone's bare feet. The flashlight scanned the toes. They were motionless.

Danica pulled her hand away from James' head and opened her eyes. Her sink and mirror replaced the images of the ground and grass and feet. She looked at the back of her customer's head. Some of those images concerned hair, but definitely some did not. Those were feet, and they looked like they were found lying somewhere.

At night.

And not moving.

Probably just a dream. Sometimes she intercepted dreams and nightmares. Channelers channeled. She didn't have a remote control to his brain. He seemed distracted when he came in. Uptight. Probably from a nightmare.

She grabbed her comb and found her clippers. She would do the sideburns first, as the clippers usually dulled the visions.

Not this time.

As she touched the side of James' head, she saw the grass again, clearer than before. The flashlight tracked the shoes as they walked. The beam found the bare feet once again. Some pink birthmark around the ankle. The beam rose up the leg, up the torn dark jeans. The flashlight rose to the shirt. A light blue button-down. Trim and sleek with short sleeves. The stomach of the shirt had a splotch of darkness. Dark brown. The light found the same color on the chest. By the heart.

The face stared at nothing, motionless. A young man. He didn't blink when the light hit him.

The beam pulled back and she saw the entirety of the young man, lying on the grass at night. Unnatural. His arms lay spread out. Whoever held the flashlight reached out his other hand and picked up the young man's wrist. It had gone limp.

The wrist had a blue bruise, but no pulse.

The hand released the young man's arm and it plopped into the grass.

Danica snapped off the clippers and pulled away. "These are the wrong ones. I got others. Somewhere. Back there." She fast-walked toward the office area in back, to the bath-room, and closed the door behind her.

The water she splashed on her face only made her wet. The images would not wash away. Danica looked around the dark bathroom, trying to find a suggestion or inspiration for any other thoughts, to springboard her imagination into another, safer, less-creepy place. A movie or a song or something else that didn't have a dead body lying in the grass. At night. Barefoot. Somewhere dark.

Facts were facts, and they needed facing. Her step-father's advice had always been annoying both in its delivery and, as she'd discovered only recently, its propensity for correctness. She had to understand what she had seen in order to deal with it.

The possibility that she had seen James' dreams seemed less likely due to the vividness of the images. Dreams didn't move that linearly, or repeat themselves. She could practically feel the grass crunching beneath her shoes — his shoes. These were not hallucinations or fantasies. These were memories, they were of a murder, and they were the murder memories of the man sitting in her station waiting to get his temples colored.

She pulled the bathroom door open a crack and looked at James. He hadn't moved an inch. He seemed very calm for a murderer, which meant he was either A.) not a murderer but someone whose brain carried the memories of a murderer, or B.) was so much of a murderer that he could sit calmly in a barber's chair and wait for his stylist to return from the bathroom. Neither option felt particularly comforting.

This spurred Danica's first plan of attack: running, out the back storage room, through the trash door, down the street and into the desert, never to be seen again. It would leave James alone with Carla and Mrs. Roosevelt, which didn't sit well with her conscience.

Calling the police seemed like a natural back-up plan. They were, after all, the police. They had training and resources. They could take it from here, and would probably tell her as much.

The cops were also a dead end. They wouldn't move their fat-blue-line butts without good reason, and good reason was just what Danica lacked. She had no way to prove what she saw, let alone explain how she saw it. The cops were useless.

Her best chance at survival seemed to be playing it cool and act like she hadn't seen images of a murder. Do the dye, get him out, then find out what she could. She rubbed the peach fuzz on her head, then dried her face and opened the bathroom door, super cool.

"Sorry," she said as she returned to her station as if nothing were wrong, and why would there be anything wrong? "I'll just use these. Couldn't find the other ones. The other clippers. So I'll use these. Those. Those clippers."

Super, duper cool. Danica prayed Carla hadn't been paying attention.

James nodded. He must have encountered babbling idiots often enough for Danica's performance to go unnoticed. Instead he raised an eyebrow when she put on plastic gloves.

"We doing the you-know-what first?"

"I'm gonna clip first."

"You do it with gloves on?"

"Sometimes. Yes. With these clippers. These. And I'll keep them on for later." The gloves also tended to make it difficult for Danica to receive visions, but she managed to keep that to herself.

She worked, keeping her fingertips away from his scalp. She felt Carla's eyes on her.

It went faster than any dye job she or anyone had ever done, and it came out much better than she suspected (which gave her another thing to worry about; bad work might have made for a one-and-done customer. Good work could bring this guy and his death images back). James cashed out with Carla at the register. He promised to tell more people about Danica's work. With a nod to the room, he left.

Once the door closed, Danica grabbed her phone and ran a quick search. The first thing she confirmed was that California held at least two billion people named "James." She tried applying additional criteria, then realized it would be a waste of battery and data, and that she was avoiding the obvious search choice.

She didn't want to search it. It felt like it would legitimize everything, and treat the visions as something that had truly happened. Or would happen. Maybe this man had made plans, had picked a victim and had focused on it so much that he was trying to manifest it, like an evil version of The Secret.

Danica had never been able to see the future, so — as gross as it seemed — that meant the killing had already happened and nothing could prevent it.

Her thumb typed in "recent," "murder," and "stabbing." She added "night" and "Los Angeles," and "young man," then submitted.

A sad ton of information appeared. Domestic disputes, a high-speed pursuit involving a knife and a few hold-ups. Everything seemed to have happened in the last month, and with varying degrees of gore. She limited her search to the night before, then expanded to the night before that, then to the full week.

Nothing useful came back.

"Congrats, by the way," said Carla. She sat in her station, and had been for quite some time, silently watching Danica try to manifest a person's identity from thin internet air. She held a small rectangular box on her leg, about the size of a necklace.

"Congrats for what?"

"Barber certification."

"Hold on," said Danica. "You cashed the guy out, right?"

"What guy?"

"That James guy."

"Yeah."

"Did he pay with card or cash?"

"Card."

"What's his last name?"

Carla tapped the box with her fingers. "That's supposed to be personal information."

"Come on."

"You can get it when you close the register out."

"I don't close tonight."

"Then you won't get it," said Carla. "What's this about? He doesn't seem like your type."

"I just need to know."

"Why?"

"Just need to." Danica recognized the expression on Carla's face that this crap was flying nowhere, no how. Not without reasonable explanation.

And since Carla was one of the few people on Earth who understood Danica's true skill set, she took the opportunity to tell the truth. Just this once.

She said, "When I was cutting his hair, I saw a dead body. A murdered one."

Carla blinked, stood up and walked to the cash register. Danica followed her. Carla put the box in Danica's hands and keyed in the code on the credit card reader.

"What is this?" said Danica, turning the box a bit. Inside, something made a thud.

"It's for you."

The credit card reader spit out a receipt. Carla read it, then said, "You're not gonna do anything stupid, are you?"

"I don't think so."

"But you aren't. You gotta be careful. Don't just..."

Danica waited for the end of the sentence. It never came, though the sentiment got delivered.

"I'll be careful. Super careful"

Carla read from the receipt: "James Van Owen."

Danica repeated the name. "Thanks." She held up the box. "I haven't passed yet, you know."

"I thought you did."

"Take the final this week."

"Open it anyway," said Carla.

She did. Inside was a straight razor. Danica had used one casually, but without her certification, she couldn't use it to make money. The handle had a nice weight, and the silver blade sat fresh and clean.

"Keep it in your station for when you pass." Carla gave a glance toward the mess. "Know what? You can keep it in mine."

Go to www.phillipmottaz.com to get your copy of "The Murderous Haircut of the Mayor of Bel Air!"

DID YOU ENJOY THIS BOOK?

You can make a *big difference*.

Reviews are a powerful tool when it comes to getting attention for my books. Unfortunately I cannot write them myself, so I'm asking you to help out!

Honest reviews help my books get attention from other readers.

If you enjoyed the book, I would be forever grateful if you could take just five minutes to leave a review. Post online, hang a poster, tell a librarian — whatever you like.

Thanks so much.

www.ingramcontent.com/pod-product-compliance
Lightning Source LLC
Chambersburg PA
CBHW032151190726
48290CB00005BB/1518